LM

"Noel, I think we should talk," Kiri said.

"We keep skirting around everything except the explosive situation on the island. I know how you feel about Long White Cloud." She swallowed, then lifted her eyes to his face. "How do you feel about me?"

Surprise showed in his eyes. Then his lips curved in a provocative smile. "You are the most desirable woman I've ever met. Does that answer your question?"

"Not really. When you first saw me, you thought I was a money-grubbing, selfish person," she said slowly.

"But I always saw something else. As for your being selfish . . . you're generous, compassionate—"

"How can you say that when you know what I planned for the island?"

"All that can wait." His finger traced a path of fire down her smooth cheek. "I think," he said softly, "that you are a warm, loving woman, struggling to get free from your shell."

"And you think you're the man who can free me?" She meant it as a challenge, but her voice sounded shaky, even to herself. . . .

Dear Reader,

The holiday season is in full swing, and most of us are busy running around buying, wrapping—and hiding—gifts for our families and friends. But it's important not to forget ourselves during this hectic time, and Silhouette Intimate Moments is here with four terrific romances for you to enjoy when you steal a few moments on your own.

First up is Emilie Richards with *Twilight Shadows*, a tie-in to her last book for the line, *Desert Shadows*. Things are never what they seem in the movies anyway, but in this case we're talking about some *real* desperate characters and bad actors. Pick up the book and you'll see what I mean!

After a long—too long!—absence, favorite author Kathleen Eagle returns to Intimate Moments with *Bad Moon Rising*. Kathleen is deservedly celebrated for her portrayals of Native American characters, and this book once again demonstrates why. And for those of you who remember her long-ago Silhouette Christmas story, "The Twelfth Moon," there's an extra treat in store. I guess this book is in the way of being a Christmas present, too!

Mary Anne Wilson's *Nowhere To Run* and Marilyn Cunningham's *Long White Cloud* round out the month. And next year (!) look for more of your favorite authors—Heather Graham Pozzessere, Kathleen Korbel, Dallas Schulze and Kathleen Creighton, to name only a few—coming to you in Silhouette Intimate Moments.

Happy Holiday Reading!

Leslie Wainger
Senior Editor and Editorial Coordinator

MARILYN CUNNINGHAM

Long White Cloud

SILHOUETTE·INTIMATE·MOMENTS®

Published by Silhouette Books New York

America's Publisher of Contemporary Romance

SILHOUETTE BOOKS
300 East 42nd St., New York, N.Y. 10017

Books by Marilyn Cunningham

Silhouette Intimate Moments

Someone To Turn To #334
Enchanted Circle #355
Long White Cloud #411

MARILYN CUNNINGHAM

lives in the high country of Idaho, which she often uses for the settings of her books. She lives twelve miles from the nearest habitation, and interruptions to her writing include the herd of elk that parade by her front window, the coyotes that pad down her driveway and the Canada geese that stop by the pond behind her cabin on their yearly migrations. When not writing, she hikes unmarked mountain trails, works in the garden with her own hero, John, or rides her quarter horse accompanied by her two poodles, Andre and Denali.

When nature palls—which it can, with snow drifting up around the cabin eaves and the gravel road blocked with drifts—she travels to visit her daughter in California, or explores Alaska with her two sons. She has used both places as settings for her novels.

Chapter 1

Suppressing a sigh, Kiri MacKay deposited her two heavy suitcases on the wooden planking and surveyed the pier that stretched out ahead of her into the turquoise waters of the bay. Her forehead wrinkled in a slight frown. What should she do next? Everything had happened so fast that she could still hardly believe she was here in New Zealand, alone, half a world away from home.

She still had a ways to go, too, so she had better keep her mind on the immediate problem of transportation, and try to ignore the confused welter of thoughts and fears that she had been wrestling with ever since she had learned of her father's death.

She flexed her fingers to lessen the cramp, then rubbed her arm against her head and pushed her straight, dark hair back from her face, as she surveyed the line of boats bobbing in slips on either side of the pier. Pursing her lips in concentration, she glanced from one to the other, wondering which she could possibly approach. She didn't see a sign of life, but surely among all these boats she would be able to locate someone who would convey her to the island.

Tilting her head backward and closing her eyes, hoping to drive away the fatigue that lurked in every muscle of her body, she inhaled deeply of the light breeze that carried the tangy scent of salt. Not entirely physical fatigue, she knew, although she hadn't rested since flying from California to Auckland where she had talked to the attorney, then taken a bus up the coastline of New Zealand's North Island. Much of her weariness was due to mental stress—the shock of learning of her father's death, the necessity of the trip, and more debilitating than anything else, the emotional turmoil that had gripped her ever since she had learned that she was the sole heir to his estate—an estate that the attorney told her consisted almost entirely of an isolated island off the coast of this luxurious resort town of Paihia.

Her immediate problem was that there was no public transportation from Paihia to the island, which the attorney had told her was named Long White Cloud. The clerk at the hotel had told her that most of the men who owned the commercial boats that would normally have ferried her across were already out in the bay escorting tourists on sightseeing excursions or fishing trips. In fact, the pier looked deserted.

But she couldn't just stand here; there had to be someone around. She lifted her suitcases again, wincing slightly at the weight accentuating the aching in her arms, and walked slowly along the pier, unconsciously shifting her hips from side to side as the structure swayed beneath her feet. The clerk at the hotel had suggested she come down here to the pier on the chance that someone would be available to take her to the island.

She scanned each boat as she passed, her spirits falling even farther as she saw no one aboard any of them. She was nearly to the end of the pier when she saw a man lounging against a piling, his face turned to the sea, and she sagged with relief. At least the place wasn't entirely deserted. Perhaps the man could give her some information.

Dropping her bags on the creaking pier, she walked a little closer, supposing that he had not heard the sound of her footsteps since he still hadn't changed his position. Although he was turned away from her, gazing out toward the open water, and she was unable to see his features, the rest of him looked presentable enough. Her mind quickly catalogued the tall rangy body, the white shorts and white knit shirt that were in sharp contrast to his bronzed arms and long, well-muscled legs. His light brown hair, streaked blond by the sun, was cut longer than she was accustomed to, but it was neat, well-styled.

He stood with nonchalance, leaning one shoulder against the rough piling, his hands thrust deep in his pockets. The overall impression was of casual, indolent grace, of quiet authority, but something about the way he held himself—perhaps a slight rigidity in his shoulders—made her think he was fully alert, although he was apparently oblivious to her approach.

She hesitated, then stretched out a tentative hand to touch him lightly on the shoulder in order to gain his attention, but drew back, sensing something about him that didn't invite a casual touch.

"Excuse me—I—"

At the sound of her voice he turned slowly, and she immediately decided he had known she was there all along. The hunch made her a little annoyed. His lean face with the startling blue eyes and sharply cut features that she immediately thought of as aristocratic betrayed not a flicker of surprise. For a long moment he just looked at her, his expression thoughtful and assessing. Her annoyance faded to uneasiness under his wordless scrutiny, and she made a supreme effort not to fidget.

"I'm sorry if I disturbed you," she said a little testily, regaining some of the confidence that had eroded under his steady regard. "I wonder if you could help me—"

Still he said nothing, his blue eyes wary and alert. Then, when she had almost made up her mind to turn away and look for someone else, he smiled slowly, transforming his rather somber expression to one of charming gallantry.

"I would certainly like to help you," he said, his tone making the words a definite compliment. "It isn't every day I meet a damsel in distress. What can I do for you?"

The smile was a definite improvement, although she couldn't help wondering about its sincerity. Something deep in his eyes belied the easy friendliness.

But perhaps she was imagining things. "I'm Kiri MacKay," she said, holding out her hand and giving him a warm smile. "I'm not exactly a damsel in distress—at least not dire distress—but I sure could use a little help."

He waited, an eyebrow cocked expectantly, and she continued. "I need a ride out to an island—Long White Cloud. Do you know it?"

He nodded briefly. "Sure. A little island on the outer ring. Out past Russell." He gestured toward the hazy horizon, which was broken randomly by hillocks of lush green rising out of blue water. "I'm going out that way myself—I'll be glad to take you."

She smiled with relief. "It isn't too far out of your way?"

"It's right on my route."

"Well, then, thank you so much." She raised her eyes to his, a warm smile still on her face. "I'll pay you, of course."

His face darkened with a frown, and she wondered if she had been too abrupt. Perhaps a blunt declaration of payment wasn't the thing to do here. But she wanted to make it plain that she didn't wish to be obligated. She made it a point to always pay her own way.

She also wondered why it was suddenly so necessary to make it clear that she wished to be under no obligation to him. Was it the confident tilt of his head, his assured voice, that made her suspect he might be used to taking things into his own hands, controlling every situation? Perhaps she was gun-shy, but she had spent a lifetime depending only on herself, and she liked it that way.

His eyes narrowed slightly. "I told you it's not out of my way. I'll be happy to take you over. Free of charge," he added somewhat curtly. "It's the least I can do for Ian MacKay's daughter."

"You knew my father?" Her eyes widened in surprise, then she shrugged. Of course he would have known her father; Ian MacKay was known throughout the world. Obviously he would be known even better on his own turf. She wondered if she had detected a trace of bitterness in his tone. If so, she would like to know what had caused it. She was fully aware that she was coming as a stranger into an unknown situation, and there might be all kinds of undercurrents she wasn't aware of. She resolved to move carefully until she had checked out the lay of the land.

"Oh, everybody around here knows everybody else," he said, smoothly answering her question before abruptly changing the subject. "I hope you don't mind a slow sail. That's my boat over there—the *Island Princess*. She's great on endurance, but I'm afraid speed's another matter."

She half smiled at the obvious affection in his voice, but before she could reply, even to thank him, he stooped to pick up her suitcases and then strode swiftly toward the little sloop rocking gently at its slip. As she scurried after him, Kiri had a quick impression of gleaming brightwork, a newly painted hull, and a tall mast with furled sails.

With a motion that set the muscles rippling in his shoulders, he tossed the bags aboard, then turned to grasp her hand to hoist her up onto the deck. For a long moment he held her hand, looking deeply into her eyes as though he were searching for an answer. Again the intensity of his gaze made her uncomfortable. It wasn't the obvious introspective look of a man wondering about an attractive woman. It was deeper. She wished she knew what lay beyond the inquisitive expression—he was obviously concerned about something. Could it be her? But since she had just met him, that didn't make sense.

Slowly, he released her hand, although he didn't move away and his eyes were still fixed on hers.

"Sorry for my lack of manners," he finally said. "I should have introduced myself. I'm Noel Trevorson."

She nodded acknowledgment. The name meant nothing to her, although he looked as though he had expected a reaction of some kind.

"I'm sorry about your father, Miss MacKay," he offered softly.

She shrugged, dropping her eyes. She was never sure how to react to expressions of sympathy about her father. No one could be expected to know the situation, of course. The truth was she hadn't even known the man. When the attorney had contacted her, telling her Ian was dead and that she had been tracked down because she was shown as next of kin on a number of legal papers, the shock had been caused by surprise, not by a real sense of loss. She had experienced his death as a culmination of a lifetime of bitterness, of pain at being ignored by one who should have loved her. How could she respond sincerely to professions of sympathy when she wasn't even sure how she felt about his death herself?

"Thank you," she said stiffly, retrieving her hand.

He kept his eyes on her averted face. "I admit I'm a little surprised, though," he said softly. "Until a few weeks ago I didn't even know Ian had a daughter."

She glanced up quickly. Judging by his tone, this man had apparently known Ian quite well, Kiri decided, but that didn't mean he knew everything. He couldn't have any awareness that his sympathy was misplaced. Ian MacKay hadn't known he had a daughter, either, if one could judge by the paltry amount of love and attention he had shown her. The familiar bitterness rose like a sour taste in her mouth as she thought of her father, a man she had never really known. And now, never would.

"We weren't—close," she said.

"I guess not. You couldn't manage to arrive in time for the memorial service."

She didn't imagine it—there was definitely something accusing, condemning, in his eyes, although his tone was as bland as water.

"No, I didn't," she said coldly. A flush of anger blazed on her cheeks. Who was this man to judge a situation he knew nothing about? She had somehow missed the newspaper reports of Ian's death, and when she had finally been contacted by the attorney, it was much too late to attend the services.

She certainly didn't have to explain that to a perfect stranger. Let him think what he wished; his opinion meant nothing to her.

Noel seemed on the verge of pursuing the subject, then shrugged and bent over to loose the *Island Princess* from her moorings. As they headed out into the translucent green water of the channel, Kiri sat quietly, watching him get underway with an economy of motion that impressed her in spite of herself. His movements were sure and graceful as he raised the sail, then cut the motor as canvas snapped in the breeze.

She glanced away, out across the crystalline water, trying to get her conflicting emotions under control. Although she had bristled instinctively at Noel's obvious disapproval of her absence from the memorial service, she had to admit he was closer to her own doubts than he knew. The truth was that she might not have come to the service even if she had known. Which brought her to the dilemma she had been wrestling with for days. Was it really ethical to accept an estate from a man who hadn't cared enough about her to send even a card or letter all the years she was growing up?

She thrust out her chin and took a deep breath, hardening her shaky resolve. Her father had given her little enough; surely he owed her this.

When Noel had completed his tasks and the *Island Princess* was skimming through the water, he moved over and perched beside her, one bronzed hand lightly on the wheel, and gave her a wide smile. The warmth of his smile was like the sun coming up, flooding her down to her toes with tingling energy. Apparently he had recovered from his annoyance with her.

"What are your plans, Kiri? Are you staying on for a while?" he asked, then continued without waiting for a reply. "You may find Long White Cloud a little different from what you're used to."

"I'm not staying long," she said firmly. "Just until I settle the estate, but I imagine I'll find the island comfortable enough. I'm used to managing." His question had been the normal one of a casual acquaintance. Why did she sense some tension behind it?

His lips tightened, and she wondered what his connection was with the island—if indeed there was a connection. She would be on her guard, she thought, returning his scrutiny as coolly as he had previously surveyed her. No doubt about it, he was an attractive man. Very attractive, if she were honest with herself—and she prided herself that she always was. He had wide-spaced, intelligent-appearing eyes, a straight nose, a mouth that seemed made to smile easily, although now it was set in a rigid pattern. Aristocratic features, cleanly and firmly molded. If he had not looked so uncompromisingly masculine, the word *elegant* would have come to mind.

"So you've come to settle the estate," he echoed, raising an inquiring eyebrow. "Has something definite been decided, then?" His tone was casual, but something about the set of his shoulders was not.

"What do you mean?"

"I heard Ian didn't leave a will—or at least, no one found it."

She glanced ahead to where the bow of the *Island Princess* knifed through the water, leaving twin trails of foam to run along the sides of the boat, and considered her answer. Could there be something more than idle curiosity behind these questions? Until this moment she had considered only how Ian's death affected her, but now she realized he hadn't lived in a vacuum. Other people were involved—people she hadn't even heard of. Was Noel among them, or was he just making conversation?

"No, he didn't leave a will," she said. "But I'm his next of kin. I inherit. Since my father didn't leave a will, the attorney says it will take a little longer to settle things. I'm not sure how long I'll need to be here, but everything is pretty much taken care of except for the court order that actually puts everything in my name. That may take awhile, so I decided I might as well stay on the island as in a hotel in Auckland."

"What do you plan to do after everything is finally settled? Have you thought of living on White Cloud?"

She didn't imagine it this time. There was definite tension in his tone. "Oh, no, I haven't considered living here. I'll look around for a buyer, I suppose. I have no idea how long finding one will take, but when everything is settled, I certainly plan on going back home."

He nodded, made a slight adjustment to the wheel, and she watched the play of muscles underneath the snugness of his knit shirt, the strong line of his throat as he tilted his head to face the breeze. She revised her earlier assessment; he wasn't just attractive, he was devastatingly attractive, and it wasn't only his appearance. He had a kind of vibrant, restless energy that was captivating, one that seemed to draw her out of her reserve.

And she was revealing more to him, a stranger, than she felt she should. She resolved to be less forthcoming.

"What do you do, Noel, when you're not rescuing damsels?" she asked lightly. "That can't be a full-time job."

"More's the pity." He grinned back at her.

"Do you live in Paihia?"

"Oh, I'm a bit of a vagabond," he replied, raising one perfectly shaped eyebrow and giving her a lazy grin. Then he turned to explain a point of interest on one of the islands they were passing, and for the next several minutes Kiri was enthralled with the panorama sliding by on each side.

It was only later that she realized he hadn't answered her question.

The time went so quickly that she was surprised to see land directly ahead. Her pulse quickened, and she impulsively clutched Noel's arm. "Look! Is that it? Long White Cloud?"

He laughed and gave the wheel a sharp turn, heading the *Island Princess* toward the pier that Kiri could now see stretching toward them. "No, that's Russell—but wellworth seeing. Would you like to stop off for a couple of minutes, look the place over, maybe have a cup of coffee?"

"Oh, I'd love to—if you can spare the time?"

Kiri had heard of Russell, a historic town directly across the bay from Paihia, and even under the present circumstances she welcomed the chance to see it. After all, she had no idea whether she would ever have another opportunity; the estate might be settled sooner than she thought, leaving her free to depart at any time, and she would hate to miss visiting the town.

"No problem," Noel said easily, bringing the boat alongside the pier and throwing off a bowline. "I have a little business to attend to here, anyway, and I was hoping you wouldn't mind a slight delay. It would save me a trip."

They strolled together up the pier, and Kiri's spirits lifted as she scanned the little town ahead of them. The buildings, white, well-kept, Victorian structures, sat decorously back behind a narrow strip of green that sloped down to meet the water, which was filled with brightly colored boats. Even from here she could see the town was old, rustic, picturesque.

Noel gestured toward an elegant frame building that fronted the bay. "That's worth the trip, all by itself. The Duke of Marlborough Hotel."

It was a striking building, Kiri thought, a white clapboard two-story structure wrapped by an airy veranda supported by narrow pillars topped with lacy trim. Above, a row of long narrow windows looked out over the water like alert sentinels.

Noel edged her toward the building, a smile on his face as he saw her rapt expression. "Would you like some midmorning tea? They're famous for it." His eyes softened. "And it looks as though you could handle a little something...I do believe those are blue circles under your eyes."

"Tea would be lovely." She had nearly forgotten how tired she was. Refreshments and a chance to relax would be welcome before she had to gather all her resources to face Long White Cloud.

They entered the hotel through an ornate double door, and Kiri looked around with keen pleasure. The lounge was decorated in the period of the late nineteenth century, heavy gold-leafed fixtures and plush scarlet carpeting. The spacious interior was panelled with dark teak, and a huge marlin was mounted on one wall.

"It's—it's spectacular," she breathed, as Noel held out a chair and seated her at a round teak table that had a marvelous view of the boats in the bay. "Do you come here often?"

"Let's just say that the *Island Princess* stops here all by herself, she's so used to the route," he said, seating himself beside her. His eyes darkened. "It was one of Ian's favorite places, too. He spent a lot of time here. Mostly in the evening, when he and the proprietor liked to hoist a few."

Kiri felt a cold little lump in her chest, and her throat tightened. How strange that she would learn such a simple intimate little detail about her father from a stranger. Another glimpse of the unknown Ian. A man who had friends, who liked a convivial drink or two. Suddenly she wondered what his friend, the hotel owner was like.

Not trusting her voice, she waited until the waitress, a pert young woman in a long skirt, took their order. Then she leaned slightly toward Noel. "Is the proprietor here now? I'd like to meet him."

He seemed to understand her sudden desire to meet someone who had known her father well, and his tone, although not his words, conveyed his sympathy. "No, Sam's not here. He has grandchildren in Australia, and he usually spends a couple of months a year with them. This year he left even earlier than usual—something about his son locating a gold mine in the outback that he wanted some help on." He frowned slightly. "Sam left just a week or so before Ian had his heart attack. He didn't even make it to the memorial service . . ."

He broke off and Kiri winced inwardly, knowing that both were aware of his unspoken words. She, Ian's own daughter, hadn't been here, either. She'd told herself it didn't matter, that it would have been just a formality anyway, a rote concession to propriety. But here, talking to a man who had known her father, sitting in a place Ian had apparently loved, the omission brought an ache to her heart.

The zest had gone out of her enjoyment of the interesting old place, and she sipped her tea silently. She was relieved when Noel left for a few minutes to take care of whatever had brought him to Russell. Later, when they walked back to the boat along the tiny little street past the Moreton Bay fig tree that dwarfed the one-man police station, she could hardly wait to be on her way. The sooner she faced whatever awaited her at Long White Cloud, the better. She wished everything was already over and she was back in California where she belonged. Back to her classes, her sculpture, her tiny neat apartment. Back to a reasonable, ordered life.

Later, Kiri lay back against a boat cushion and closed her eyes, letting the time slip by. A combination of exhaustion and fresh sea breezes put her quickly to sleep. She wasn't sure how long they had been sailing—perhaps a couple of hours—when Noel touched her lightly on the shoulder.

"Wake up, Kiri. There she is. You can just barely make out the outline of the island now."

Kiri opened her eyes, momentarily disoriented, then came slowly to her feet, her gaze following his pointing finger. Her breath caught in her throat. The island floated on the horizon like a long, low cloud, its form shifting and ephemeral in the mist rising off the pristine water. Rising like a jewel out of the turquoise sea, it appeared unreal, a mirage, a bastion of serenity in a turbulent world.

"Oh, Noel, it's beautiful," she murmured. "So quiet, so peaceful..."

Noel shrugged. "It's beautiful, all right. But peaceful? I'm not so sure about that." At her inquiring glance, he grinned, as though to lighten the intensity of his words. "You have to look below the surface of things, Kiri. Don't take them at face value..."

Was it a warning? She smiled up into his face and spoke lightly. "You mean it's all a facade, like a Hollywood set, with waving palms and happy natives? Don't worry—I'm not usually misled by appearances." She turned away, her gaze on the swiftly approaching island.

She was close enough now to make out some of the details and she surveyed the island with keen curiosity. She could see that it was thickly forested; the vibrant green of the *rata* trees came down to the tiny strip of white sand where the green gave way to the scarlet of *pohutukawa* trees lining the beach.

As they came ever nearer, she tried to remember everything her father's attorney had told her about the island: It was approximately five hundred acres of undeveloped land, purchased by her father years ago from the profits of his first successful books. Neither the original owners who had received it from the Maoris by treaty nor their heirs had ever done anything with it, and it had remained in a nearly pristine state. The house her father had built and a few Maori huts were the only dwellings on it.

Excitement bubbled up inside her as she surveyed the island. All of this was hers. This legacy would make so many things possible; so many of her dreams could come true.

Her excitement was followed almost immediately by a rush of anguish, and she was in the grip of the same torment that had plagued her ever since she had learned of the inheritance. Her father had given her nothing while he lived. Even in death he hadn't changed his mind; she had gained this beautiful little island by default, inheriting because he hadn't made a will. Where was her pride, to permit her to accept it on such terms?

On the other hand, didn't he owe her something, something to make up for his lifelong neglect?

The inner debate was sapping her will, and a tiny shiver of uneasiness rippled down her spine. It had all seemed so simple when she was in California, but she was beginning to feel differently now. She hadn't fully realized what the island would be like, or that she would be so isolated.

She was tired; that was all. Closing her eyes, she tilted her head back to inhale the air that floated from the island, carrying the fragrance of exotic flowers and green forests mixed with the crisp fresh smell of saltwater. The breeze had freshened, billowing out the sails, and now it made little snapping sounds in the canvas. It lifted her straight dark hair from her shoulders, and flattened her blue cotton shirt and white slacks against her slender body, as she tried to prepare herself for the unknown that lay ahead.

She was jolted from her musings by the crunch of the sloop scraping against a piling of a pier built out into the deep water, and a spasm of nervousness tightened her throat. She hesitated as Noel stepped over the side of the boat and deposited her bags on the smartly maintained wooden planking. Then, taking a deep, steadying breath, she jumped out after him. She was here; she would face whatever needed to be faced.

Kiri paused long enough to accustom herself to the sudden lack of motion, then stretched out her hand.

"Thank you so much, Noel. I don't know how I'd ever have gotten here without you. If there's anything I can do to repay you—"

He held her hand, still making no move to leave, as he glanced up the pathway behind her, then back, a slight frown on his face.

"I hate to just leave you here on the dock. Do you want me to walk up with you? Although I'm sure they know you're coming..."

They must refer to the occupants of her late father's house. The attorney had told her that a Maori woman and her son were still living on the island, but she hadn't given it much thought, and the attorney hadn't said much more than that. Now she wondered about them, suddenly anxious. Exactly who were they, and how had they fit into her father's life?

"Oh, I'll be fine," she hastened to assure him. "I won't impose on you anymore. I'm sure the attorney got word to them and they'll know I'm coming."

It took considerable mental effort to remove her hand from his warm grasp. If she'd been a more fanciful woman, she'd have said she was hanging on to him as if he were a lifeline, which was really quite ridiculous. She didn't know him at all; he was just a man she had met by chance who had given her a ride to the island. No, she was reluctant for him to leave because he had known Ian, and he'd shown flashes of kindness despite his faint hostility. It was merely that she felt so alone and he was more familiar to her than anything else in this strange place.

She bent to pick up her bags and half turned away, but was stopped by his voice, oddly hesitant after his usual confident manner.

"Kiri, I really am sorry about your father. Everyone around here thought a lot of him. He was the kindest—"

"Thanks again," she said brusquely, cutting off whatever else he had been about to say about Ian. Perhaps she was being rude, but she couldn't bear hearing any more about what a wonderful person Ian had been.

A bag in each hand, she started up the trail toward the house, her heart beating more quickly than the elevation justified. It was most disconcerting; everyone around here probably knew more about her deceased father than she did. Or at least, they knew one side of him. All she knew about him, she had read in the papers, she thought, a rush of anger coursing through her.

Oh, sometimes she thought she remembered him. She had a vague recollection of a huge, laughing bear of a man who threw her up in the air and caught her in strong hands. Then, when she was a little over three years old, he was gone. After that, the only information about him came from her abandoned mother and the newspapers.

Her mouth twisted in a bitter smile. Everyone around here might be surprised that he had died without leaving a will and that his entire estate had gone to his only living relative, his daughter, but they were certainly no more surprised than his daughter was!

Although she didn't turn, she was aware that Noel watched her walk up the path, and she straightened her spine in a gesture designed to show self-confidence. Noel was another surprise. Handsome, charming, he obviously knew a lot about what was going on at Long White Cloud. It had certainly been a fortunate coincidence that he had happened to be waiting on the dock at Paihia....

The thought made her uneasy. Too fortunate, perhaps. There had been something about him, something she couldn't quite put her finger on. Oh, he had been perfectly polite, urbane, a gentleman giving a lift to a stranger in his country. He'd been friendly, bantered impersonally. Why had she sensed hostility, an aura of disapproval? Was he disapproving because she hadn't attended her father's memorial service? But who was he to judge her?

She winced inwardly. She was quite capable of that herself! But was she judging herself too harshly? Why shouldn't she have the estate?

She pushed the thought of Noel out of her mind as she continued up the pebbled path toward the house, glancing at the greenery that lined the trail. Ian had apparently loved beauty—another thing she hadn't known about him. She was surrounded by clouds of blooming lavender and rosemary, and drooping bunches of wisteria grew from the trunks of *pungas,* sturdy palmlike trees that grew profusely all around her. The nearly cloying fragrance of sweet william mixed with the heady scent of roses permeated the air and a bewildering variety of varicolored birds skittered away as she approached. Then the path made an abrupt turn, and she paused for breath, then took a good look at the house that was finally fully in view.

In spite of her resolve not to be impressed, she nearly dropped her suitcases. She had expected that a world-famous author and renowned conservationist such as her father would own a showplace, but this structure was not nearly as pretentious as she had expected—and it was twice as beautiful. A low, white, villa-type building, it rambled over its site like a living creature, adjusting to slight variations in elevation, seemingly built without a unifying plan, but with each separate wing coming together in a harmonious whole.

The impression was of lightness and gaiety: a wall of windows looked down into the bay, some of them nearly obscured by a riot of scarlet vines. A veranda meandered halfway around the house—did every New Zealand house have a veranda?—its roof supported by delicate white columns adorned with filigree; a patio fringed by high shrubs was off to one side, barely visible from where she stood, and from someplace close came the sound of running water, probably a hidden fountain, she decided.

She stood still, awestruck in spite of herself. Paradise.

Her heart began to beat a little faster, and a sheen of perspiration moistened her skin as another thought occurred to her. When the attorney had first contacted her, she had been so excited and then so torn about inheriting, that she had given little thought to the people she would meet here. Now she remembered the slight hesitancy in his voice when he had talked about the people who lived here. A Maori woman and her son. Now, faced with the certainty that she would soon meet them, she wondered if he had been less than candid? But what could he have left out? She knew her father had never remarried, so what was this woman to him, and why was she still living in his house?

Well, she would find out soon enough. She took a deep breath and continued up the walk. Perhaps the Maori woman was a housekeeper, or maybe someone who had had a more intimate relationship with her father and who might possibly feel resentment? If so, she would resist any sentimentality. She had every right to be here; she wasn't a carpetbagger. She was the closest relative. And she would make good use of the money.

She bit her lip to quell the familiar hurt, but the ache was still there. Money couldn't take the place of love, but it was better than nothing. And in this case, it was a *lot* better than nothing. When she sold this place, she would have the money to do what she had always dreamed of doing—devote herself full-time to her sculpture. Ian owed her that, she repeated firmly to herself, more firmly because she wasn't totally sure she believed it.

The familiar litany of childhood memories ran through her mind; of her mother picking up the latest *Geographic World* and pointing scornfully to an article. "I see *he's* been in Afghanistan, saving the world as usual. Nothing for his family!" Or when he had written his first bestselling novel and her mother had looked at it contemptuously, "I see *he* is in the horror business now."

As Kiri grew older, she had followed his career with bitter fascination. He was the best-known New Zealander since

Sir Edmund Hillary, it was said. Money from his novels provided the means for him to pursue his burning interest in the planet's ecosystem, and she read that his interest in ecology took him all over the world.

She had finally accepted the fact that he had no interest at all in his own daughter. When he was a young man he had come to California, married her mother, sired a child, and then decided it was time to move on. As far as Kiri knew, he had never looked back.

A low snarl jerked her back to the present, and she glanced quickly up at the veranda. Immediately she tensed, every muscle rigid, her heart in her throat, as her hand tightened convulsively around the handle of her bag. Standing on the lower step and staring back at her, his eyes glowing red in the reflected sunlight, was a huge, obviously belligerent black dog.

Her mouth was suddenly dry and she made an effort to swallow. Usually she wasn't afraid of dogs, but usually they didn't look like this half-wild cur—legs braced, hair rising stiffly from a powerful neck, lips drawn back to bare rows of long white sharp teeth.

She forced her eyes from the menace of the dog to look at the man restraining the beast, and swallowed again. He didn't look all that dedicated to the job.

She met his eyes from a distance of about twenty feet, willing herself not to drop her gaze as she looked him over. Bracing himself on the veranda with wide-spread legs that appeared as solid as tree trunks, he held the dog's collar with one powerful hand. Probably somewhere in his early thirties, he was bare from the waist up, exposing a thickly muscled torso and massive shoulders. A shock of coarse black hair grew low on his forehead, his face was smooth and bronzed, his nose slightly flattened, his mouth full and wide.

With disbelief, she noticed that he held a spear in the other hand.

But it was his eyes that nearly mesmerized her. As black and flinty as obsidian, they radiated hate. A hate so palpable that she gasped and took a trembling step backward.

Unable to move, she watched in mounting fear and astonishment as he stuck his tongue out and began rolling his eyes, an absolutely ferocious expression on his heavy face. What was going on with him—was he crazy? Crazy or not, he sent shivers of fear all along her spine as he began a rhythmic, stamping dance. She didn't dare move, as he increased the rhythm, his gestures becoming more and more frenzied, a wild chant coming from his contorted mouth—a chant so eerie that the hair on the back of her neck prickled.

Suddenly he lunged toward her, spear at shoulder height. Her heart nearly stopped beating, then raced wildly. She felt the color drain from her face, and knew her legs weren't going to hold her. That she didn't run wasn't due to courage; she had frozen into immobility. She couldn't even scream.

The spear stopped about a foot from her face, then plunged into the ground at her side. The man pulled it easily from the earth, glared at her again, then he and the dog turned and disappeared around the corner of the house.

She stood there until she could breathe again and get her trembling muscles under control. She didn't believe what had just happened. Who was this man and why had he made that hideous threat?

One thing was certain; she no longer need wonder about her reception. Someone had just made his feelings perfectly clear.

Well, she had news for him. She wasn't a child to be frightened away. She clenched her jaw with renewed determination. When she was sure her legs would hold her, she took a deep breath and moved up onto the veranda, then raised her hand to knock on the door.

Chapter 2

Before the ornate brass knocker could touch the wood, the door opened silently. Kiri, hand still raised in the air, stared at the woman in front of her—a woman who stared right back with dark, noncommittal eyes. She had opened the door so quickly that she must have been aware of Kiri's progress up the path—perhaps she had even watched from a window.

Although still shaken by her encounter with the half-naked man, Kiri made a quick assessment. The woman was possibly in her fifties, although it was difficult to tell; she looked ageless. She was slightly shorter than Kiri's own five foot seven, and the flowered cotton dress she wore flattered her slender figure, which, although thickened somewhat around the waist, was still supple and attractive. Her soft brown skin was unlined, her black hair showed not a hint of gray, and her expression, as she watched Kiri's face, revealed nothing.

She certainly wasn't a chatterer, Kiri decided, feeling somewhat at a loss, as the woman waited silently for her to speak. This must be the woman whom the lawyer, Mr. Marston, had said lived on the island. She revised her supposition that the woman might be a housekeeper; she appeared poised and at ease, an extremely reserved hostess greeting a guest.

"Hello," Kiri said, holding out her hand. "I'm Kiri MacKay. I hope Mr. Marston told you I was coming, I certainly don't want to just barge in. Perhaps I should have called you myself, but I wasn't certain just what the situation was here...."

Her words trailed away as the woman gave her a slight, ironic smile and took her hand in a cool grasp, releasing it quickly. "There's no problem about that, Kiri. I hope you had a pleasant trip. Please come in. I'm Neiri—" The woman gave her an intent look. "You look a little upset. Is something the matter?"

Was there genuine concern in the woman's voice, Kiri wondered, as well as slight maliciousness? If Neiri had been standing by the window watching her arrival, she'd probably seen everything that had happened. Kiri realized that she was still trembling slightly from her recent encounter, and supposed she looked a little pale. "I was just a little surprised, that's all," she managed to say. "There was a man on the porch, and he made, well, I guess you'd call them threatening gestures—"

She broke off at Neiri's quick smile. "Oh, that's just Rapauru, my son. Don't pay any attention to him. I'm sorry he frightened you, but he really didn't mean anything. Those threatening gestures are just the traditional Maori challenge to visitors, a reenactment of an old-time welcome ceremony, but Rapauru should have realized you wouldn't know that."

Kiri repressed a shudder, remembering the anger in the man's eyes. He knew, all right; he had meant to frighten her. But she managed to smile at Neiri.

''Perhaps—but I think it might give any visitor pause, if that's the usual greeting. Anyway, I guess Mr. Marston definitely told you to expect me!''

Neiri laughed softly, but Kiri thought she caught a hint of sadness in the tone. ''Oh, yes, we've been expecting you. I think you'll find everything in order.''

Kiri wasn't at all sure how to phrase the next question, but Neiri was volunteering very little, and she was curious about the woman's status. She spoke hesitantly. ''I didn't have a very long talk with Mr. Marston, mostly signing papers and instructions on what I should do next. Perhaps there are things I should know. He mentioned that you and your son were living here, but he didn't tell me much else. . . .''

The woman shrugged delicate, expressive shoulders. ''Perhaps he wasn't sure just how to explain us. After all, we have no legal status, and I suppose to a lawyer, that causes problems. Rapauru and I came here with your father twenty years ago. . . I loved him very much.''

She turned to look at Kiri, her eyes moist with tears, and suddenly she understood everything. This was her late father's mistress! No wonder she seemed so much at home. This *was* her home! She caught her breath, unable to think of a thing to say, but what was unsaid was in both their eyes, lingering in the air like a dark cloud. Kiri had arrived to take away the woman's home.

''Is—is Rapauru his son?''

Neiri shook her head. ''I was married before I met Ian—to a Maori. But Ian treated Rapauru as his son.'' The words were definitely a challenge.

Kiri stared at her. Here was an entire family she hadn't known a thing about. And a family who had every reason to hate her.

Neiri broke the uncomfortable silence. ''Your father spoke of you sometimes, Kiri. I'm glad to have the chance to meet you.''

Kiri felt the familiar flash of bitterness, perhaps more acute because of the twinge of guilt she'd experienced when she understood Neiri's relationship to her father. Unspoken words raced through her mind: *What did he say about me? That years ago he left some unclaimed baggage in another land?* She managed to keep her voice cool and even.

"I hardly knew him, but please accept my sympathy, Neiri. I do hope I'm not inconveniencing you terribly. I'd hoped to stay here until things were settled, but I hadn't realized exactly—"

"It's not at all inconvenient," the woman cut in. "And it is your home now. I've already arranged to leave—in fact, I'm expecting my brother here any minute to take me to Rotorua. My family lives there," she added.

Kiri suspected that the woman was making every effort to keep her face expressionless, but Neiri couldn't quite control the shadow that passed over her features, and Kiri felt a swift flash of compassion. Neiri's life must be turned upside down by her arrival. She had lived with Ian for twenty years, certainly had a right to expect something from him when he died, and now a complete stranger had arrived—an intruder—and her life was shattered.

"Don't do anything hasty," Kiri said impulsively. "We'll need to talk about things, make some arrangements." She wasn't sure what there was to talk about—certainly she didn't plan to renounce her inheritance, but perhaps she could do something for Neiri. Kiri wasn't a monster. Naturally, she wouldn't just turn the woman out with nothing.

As her father had done, she thought, unable to meet the woman's eyes.

The woman shrugged, cutting off the discussion, and motioned her on into the marble foyer. "Forgive my manners—I shouldn't have left you just standing in the doorway. You'll want to look the place over, inspect your room." Her voice was cool; the moment of intimacy was gone.

She would have to wait until later to talk to Neiri, Kiri decided. Obviously it would be too painful to discuss everything right now, and the woman was right—the doorway wasn't the place in which to do it. She glanced around the foyer, getting an impression of glowing color and polished wood. Neiri was acting the perfect hostess, but Kiri now suspected what it must be costing her. She followed the woman's erect back, as Neiri moved away down the corridor that apparently divided the house.

Neiri paused in front of a door and stood aside for her to enter, but Kiri hesitated. She couldn't drop the subject just yet.

"Neiri," she said slowly, carefully choosing her words, "all of this is new to me, too. His death was so sudden—there have been so many surprises. But we'll talk as soon as we can about your situation...."

The woman's black eyes snapped and Kiri realized her choice of the word *situation* had been tactless. "My plans are made," Neiri said stiffly. "There's no reason to concern yourself."

"Neiri, please don't make any immediate decisions. I'd really like you to stay awhile."

Her voice must have conveyed her sincerity, because Neiri's expression softened, but she was still adamant. "I've no reason to stay now," she said. Kiri, who had expected bitterness, detected only infinite sadness. She gave Kiri a half smile, and her eyes glinted. "My son feels differently, though."

"I'll bet he does." Kiri said dryly, remembering the hate that had radiated from the young man's eyes.

"Don't worry about Rapauru," Neiri said softly. "He's like a lot of the young people these days, obsessed with finding his roots, trying to turn back time to the old days. As I explained, that posturing you saw was just the old Maori welcome, the way the warriors greeted visitors. It doesn't mean anything these days."

If that was a welcome, Kiri wondered what the young man would have done if she were unwelcome! The thought sobered her. She *was* unwelcome; she was just beginning to realize how unwelcome, and she really couldn't blame them. Nevertheless, she wasn't the culprit. It was Ian who had apparently left them high and dry. And left her to inherit only because he had procrastinated and hadn't left a will.

"Naturally, Rapauru can stay on in the house, too, until—"

"Oh, he doesn't stay in the house," Neiri interrupted. She took a deep breath, as though putting aside unhappy thoughts, and spoke with determined cheerfulness. "But come, take a look at your room. I made it up especially for you. I hope you like it."

Neiri flung open the door to a light, spacious room, and for a moment the sight drove the uncomfortable conversation and her curiosity about where Rapauru stayed from her mind. She felt as though she were stepping into a flower garden. A riotous mix of blooming plants hung on both sides of a long row of windows that opened out onto a private patio. The flowers were repeated in the furnishings of the room, with inside and outside blending into one charming vista.

Dropping her bags, Kiri crossed to the wide bed that was covered with a delicate floral print in various shades of pinks and greens, and ran her hand over the satiny finish. She looked slowly around, taking in the soft chair covered in the same material, and admiring the elegant kauri-wood desk along one wall. Mirrors covered a third wall, reflecting the soft pink of the rug and the green of the foliage, creating the impression that the room was double the size.

Correctly reading the expression on her face, Neiri gave her a genuine smile . "I had hoped you would like it."

"Oh, yes, it's beautiful," she breathed. She didn't mention the wistful emotions the room evoked in her. It was lovely, but it didn't fit her personality. It was made for someone much more feminine, more pliant, than herself. Her assessment of herself was that she was all angles and intensity, her taste running more to the severely tailored, and this was a dreamscape. In a seductive setting like this, she would have to be careful to keep both feet firmly on the ground.

As Neiri started toward the door, Kiri remembered the interrupted conversation and stopped her with a question. "Where does Rapauru live, if not here? I didn't know there was another house on the island."

"There isn't—it's not exactly a house." Neiri's eyes were suddenly veiled. "Ian allowed Rapauru to build several little huts, a replicated Maori village really, along the beach. He lives there most of the time and on weekends he's joined by several other young men." She smiled wryly. "They are all determined to return to the old ways. That's all they can talk about. I think it's a losing battle, although I understand how they feel."

A replicated village. Kiri frowned thoughtfully, trying to remember what she knew of the Maoris. A warrior culture, she thought, never completely subdued, although she didn't think they were violent anymore. As far as she knew they had been all—or almost all—successfully absorbed into modern culture. She'd have to learn more about them. Suddenly she remembered Noel's cryptic remark about things not always being as peaceful as they seemed, and she wondered if he had been referring to Rapauru's village.

She brought her attention back to Neiri; she was her first concern. There was no disguising the anguish in the woman's eyes, and she supposed she could think of something to do for her. At least, she couldn't allow her to leave immediately, not until they had talked things over. Impulsively, she held out her hand.

"Neiri, please, you mustn't do anything in a hurry. Won't you stay for a few days, just until we can sort something out?"

Ignoring Kiri's hand, Neiri glanced around the room, as though memorizing the scene for darker days, then looked back at Kiri. "There's no reason to prolong things," she said softly, but Kiri detected a hesitancy in her voice. "My brother expects me, and postponing my departure will just make it worse...."

"This has happened so suddenly, for both of us," Kiri protested. "You must take your time..." She was becoming increasingly uncomfortable. She had been so excited when she heard about the inheritance that she hadn't thought about the ramifications, hadn't dreamed there might be other people intimately involved. She had certainly never expected to evict anyone.

Neiri's bottom lip trembled, and Kiri pressed her advantage. "Just a few days. I'd really like to have someone here to show me the ropes, and you can tell your brother you're just putting things off for a while, not making a firm decision."

Again Neiri glanced around the room, and Kiri understood her conflict; the fierce pride that wouldn't let her stay where she had no legal right, the anguish that came from leaving the home that had been hers for so many years.

The silence dragged on; finally the woman shrugged. "Well, perhaps I'll wait for a few days. Just long enough to settle you in, show you where things are..." She made a helpless little gesture and turned to walk away down the hall.

Watching her, Kiri felt as though she had kicked a harmless puppy. Why hadn't that darned lawyer prepared her for this? She thought of Mr. Marston, a tall gray man in a gray suit, a voice that sounded like paper crackling, and supposed she knew why he hadn't told her about Neiri. He knew the law, the law was his life, and he probably didn't quite know how to categorize relationships such as Ian's and Neiri's. Perhaps, to him, she *was* just a woman living on the island.

Unfortunately, Kiri couldn't feel that way. There had been too much emotion in Neiri's face when she spoke of her home, too much love when she mentioned Ian's name.

Had Marston neglected to mention anything else? Might there be other surprises in store for her? This one was a doozy.

Sighing, she began to unpack, trying to sort out her confusion along with her clothes. Why wasn't anything ever simple? Her emotions had been chaotic enough as she tried to come to terms with accepting the estate from a man she had never known, a man who had ignored her, and whom she *knew* would not knowingly have left her a thing. Now she found another complication. He had left nothing to the woman who obviously loved him and whom he had presumably loved. Why else would they have lived together so long? And why had he done such a callous thing?

She straightened her shoulders and set her mouth in a thin line. Because he was the man he was. Irresponsible. He had left her when she was a child; why should she expect him to treat anyone else differently? Family, people who loved him, all that meant nothing to him. He didn't even care enough to make a will.

If only he *had* left a will, she thought, setting her mouth in a thin line at the pain that surged through her. If she could believe that he wanted her to have Long White Cloud, she would feel differently, perhaps. Now, she had inherited by default, and was displacing people who undoubtedly felt bewildered and angry. Was it fair?

But was it fair that she have nothing? The money would mean so much to her—the only chance she might have to follow her dream. Sculptors didn't make much money. To be a serious sculptor, she needed the means to live while she devoted her energy to her art. She deserved happiness as much as anyone.

Another niggling little thought pushed its way in. Was there another reason she wanted the money? Revenge, perhaps? To wrest something from her father who had given her so little? But she couldn't be that kind of person! Giving up for the moment, she flung herself face down on the bed.

The remainder of the day did little to alleviate her uncomfortable feeling that she was an intruder. Under Neiri's direction, she toured the house, talked to Mrs. Armi, the rotund and pleasant cook, then took a quick look around the grounds. She didn't see Rapauru, but from the occa-

sional tingle that skittered down her back, she suspected he
knew exactly where she was. The thought was unsettling. He
was a different sort of problem to the one she faced with
Neiri; when and how could she deal with him?

Neiri left her to go to her room, and for a few moments
she wandered aimlessly around the house, picking up an
object, putting it down, wishing she hadn't come here until
everything was settled. Then, deciding she needed to get
outside and let the wind blow away her depression, she
walked out into the yard. It was still early afternoon and the
sun was high in the cloudless sky. She would have plenty of
time to explore the island before darkness fell.

Relieved at the prospect of some strenuous activity, she
struck out briskly, following a well-marked trail that led
from the house, and soon found herself in the midst of what
seemed like a jungle. Everything was lush and green. She
brushed against giant ferns that reached out to her from
each side of the trail, and paused occasionally to stare upward at huge trees that climbed to block out the sun, leaving the path in deep shade. The din was nearly deafening, as
cicadas called shrilly to one another, and unknown birds
shrieked alarm at her approach.

Ignoring slight feelings of claustrophobia as the path led
ever upward, she followed it blindly, trusting it would soon
lead to a clear spot where she could get her bearings. For
over an hour she walked, at last falling into the rhythm of
physical activity, although the exercise did little to raise her
spirits. The internal debate raged. If she hadn't actually met
Neiri, she wouldn't have felt so badly about being the one
responsible for the woman losing her home.

Then she rejected the thought angrily. She wasn't responsible; it was Ian. She wouldn't give in to sentimentality. Legally and morally, the estate was hers.

She was breathing heavily when she reached the outcropping of stone at the very crest of the mountain. From this
vantage point she could see the entire shoreline of Long
White Cloud. Long and narrow, it was roughly the shape of

New Zealand itself. To the east the gentle sea lapped against white sand. Farther along, deep inlets cut into forested hills, making perfect harbors for boats. The western side where she stood was much wilder; the rocky cliff dropped nearly one hundred feet to where water dashed against dark rocks in endless, angry frustration.

Although the sun was still high, a shiver made her clasp her arms across her chest, Noel Trevorson's comment coming suddenly to mind: Long White Cloud had both its light side and its dark side.

She peered into the forest, trying to discern the huts that Neiri told her were on the shoreline, but they were effectively camouflaged with dense vegetation. Then, as her gaze wandered along the shoreline, she stiffened.

A white sail bobbed in a cove a few hundred yards away. Although she couldn't make out the details from this distance, and although she wasn't too familiar with boats, she recognized this one instantly. The *Island Princess*.

Her pulse quickened with pleasure, which she almost instantly suppressed. She had never expected Noel's boat to be here; she was certain he hadn't said anything about anchoring off the island.

Someone was moving around on deck. She took her binoculars from her pocket and raised them to her eyes. That brought him so close that she had a momentary illusion that she could reach out and touch him. Even the intent expression on his lean, bronzed face was perfectly clear. He was frowning slightly as he bent to coil a rope, then straightened and fastened it to a hook. The sight of him bending like that, outlining muscles along his back and legs, pulling his shorts tight across his thighs, caused a strange tightness in her throat.

She tossed her head, shaking away the momentary lapse of sanity. It was definitely Noel Trevorson. Why was he anchored just offshore? Although he hadn't said specifically when he'd dropped her off at the pier, she'd had the definite impression he was leaving the island.

She wrinkled her forehead, trying to recall the exact conversation. An impression that he was leaving was all she'd had, she realized. In fact, she knew very little about him. In the short time they had been together, he had learned much more about her than she had about him, she thought, suddenly uneasy.

Wrestling with the puzzle, she continued to watch him, although she knew she probably should leave or somehow make her presence known. Still she didn't move. She felt a little like a voyeur. It gave her a strange, tingling feeling, a feeling of intimacy, to watch him move about the boat, intent on his chores, completely unaware that he was being observed.

And she enjoyed watching him. He was lean, she thought, her gaze going over his long, well-muscled legs, his bronzed chest, his bare brown feet that moved smoothly over the deck. She wondered where he had put his knit shirt, then saw it slung casually over the wheel; apparently it was just for when he had company. Again she felt the tug of his attractiveness. He was a type she didn't see often. No bulging muscles, no masses of chest hair, he had the body of a runner, built for strength and endurance, not weight lifting, she thought, smiling slightly. He moved about the boat with easy confidence, making her suspect he was accustomed to doing things his own way.

Immersed in her assessment, she was startled when he suddenly looked up. She caught the flash of his electric-blue eyes and felt a definite shock, as though she had been singed with an intense electric current. Instinctively, she jumped back. The contact seemed almost physical. Her cheeks burned, and she stumbled backward into the concealing trees. He couldn't have recognized her from that distance. He was much too far away, and she must have imagined that intimate look.

Sure that she couldn't be seen now, she glanced at her watch. She didn't want to stay here; even though she was well-concealed, she still felt vulnerable. She had a feeling he might sense she was here. Still, she didn't need to start back to the house for another half hour or so; she might as well continue exploring—on the other side of the island. She didn't want Noel to think she was spying on him.

But who was he and what was he doing anchored just off the island? There was no reason he shouldn't be here, she supposed, but why hadn't he casually mentioned it? Perhaps he had just stopped on impulse, decided to stay the night before sailing on to wherever he belonged.

Just where did he belong? She had asked him where he lived, she remembered, and he had said that he was a vagabond, then casually changed the subject. Had he deliberately evaded her question?

Perhaps she shouldn't read too much into his unexpected appearance. Although the island was private property, there was no prohibition against anyone anchoring in the innumerable little inlets and coves, as far as she knew. This was just a chance encounter; she probably wouldn't see him again.

Another chance encounter. The thought was sobering. He had been available in Paihia to ferry her to the island, but that wasn't necessarily incriminating. She had never heard of him, and he had no reason to suspect she would show up in Paihia at that particular time. Even supposing he *had* maneuvered to be there when she arrived, she couldn't see what he had gained.

She skuffed her toe in the moist earth, and frowned. His being on the dock at exactly the right time was just a fortuitous coincidence. Another coincidence. She bit her lip, glancing back over her shoulder to the small inlet, now hidden by foliage. She wasn't sure what caused the uneasiness that curled along her nerves to the pit of her stomach; was it because of her doubts about his motives—or her unsettling pleasure in seeing him again?

Noel Trevorson was aware of the exact moment that Kiri stepped back from the promontory into the cover of the trees. Squinting into the sun, he lounged against the railing of his boat and thoughtfully surveyed the spot where she had been. He had known she was watching him for some time, but his glance in her direction must have frightened her off.

Although he'd had only an impression of a slender, dark-haired woman silhouetted against the sky, he had recognized her at once. In her proud stance, the quick way she moved, he detected a vibrant energy, a pent-up force of some kind, that was unmistakable. A force that might be interesting when released, a force that almost tempted him to find out for himself.

Although he couldn't make out her features from where he stood, they were etched in his memory. Interesting. Alive. Changing with each emotion. Under any other circumstances, he might have been moved to explore the possibilities.

But he certainly didn't intend to explore anything about her. He wanted nothing to do with her. Marston had notified him that she would be arriving, and, with uncharacteristic impulsiveness, he had decided to get a good look at her without revealing who he was. Size her up, see what decisions he must make. The lawyer might have known what her plans were, but he hadn't informed Noel. If she were the kind of person he suspected she was—a cold heartless woman who hadn't even come to her father's funeral, arriving on the island only when there was money to be had—he would just move on, cut his losses. There was nothing he could do.

He shook his head in total disbelief. How could his old friend have done such a thing? For the hundredth time since Ian's death, Noel tried to fathom why the man hadn't made a will. It wasn't like him; he was organized to the point of obsession. Had he realized that without a will everything would go to his daughter? It seemed unlikely; he hadn't even mentioned a daughter until shortly before his death, and then, although his voice had been slightly wistful, he hadn't mentioned any plans to see her. There was certainly no love on her side; she had neglected him for years, didn't even come to his memorial service.

He had wanted to assess her, and he had done so. Although she wasn't quite what he had expected—he was still perplexed by that haunted, vulnerable look that occasionally appeared in her eyes—he had learned enough to know there was no reason for him to remain on the island. She planned to sell, and that was that.

His jaw tightened. What a calamity, what a blow to his hopes. This island shouldn't belong to any one person. It was the heritage of every New Zealander, Maori and *pakeha* alike. He and Ian had agreed on the dream: turn the place into a wildlife preserve, keep it pristine and unpolluted for future generations. Ian had been excited about the idea, and Noel knew very well that if his friend had made a will, that is exactly what it would have decreed. Instead, the island would be sold and a carpetbagging stranger would make off with part of his birthright.

Yet she didn't seem as crass, as hard, as he had expected, he thought, suddenly uneasy. And she was an attractive stranger. He had watched her start down the pier at Paihia and had deliberately turned away so she wouldn't suspect he was waiting for her. At that first sight, she had seemed unprepossessing. Then she had raised her head, and he had a look at those emerald eyes. Something hit him in the pit of the stomach, and he had immediately changed his assessment.

He shoved his hands into the pockets of his shorts and stared angrily at the gulls squawking and squabbling around the rocks at the foot of the cliff several yards up the shoreline from his anchorage. What difference did it make whether she was attractive or not? She was still an interloper. The sensible thing to do was weigh anchor and get out of here, forget all the hopes he'd had for the island and start anew, as Neiri was doing.

He glanced into the forest, unable to see the huts along the shore, but knowing they were there. Another dream gone. Ian had been as excited as Rapauru when the young Maori had conceived the idea of replicating an old Maori village and reviving some of the crafts of his people. Whoever bought the island would hardly take the same point of view.

A frown wrinkled his forehead. Rapauru wouldn't give up without a fight. His hot temper would fuel his determination and he would have plenty of backing. Among the younger Maori, the movement to reclaim the land was gaining strength. So far it had been a peaceful protest, and Noel hoped it always would be, but he knew there were fringe elements who stood ready to exploit any situation. Would Kiri's arrival and her threat to the island push Rapauru over into their camp?

Sighing, he shifted his weight as the *Island Princess* moved in the freshening breeze and the deck tilted. The sun would soon be down. He should open a can of something for supper, although he wasn't enthusiastic about it. In the years he had worked with Ian it had become a habit to have his evening meal with his mentor at the main house, but now his friend's place had been usurped by a stranger.

His throat tightened and he felt a suspicious stinging behind his eyes. How he missed the old man. Ian MacKay had been more of a father to him than his own biological parent had ever been.

He knew Ian wouldn't approve at all of what was happening. Did he have the right to run away, or should he stay and do what he could to see that his late friend's wishes were respected? Should he confront Kiri, test her resolve?

It was the least he could do. The decision made, he climbed through the hatch and down into the spacious cabin. Whistling softly, he stepped out of his shorts and headed for the miniscule shower. He turned on the water just long enough to wet himself, then soaped, rinsed off, turned off the shower head and reached for a towel.

He rubbed himself briskly, a half smile on his face, his mind far away at the villa. He was inviting himself for dinner.

She probably didn't expect any opposition at all to her takeover, and he would let her know it wouldn't all be clear sailing. He wasn't sure what he could do, but he had to try. Besides, he looked forward to seeing the expression on her face when he unexpectedly appeared; it should jolt her a bit, cause those magnificent eyes to widen in surprise.

The thought of her eyes made him suddenly uneasy, almost made him question his motives in going to the house. Deep, glowing emeralds, they shone in her face with warmth and intelligence. They didn't tally with what he knew of her, made her a puzzle he wanted to solve.

Made him want to see her again.

Chapter 3

Kiri paused in the archway that opened into the dining room, her eyes going immediately to the tall man standing by the fireplace. She barely stopped her hand from flying to her throat, and her eyes opened wide. Noel Trevorson. Lean and assured and devastatingly attractive. And becoming more and more of an enigma. Was he going to turn up everyplace?

She was suddenly, absurdly glad that she had changed before coming to dinner, and that her silk pantsuit was in the vibrant shade of emerald green that matched her eyes.

Immediately, she brushed the thought away, determined to be on her guard. She doubted very much that he was here to look at her eyes. Running into him three times in one day was a little too often to ascribe to even the most blatant chance.

She had expected only Neiri would join her for dinner, and seeing Noel was a definite shock. In spite of her wariness, her heart raced, as her gaze locked with that of the tall man who regarded her with eyes that gave nothing away. He seemed completely at ease, one elbow propped nonchalantly on the marble mantelpiece, as he swirled pale amber sherry in a delicate stemmed glass. Her throat tightened a little as she noticed the contrast of his strong bronzed fingers against the fragility of the crystal. Fingers that might trail lovingly, tenderly over delicate white skin, fingers tipped with fire...

She shook her head slightly, as though the physical action would rid her of the uncomfortable thought. What kind of a subconscious did she have, anyway, to have such fantasies about a man she didn't even know? She forced herself to look at him objectively. It didn't help much.

He was dressed much more formally than he had been on the other two occasions when she had seen him, but he looked every bit as sexy in his perfectly tailored beige twill trousers and white dress shirt open at the throat. She returned her gaze to his eyes, and saw that under his studied casualness, he was watching her warily.

She was the one who should be wary, she thought, with a wry inward smile, wary of that indefinable current of awareness leaping between them. She had felt it when he ferried her from Paihia to the island, although she had nearly convinced herself she was imagining it. It had sizzled between them when she had caught his eye as she looked down on his boat, and it had caused her to draw back in confusion and hide herself in the foliage. She was determined to ignore it; physical involvement was the last thing she needed in her present situation.

The inexplicable attraction wasn't the only reason to beware of him, either. The other two times she had seen him could have passed as coincidence. This was not. The implications were unnerving.

No one had ever been aware of Kiri's emotions unless she wished it so; she was proud of that fact. She arranged her face into a pleasant smile and took a step into the room, still holding his gaze.

"Hello, Noel, this *is* a surprise. Neiri should have told me we were having company for dinner."

Noel placed his glass carefully on the mantelpiece, glanced at the glowing kauri table which was set with three places, and smiled. An assured, confident smile, a prince holding court. His attitude triggered an unexpected rush of animosity in Kiri. He was much too sure of himself. When he'd left her on the dock this morning, there had been no indication that she would ever see him again. What was he doing here now, lounging in her dining room, completely at ease?

"Oh, I'm hardly company," he assured her, a slight edge to his voice. "Neiri is used to having me here nearly every evening—she probably just forgot to mention it. And you can see your cook set a place for me. I hope you don't mind."

"Of course I don't mind." He didn't care whether she minded or not, she thought. He was telling her he belonged here. His smile, on the surface so warm and inviting, was belied by his eyes, which weren't warm at all. She had a sudden sense that she, not he, was the intruder, and it shook her hard-won poise.

If it killed her, she wasn't going to let him see that his unexpected presence upset her.

"To tell the truth, I was beginning to feel a little lonesome," she continued, "and you're certainly welcome. Neiri disappeared early this afternoon, and Mrs. Armi has been busy in the kitchen."

She walked into the room, conscious that his eyes followed her every move. When she was within arm's reach of him she stopped and pulled herself to her full height, meeting his eyes with a look of challenge.

"But I *am* surprised. When I saw you last, I got the definite impression you were sailing on to wherever *vagabonds* sail to."

He really had some explaining to do, and she was determined to get an answer this time. He had mentioned this morning that he had known Ian, but had never indicated that he was on such familiar terms with the household. She suspected he had deliberately misled her, although she couldn't think of any reason he should want to do so.

He couldn't know she had seen him anchored off the little island this afternoon, and she hoped he didn't find out. She still felt a little squeamish about having observed him when he'd been unaware of her presence, and she'd nearly convinced herself that the jolt she'd experienced when his eyes had met hers was all imagination. Until now.

He gave a graceful shrug. "I didn't mean to be mysterious. I probably should apologize for breaking in on you this way. I had dinner with your father on so many evenings, it just seemed the natural thing to do."

His eyes met hers in obvious response to her challenge. "I'm sure he wouldn't mind," he said, his voice reminding her of rich warm cream, and his expression of the cat who ate it.

She noticed again that he had a definite accent. His pronunciation—broad a's, neglected r's—betrayed a cultured background that reminded her of the enunciation of British people she had heard being interviewed on TV. Hardly a boat bum.

But it was certainly confusing. The lawyer hadn't mentioned anyone named Noel Trevorson, but that didn't necessarily mean anything. The lawyer had left a lot unsaid. What did mean something was the fact that Noel had obviously let her make a number of assumptions that weren't true. His status on White Cloud must be informal, although he certainly seemed comfortable enough here, she thought, as Noel turned to retrieve his glass of sherry from the mantel and raised it to his lips, his eyes never leaving hers.

"Will I do?" he asked, a knowing smile on his lips.

A little flustered that her assessment had been so blatant, she turned away.

"I'm sure dinner will be ready soon," she said, ignoring his comment. "Why don't you just make yourself at home?" she added dryly.

His eyes mocked her attempt to ignore whatever was smoldering between them, but his voice was as neutral as hers.

"Why thank you, Kiri. And you might as well sit down and relax, too. Neiri usually doesn't show up until right at dinnertime, and Mrs. Armi won't serve for another half hour."

Again he had moved ahead in the game. Annoyed at being asked to sit down in her own home, she bit her lip, torn between confusion and anger. Of course, it was only her home in a legal sense, but it wasn't his, either, was it? There didn't seem to be anything to do except to follow his suggestion and sit down.

She chose a comfortable wingback chair upholstered in a soft flowered fabric, and Noel sat across from her, long legs crossed at the ankle, one arm resting lightly on the chair.

"I suppose there's no use asking whether our meeting this morning was accidental," she murmured, reaching for the sherry he had poured for her and taking a small sip.

He smiled, and she was struck again by the way his smile changed the cool elegance of his features to pure warmth.

"My, you are suspicious," he replied softly. "Didn't it occur to you that I might be here tonight because I enjoyed your company so much?"

"I'm afraid that explanation never occurred to me," she replied, amused and a little flattered in spite of herself.

"I didn't learn enough about you this morning," he continued easily. "You're a teacher, I believe you said."

"At a community college," she replied. "Painting, sculpture, art appreciation." *But only because I don't have enough money to do what I really want to do,* she added silently. *But now all that had changed.*

"Art appreciation?" Noel smiled. "Do you have to be taught that? I thought you either appreciated beauty or you didn't."

Kiri felt her cheeks flush with anger. To judge from his manner, his accent, Noel was probably born with a silver spoon in his mouth, and he had no idea of the struggle some people went through to better themselves.

"Appreciation is always helped along by a little knowledge," she said stiffly. "I like to think I open avenues to people whose minds might otherwise be closed."

She knew she was being overly stiff and formal, but it was hard to keep the conversation impersonal when he kept staring at her. She rose abruptly from the chair and crossed to the sherry decanter. She didn't want anything more to drink, but it gave her something to do with her hands.

"Sit down, Kiri," he said gently. "I'm sure you're very competent at your job."

She swung to face him, suddenly tired of the intricate dance, the evasions, the unspoken words. She had never believed in indirection. It was best to come straight to the point.

"Noel, what's going on? I'm not at all sure our meeting this morning was an accident—"

"In the larger sense, is anything ever an accident?" His tone was mocking.

"And don't be metaphysical." She shot him an indignant glance. "Just exactly what is your interest in me?"

"My interest in you?" He raised his glass in an ironic gesture. "You don't buy the answer that I'm overwhelmed by you, can't stay away?"

"No." Although wouldn't it be nice if that was true? she thought, before she could stop the errant idea. She had never overwhelmed anyone. She'd always known that her intensity, her direct manner, her uncompromising integrity, was a turnoff to the men she met.

"Well, you'd be right," he admitted. "I'm more interested in what you intend to do to Long White Cloud, now that you've inherited Ian's estate." He stared moodily into his glass. "You're really somewhat of a surprise, you know. I didn't even know Ian had a daughter until a few days before he died."

"Neither did Ian." Immediately she wished her tone had been less bitter.

He sat straight up in his chair and leaned toward her, his eyes widening slightly. "You mean he didn't know about you until recently?"

She saw the suspicion flare in his eyes and answered quickly. "I didn't mean he didn't know I existed. Just that he ignored me for years, and to suddenly leave me his estate—"

"He didn't exactly leave it to you," Noel cut in. "He told me he planned to make a will. I think he made one. I don't know that you figured into it at all."

"He told you!" she exploded. "I'm getting tired of everyone knowing more about my own father than I do. Just who are you, and don't give me any more evasions. How are you involved? No one has ever mentioned you to me."

He shrugged. "We're pretty close to even, aren't we? I've known and worked with your father for years without hearing you mentioned until very recently. Three years ago, when he got the idea of turning the island into a wildlife preserve, he asked me to come and help him. I'm a wildlife biologist and I have several studies going on Long White Cloud. Ian and I were working together."

So that was why he was anchored just off the island. It wasn't just Neiri and Rapauru; Noel lived here, too. Another complication. Perhaps a problem.

She gave him a slight smile. "Somehow, you don't seem like a wildlife biologist."

For the first time his laughter reached his eyes. "That's exactly what my father said when he wanted me to go into the family business. Only he put it more forcefully."

"Your father? Tell me about your family." It appeared that this man might become an adversary, and she needed to know as much about him as she could.

He shrugged. "Pretty uneventful, I'm afraid. They own a shipping business in Auckland. I'm the oldest son, educated in England, groomed to take over. But my interests were elsewhere and they finally accepted it." He paused, his eyes shadowed with memory, then grinned. "Besides, my brother is much better at making money than I am."

She regarded him gravely, adding the things she suspected he had left out. Old New Zealand aristocracy, probably. A family fight when he refused to fit the established mold. It must have taken dedication to pass up a privileged life he had apparently been born to. He had depth, character. Suddenly she liked him more than she had expected to.

Perhaps he couldn't help that attitude of his that bordered on the arrogant—it was innate! And she was touched by the genuine affection in his voice when he spoke of her father. A sense of loss suddenly enveloped her, a wave of painful envy. There had been a closeness between the two men that she would never know.

"You liked Ian," she said simply.

"I loved him." He was silent a moment, then gave her a hard stare. "And I can't believe he would have wanted what you are going to do to this island."

The die was cast. They were at war. "How do you know what I'm going to do?"

"It's obvious, isn't it?" He turned from her to watch the amber liquid swirl in his glass, tilting it gently to catch the light from the candelabra, a faint smile on his lean face.

Not a friendly smile, she decided.

"But then, how could you have any feeling for this place," he continued, almost as though he were speaking to himself. "You'll sell, of course. Take the money and run."

"Exactly," she said shortly, stung at his assessment, even though it was true. "Mr. Marston says I will have the entire estate, whatever you may think about a will." She lifted her chin in cool defiance. "I can do whatever I wish."

"And what you wish is to destroy an irreplacable treasure for money," he said harshly, springing to his feet in one long motion and glaring down at her. "How can you live with yourself? It's a betrayal of your own father. Ian MacKay thought more of posterity than that!"

"He may have thought a lot of posterity," she retorted, "but he didn't think much about his own family."

For a long moment they stared at each other, each unwilling to be the first to look a way. Noel's opinion of her was obvious in his expression and it angered her. He thought her a crass, insensitive woman, grasping for an inheritance that she had only acquired by default. He obviously thought it grossly unfair—and in a way she agreed with him.

But that didn't matter. Even to herself she couldn't explain what the estate represented to her. Justice, perhaps. Vindication. The freedom to follow her dream.

"I see you two are getting acquainted."

Kiri whirled at the sound of the soft voice, and saw Neiri poised in the archway, a faint smile on her handsome face. Dressed in a long slim skirt with geometric patterns along the hem, and a matching scarlet blouse that bared her smooth brown shoulders, she looked as exotic as one of the strange flowers Kiri had noticed blooming along the trail this afternoon.

Immediately, Noel strode forward and grasped her hand between his two large palms, then dropped a light kiss on the crown of her head. Even to a stranger, the affection in the gesture was obvious.

When he released her hand, Neiri touched his cheek gently, moving her finger along the clear line of his jaw. It was an easy, fond, familiar gesture, and Kiri's chest tightened. She had never experienced such warmth from her own mother, even when she was a child, and now that Lois was married to a stockbroker and living in an affluent neighborhood, several miles away, she rarely saw her except for holidays.

Kiri remembered the phone call she had made to Lois just before she had left for New Zealand. Predictably, her mother had reiterated her disapproval of Ian, tempered somewhat by the hope that Kiri might get some money, but there had been no real interest.

"Neiri," Noel was saying, as he put his arm around her and drew her into the room, "I'm glad you decided to stay."

"Nothing's decided," she murmured.

"I know. I ran into your brother as I was coming over this afternoon, and he said he wasn't sure just when he was coming back for you."

Neiri slanted a glance at Kiri. "I'm not sure, either. It all depends."

Kiri never did find out exactly what it depended on, as just then Mrs. Armi scurried into the dining room. She had met the cook this afternoon and had liked the short, round, unpretentious little woman. She bore a platter containing a steaming hunk of roast beef surrounded by roasted onions, potatoes, and carrots, and placed it with a flourish in the middle of the table.

"Dinner's ready," the woman said, reaching up to push back a gray sausage curl from her flushed faced. She darted a look at Neiri, then glanced at Kiri, uncertainty written all over her countenance. "I hope everything is all right."

"I'm sure it is," Kiri said, after a lengthy wait in which Neiri did not reply. Darn the woman. Did she have to make it so obvious she was no longer in charge? She already felt guilty enough for two people.

To Kiri, the dinner went on for an agonizing length of time. She was mostly silent, as Noel and Neiri laughed and talked together, telling anecdotes about Ian, fondly recalling times past. It wasn't that they were rude. She knew they tried to bring her into the conversation, but she still felt like an outsider and it hurt more than she would have believed possible.

She was relieved when Mrs. Armi came to stand in the kitchen door, a worried look on her face, as she twisted her hands in her apron. Neiri looked up.

"Is something the matter, Martha?"

Mrs. Armi glanced at Kiri, then back at Neiri. "Rapauru wants to see you."

"Well, tell him to come on in. There's plenty." Neiri gestured at the half-eaten roast.

"He says he wants to see you alone."

There was a moment of silence. Then Neiri sighed and Kiri glanced down at her plate. The reason for Rapauru's refusal to come into the house was obvious. She remembered the fierce anger she had seen on his face when he had accosted her this morning, and found she was just as glad he planned to stay outside.

"That boy," Neiri said, shaking her head and rising from her chair. "I wish he didn't take things so—so personally."

"That boy" was over thirty years old, Kiri thought. And making his displeasure with her known. She glanced across the table at Noel. "I guess I'm disrupting a family dinner."

"Rapauru doesn't always eat with us," he said quietly. "He has his village, his friends. That's where he spends most of his time. He's more comfortable with his own people. He loved Ian, tolerates me. But that's about as far as it goes."

"His tolerance certainly doesn't extend to me," she said shortly. "I'll be happy if I never see another Maori welcoming ceremony."

He game her an amused look. "I heard about that. You stood your ground."

"I didn't faint, if that's what you mean."

She caught a glint of admiration in his eyes, and it sent a warm glow coursing through her. Kiri's reaction to him confused her. Only Neiri's entrance earlier had stopped what might have become a full-fledged battle between them. The sides were drawn; Noel hadn't actually said so, but she suspected he was going to do everything in his power to thwart her plans for the island. In spite of his charm, and the way her heart raced when he was near, he was the enemy. The man who would try to sabotage her dream.

So why did she welcome his approval?

As though aware of her ambivalence, Noel leaned toward her across the table, his intense blue eyes suddenly gentle and sympathetic. The look was almost a touch, a caress. She couldn't look away. She had never felt this sensation before; light-headed, breathless, her attention a pinpoint of energy directed only at Noel.

The moment was broken by the sound of raised voices coming from the kitchen. Swirling back to reality, Kiri caught the rumbling, angry tones of a man, and the lighter voice of a woman. She couldn't make out the words, but there was no doubt in her mind about what was happening. Neiri and Rapauru were involved in a heated argument. Probably about her.

Noel pushed back his chair. "Maybe I'd better go see what's going on."

Kiri half rose, too, but he motioned her back to her chair and strode from the room. She wasn't sorry to be left alone; she felt as though she had been holding her breath, and now could release it. All evening she had been battered by conflicting emotions—by outrage, sorrow, envy, a piercing sense of loss.

As for Noel—she was glad he was out of the room. He was too vital, too alive, too overpowering for comfort. He kept her emotions on a seesaw. Logically she knew that she should stay as far away from him as possible, that she would get burned if she danced near his flame. But when he had looked at her with eyes so full of understanding, had reached out his hand, when she had nearly drowned in that last long look, she came very near to forgetting that logic.

She glanced at her watch; Noel had been gone for over fifteen minutes. No sounds came from the kitchen, so obviously the quarrel was over, or it had been moved to another site. There was no reason at all to remain here in the dining room; she would go to her room, have a nice soak in a tub, and forget the entire crazy bunch for a few blessed moments.

She had pushed back her chair and was rising to her feet when Noel strode through the door. She caught her breath; she wasn't imagining the crackle and snap of electricity that came with him. His presence charged the entire room.

"Sorry to leave you so long," he said, coming toward her and putting his hand on the back of her chair. "Rapauru was a little upset: I think everything's under control now."

"Where's Neiri?"

"She went to her room."

"I was just going to mine, too." She gave him a wan smile. "It's been a long day. I suppose you can let yourself out?"

He put his hand on her shoulder and turned her slowly to face him. The warmth from his fingers came through the silk, flared along her skin, and tingled along her nerves until it reached deep inside her, suffusing her with trembling uncertainty. When she lifted her eyes to his, she saw that he was regarding her with a mixture of puzzlement and compassion.

He sighed, seemed about to say something, then changed his mind. "I guess I'd better be going, too."

Going where? To his boat, or sailing away? A man on a boat was about as mobile as you could get. "What will you do now?" she whispered.

He dropped his hand from her shoulder, although he still held her gaze. "Now that you're going to sell the island? I'm not sure." Something blazed in his eyes and she suddenly knew how frustrated his father must have felt when he had tried to deflect him from his ambition. "Perhaps I'll stay and try to change your mind."

She was dismayed at the sudden tightness in her chest. His gaze was so intimate that she felt it like a physical touch. Warmth spread over her face, and the palms of her hands were suddenly damp. Just how did he plan on trying to change her mind? The idea involved a number of possibilities. Some delicious.

She took a deep breath, regaining control. It really didn't matter. Her strong affinity for Noel had taken her by surprise, but when she had time to think about it, she knew she was immune to male blandishments. She had learned a long time ago, first by her father's abandonment, then by a man she had dated who had seen her as a challenge, that men were not to be trusted.

"I won't change my mind."

"Well, allow me the pleasure of trying, Kiri." His grin was absolutely wicked. "Kiri. That's an odd name for an American woman. Isn't it Maori?"

"So my mother said. My father insisted on the name." Her lips curved in a bleak smile. "The first and last interest he showed in me."

"I'm sorry, Kiri," he said gently. "It seems so unlike the Ian I knew."

Tears strung at the back of her eyes, but she kept the smile on her face. She had stopped crying about her father years ago; she wasn't going to start now.

"I guess we knew a different man," she said calmly. "But it's getting late. I'll walk with you to the door."

A few minutes later she stood on the veranda and watched Noel disappear into the darkness. There was a poignant softness about the night that brought with it a flash of homesickness. The evening seemed to intensify the fragrance of the flowers and she raised her face and closed her eyes to concentrate on their sweetness. Night sounds were beginning; soft chirping of birds and animals she couldn't identify, the rustle of leaves dancing over her head.

What was she doing here, alone and so far from home?

When she opened her eyes, Noel's tall form was no longer discernible among the shadows of the trees and she turned back into the house, as lonely and confused as she had ever been in her life. What had seemed so simple when she left California was becoming more complicated by the minute.

Had her father really intended to leave the island to the state for a wildlife preserve? Why hadn't he made any provisions for Neiri and Rapauru? Why hadn't he left a will?

Or had he? But if so, where was it? Certainly it wasn't with his lawyer. No, the likelihood was that Ian had been a thoughtless, selfish man, too involved with saving the world to worry about things like love and family.

Idly, she wandered through the quiet house, loath to go to her own room. Everything was different at night. In the daylight, she had been impressed by the lightness and gaiety of the ambiance: highly polished hardwood floors throughout the house marked by glowing oriental rugs that echoed the blooming flowers of the drapes; doors and windows everywhere that opened out onto private decks or gave sweeping views of the bay.

Now the polished floors reminded her of dark deep water, the rugs of little islands. And the windows, which in the daylight opened the house to light and air, now seemed striving to keep out the encroaching darkness of the night.

Perhaps her uneasiness was a result of the resentment she felt all around her. It enveloped her in a gray cloud. But she wouldn't let the opinions of the others bother her.

She ran her hand along the smooth surface of a rosewood desk, fingered the intricate carving on a greenstone Maori statue that presided over the coffee table, then left the living room to move slowly down the hall to her bedroom. There was no reason to be ambivalent; she needed—she deserved—the money that the sale of Long White Cloud would bring. It was the key to her lifelong dream.

It was more likely that Noel was the reason for her unsettled emotions. She had heard of instant attraction, of looking once into someone's eyes and recognizing a potential lover, but she had never really thought the phenomenon was real. Now she knew it was, probably the result of a haphazard collision of chemicals and hormones. And just as meaningless. Nothing to take seriously.

Shaking her head impatiently, she walked back into her room, closing and locking the door behind her. She really would take that long hot soaky bath. There were times when showers just didn't make it. A bath, and a good night's sleep, and she could face tomorrow and do whatever needed to be done to conclude her business.

The lawyer hadn't been able to tell her how much time she'd have to spend here. The impression he'd given her was that things moved slowly when a man died without a will, even if there was only one heir.

Only one heir. She jerked her thoughts back from Neiri and Rapauru. And Noel, who might also be considered a foster son. She couldn't face those thoughts now; she would think about them tomorrow.

She switched on the lamp on the bedside table and reached for the robe that she had flung across the bed earlier. The room blazed with light.

A spasm of terror froze every muscle in her body, as she stared at the object on the bed.

For an endless moment she couldn't breathe. Her pulse pounded in her ears like a war drum. It couldn't be. It was too grotesque. Impossible.

Finally she broke through her paralysis and moved gingerly toward the object, still refusing to believe she saw it. It couldn't be. Lying obscenely right in the middle of the flowered spread. A severed head.

She fought back a tide of nausea, forcing herself closer to the dark object. Her legs were trembling; she wasn't sure how long she could stand.

Then, as she recognized it, she let out her breath in a long quivering sigh of relief. It wasn't an actual head. It was a mask. A very realistic-looking likeness of distorted human features, but a mask.

It must have been fashioned by a master craftsman, she thought, her skin crawling. It was remarkably lifelike, with its tattooed skin and staring eyes, its expression forever frozen in a grimace of pain and fury. Attached to the wooden skull were strands of long, coarse black hair that looked all too real spread out over the pastel pink and green of the bedspread.

As she examined it carefully, her panic subsided, replaced by anger. Who had done this? The thing didn't look quite so real now. It had been the unexpectedness of the sight, the contrast of the dark hair against the soft, flowered material that had elicited the shock of horror. Now it was obviously only a mask, a common artifact among the Maoris. She'd seen pictures of them, and had seen the originals in the museum in Auckland, which she had visited while she had waited for transportation to Paihia.

Her father probably had collected the things. Everyone had said he was interested in preserving Maori history and legend. In fact, now that her heartbeat was approaching normal, she realized she had glimpsed something like it in her father's study when Neiri had taken her on a quick tour of the house earlier, but it had been in the shadows and she'd had only a fleeting glance.

Yes, its presence could be explained. Except for one thing, she thought, her stomach churning. It had been placed there to frighten her, scare her away from the island. Who resented her enough to remove the mask from her father's study and put it right in the middle of her bed?

She controlled a hysterical giggle. Who didn't?

The thought was immediately replaced by another, even more sobering one. Who had had the opportunity? Almost everyone. Neiri had come into the dining room much later than Kiri had, and could easily have removed the mask from the wall and placed it on her bed. Rapauru had been at the house tonight, and she was under no illusions as to how he felt about her.

Even Noel. The thought was like a cold hand clutching her heart. Noel had left the dining room for at least fifteen minutes tonight, plenty of time to go from the study to her bedroom.

Gingerly, she picked up the mask with the tips of her fingers and deposited it on a chair at the far side of the room. She hated to sleep with the thing so near, but she wasn't about to go wandering about the house tonight.

She checked the door to be sure it was locked, then slipped the catch on the French doors that opened out on the patio, realizing for the first time how exposed she actually was. Then she switched off the light and collapsed on the bed, but it was a long time before sleep came.

Chapter 4

If he not been concentrating so intently on the scene he had just left, Noel would never have allowed himself to be taken by surprise. As it was, he jumped back, startled, as the man leapt out of the shadows and planted himself like a tree trunk in the trail in front of him.

"What the hell?" Anger laced his voice, tightened his fists.

Then, even in the dim starlight, he recognized the stalwart figure, and relaxed. Rapauru stood like an ancient warrior barring the way of marauding war parties. A scowl cut across his heavy features, and his meaty hands were clenched belligerently. He wore the ancient Maori dress, a kiltlike affair that ended just above his knees, and his powerful naked chest glistened in the faint illumination.

Noel sighed. Rapauru sometimes carried things a little too far in his effort to roll back time. Noel liked the man, but he sometimes thought the Maori indulged in theatrics.

"Hello, Rapauru," he said mildly. "What are you doing here? The last I saw of you, you were trying to convince your mother to move out of the villa and stay at your village."

"She won't do it," Rapauru growled. "Says she'll visit, but she won't move."

"Maybe she likes running water."

"Ha! What do you know, *pakeha?* She belongs with us."

"Pakeha?" That was the term used for Europeans, and by using it now, Rapauru had put himself and Noel on opposite sides of the fence.

"Ah, Noel, I know you're not like some of the others." Rapauru shifted uneasily. "But this land is Maori land. We were here first."

Noel sighed. "If you're going to turn back time, you can't be so selective. Your ancestors didn't find a vacuum when they came here. They were relative newcomers themselves."

"The land was theirs by right of discovery," Rapauru maintained.

"They fought their way in," Noel replied. "It didn't take them long to eliminate the Moriois." Noel knew that any reference to the primitive peoples that anthropologists believed had inhabited the island before the arrival of the Maoris would enrage Rapauru.

"A lie made up by the *pakeha!"*

Noel shrugged. There was no use arguing. Rapauru was a single-minded activist, intent on a glorious return to the old ways, dedicated to the movement to reclaim the land. Noel knew there had been injustices, and he sympathized with Rapauru, even though he knew the man's goal was unrealistic.

"What are you doing here?" he repeated. "You surprised me, jumping out of the brush like an avenging warlord."

"You should be more alert," Rapauru retorted. "No Maori would allow anyone to slip up on him like that. I've been following you since you left the house."

When Noel was silent, Rapauru shifted impatiently. "Well, what's she like? What did she say, this *pakeha* that's come to take the island?"

Noel hesitated. What was Kiri like? Like a jab in the solar plexis, a woman who seemed able to get right through his defenses without even trying. A woman who couldn't hide the passion that blazed beneath her cool facade. A woman both intense and assertive, who didn't even know that occasionally her eyes betrayed a hurt that made him want to take her in his arms and make everything all right.

But that wasn't what Rapauru wanted to know.

"Just about what you'd expect," he said slowly. "A little confused by the unexpectedness of everything, but basically sound—and plenty stubborn, I'll wager."

It wasn't a satisfactory answer to what Rapauru was asking; it left too much out. Noel had been mulling over that question since he'd left the house and his inability to come up with a definite answer was the reason he had been so deep in thought that he hadn't heard Rapauru's approach.

He shifted his weight and leaned back against the trunk of a kauri tree, vaguely aware of the ridges of rough bark through his thin cotton shirt, and shoved his hands into his pockets. What was Kiri MacKay like? When he had first seen her tonight, standing irresolute in the archway of the dining room, he'd felt such a current of sexual energy crackling between them that he had almost dropped the sherry he was cradling.

Suddenly, he was viscerally aware of her, aware on some elemental primitive level that she was a woman and he was a man.

It wasn't that she was beautiful in the conventional way, with her narrow face, high forehead, prominent cheekbones, wide mouth. She was all angles and smooth planes. That green silk thing she had on accentuated her height, uncompromisingly outlined her small high breasts and narrow waist.

No, it wasn't her physical appearance. Something shone through; she conveyed a sense of presence, a keen intelligence, a cool poise that would have made her stand out in any crowd.

She wasn't his type. He liked women to look like women, curvy and cuddly, liked them to flutter a little. The softness of their figures indicated their temperaments, he suspected—easygoing, lighthearted, amenable to masculine guidance.

This one looked as prickly and assertive as a bunch of Scotch broom.

He'd been attracted to her before, when he'd first seen her on the dock, although he couldn't have said exactly why. But tonight, when she had raised her eyes to meet his, he felt as though he had been slammed against a wall. Perhaps they were intensified by the clothing she wore, but he had never seen anything like her eyes. Emerald green, fringed with long black lashes, they glowed in her narrow face, transforming plainness to beauty. Almost magnetic in their intensity, they flashed with energy and intelligence.

But it wasn't something he could relay to Rapauru. "She's smart," he said. "And determined."

Rapauru grunted, turned, and started walking back down the trail. "We've got to get rid of her."

Uneasy at his tone, Noel moved onto the trail and fell into step beside him. "What do you mean, get rid of her? Don't do anything foolish."

Rapauru snorted and gave him a dark glance from under heavy brows. "She'll ruin everything. Everything I've worked for, planned for, for the island. I would think you'd be with me on this."

"I want her gone, of course. You know how I feel about Long White Cloud. But there's only one way to do it. Find the will."

"You're sure there was one?" Rapauru gave him a sharp glance. "Anyway, that's not the only way to get rid of her."

"It's the only legal way," Noel retorted.

"Legal! *Pakeha* law. Think about it. She's the only heir, and if she were gone the estate would revert to the government."

Noel shot him a quick glance. It sounded like a threat, and although Noel was sure Rapauru would never carry it through, it bothered him.

"You haven't done anything, have you?"

There was a short pause, definitely not reassuring. "Of course not," Rapauru finally said. "But someone should."

"Don't talk nonsense," Noel said sharply. "She's here, and I don't think she's the running type. Even if she did run, she'd still have the island, unless she renounced ownership of it. Besides, there has to be a will. Didn't Ian assure you that you could live in your village forever?"

"Just like you figured you could keep on with your studies," Rapauru grudgingly agreed. "But where is it?"

"Not with his lawyer in Auckland."

"It must be somewhere in the house."

The men walked silently through the night until finally, spotting what seemed to Noel an invisible trail, Rapauru plunged abruptly into the dense forest and was lost to view. Noel continued on until he caught sight of the *Island Princess* floating serenely in the sheltered cove.

As he swung aboard, he realized that he no longer felt the animosity toward Kiri that had consumed him before he met her. Nothing had changed—and everything had changed. Attraction was a pale word for what she aroused in him.

Yet he couldn't let it affect his actions. There were things much more important than his feelings about a woman. Long White Cloud. His in trust. Ian was gone; now it was up to Noel to save it.

He would definitely stay on the island, and do everything he could to persuade Kiri not to sell.

He smiled briefly, a smile that wouldn't have reassured anyone. He wasn't given to false humility. He would do his best—and his best was pretty damn good.

* * *

Kiri stirred uneasily in the unfamiliar bed, momentarily not sure of where she was. Somewhat apprehensively, she opened her eyes and glanced around the room. Sunlight flooded in through the long windows. From the fountain on the patio just beyond her door, the melody of splashing water mingled with the morning cry of birds, and the scent of lavender and wisteria floated in through an open window.

Memory came flooding back, and with it a rush of anxiety. She swung her legs over the side of the bed and stretched out the tips of her toes to reach for her slippers. She didn't look forward to this day. This little island might be the paradise everyone claimed it was, but last night she had seen the Serpent.

She put on a white, terry cloth robe and tied it snuggly around her waist and crossed the room to the chair positioned against the wall. Her fingers trembled slightly, as she pulled off the blanket she had flung across it last night. Her mouth curved in a little grimace of distaste. The carved mask with the tortured features looked terribly incongruous against the peach and green of the satin upholstery.

Gingerly, she picked it up to get a better look. It was intricately carved, a real work of art. Probably every one of those lines meant something. She knew very little about Maori art or history, but she suspected this artifact was ancient indeed.

Holding the mask well away from her body, she walked through her door, down the hall and into her father's study. For an instant she hesitated, gazing around the room. She considered herself a pragmatic, rational woman, but she wasn't immune to the vibrations of the place. Did a person's essence linger on, she wondered, in a room that had been so much a part of him?

For a brief moment she thought she sensed her father's presence. This room, with its shelves of books, warm dark carpet, large rolltop desk, looked as though its owner had just stepped outside for a few minutes.

She had paid only cursory attention when Neiri had toured her through the house yesterday; now she took her time and surveyed the room carefully. A comfortable, masculine room, with a heavy fieldstone fireplace situated in the center of one wall, flanked by a mammoth globe, and a computer station placed to face a window that looked out over the bay.

She swallowed the lump in her throat. The man who used this room must have been complex and fascinating. The old mixed so elegantly with the new, and everything combined to give a feeling of strength and solidity.

A strength and solidity she would never know. He was forever lost to her. She lifted her chin and took a deep breath, ignoring the sting of unshed tears. She had thought she was far beyond that hurt, but being here where he had lived and worked was opening all the old wounds.

She glanced at the walls; a niche between two bookshelves was empty. The space was darker than the surrounding wallpaper and just the right size for the mask. She moved to the wall and hung the mask on the nail that still protruded from the wallpaper. It fit exactly.

So she knew where it had come from, and she could guess why it had been taken from there and placed in her room. Someone wanted to scare her away. At this very moment, that person might be nearby, waiting for her reaction. Waiting for her to panic, to accuse. Well, he would wait a long time. Until she could get some idea of what was behind it, she wouldn't mention it to anyone. Let the culprit sweat a little.

Maybe she'd feel better after she had some breakfast. She entered the kitchen just as Mrs. Armi hoisted a kettle from the stove and began pouring boiling water into a delicate china cup on an engraved tray.

The woman turned to her with a smile. "You're up, miss. I was just going to bring you some tea. Unless you'd rather have coffee?"

Mrs. Armi looked so doubtful at the prospect that Kiri smiled. "Tea will be fine. But you don't have to bring it to me—I'll have it in the kitchen."

Mrs. Armi nodded approval and bustled about the kitchen. Kiri regarded her thoughtfully. She couldn't see this cheerful little woman involved in anything like the mask episode. But she might know a lot about what went on around here.

"Have you worked here a long time, Mrs. Armi?"

"Call me Martha." Her face crinkled in a sweet smile. "I've been here ever since Ian MacKay came to the island, twenty years ago. He and his lady and the boy." She swung to face Kiri. "He loved this place, he did. He'd been around enough to see other parts of the world, and he said he wanted to save one little part of it from destruction. He said Long White Cloud would be kept so our grandchildren could all see what the world used to look like."

Kiri's expression hardened. If Ian had had any grandchildren, he wouldn't have given them any more attention than he'd given her. It was other people's grandchildren he worried about. He could only love people in the abstract.

"Long White Cloud—that's a strange name for an island," she said, anxious to change the subject.

"It's what the Maori call New Zealand," Mrs. Armi replied. "The Land of the Long White Cloud."

"Do the Maori think New Zealand floated down from the sky?"

Mrs. Armi laughed. "Just the opposite. You've heard of Maui, the old hero-god? The one who lassoed the sun to make it go slower? Well, he fished the North Island out of the sea. According to legend, it was originally a giant fish."

Kiri smiled. She had always been fascinated by old legends, especially creation stories, and the Maori myths seemed very interesting. Investigating them would give her something to do while she was on the island—which she hoped wouldn't be very long.

"Where is Neiri this morning?" she asked, as she rose from the table and put her cup in the sink.

"Oh, she was up and out of the house hours ago," the cook replied. "I think she went over to Rapauru's village."

"Then I guess I'll take a little walk around the garden." With Neiri away, Kiri was on her own, and she had no idea how to fill in the day. She stepped out the back door and stood on the veranda, looking into the obscuring density of the woods that crept to within a few feet of the house. Since she would undoubtedly be here for a while, she should figure out a routine of some sort....

She raised her arms in a long, lazy stretch, and then, attracted by movement glimpsed from the corner of her eye, swung toward it. As she recognized the figure, she had a moment's difficulty with her breathing. Noel emerged from the tangle of palms and vines and strode smoothly down the path toward her.

It was strange how the sight of him unnerved her. He looked like a young English lord might have looked, assured, confident, striding over his land—a man who would take what he wanted—in the days before democracy reigned, and such men existed. His hair gleamed in the sunlight, his skin tone was even more darkly bronzed than she remembered it. Bare, well-muscled legs emerged from khaki shorts and he wore a faded blue T-shirt that showed the effects of many washings.

She had seen the muscled chest that was under the shirt, and a thought flashed through her like the flit of a swallow. What would it be like to run her hand over the contours of his bare chest? Unconsciously, she clenched her hands as though they might decide to find out on their own.

She hadn't imagined it; it was all there—the primitive instinctual feeling that she knew this man on some level deeper than intellect. The force of his potent masculinity held her motionless, although she was trembling inwardly. She nearly forgot to breathe, as she watched him come toward her.

With a supreme effort, she jerked her thoughts back into line, trying to ignore that moment of timelessness. She noticed the backpack he had slung over one shoulder, as his easy confident stride brought him closer. Even his casual clothes did nothing to detract from his air of easy elegance.

He flashed her a smile, and she arranged the expression on her face to bid a casual welcome. She must be on her guard. He was too assured, too confident, used to controlling any situation. And he didn't approve of her.

But she was inexplicably glad to see him, just the same.

Noel was thinking nearly the same thing, as he strode along the path toward the veranda. The sight of her standing there, a slender, erect figure in a simple white robe, sent a flash of excitement through him. His chest constricted, his groin tightened. With her dark hair falling loose around her narrow face, her translucent skin innocent of makeup, she looked more vulnerable than she had the night before. She looked like someone he would like to take to bed....

Such thoughts weren't at all welcome. If he was to influence her decision about the island, he had to keep control of his emotions, play her like a violin. Although he didn't think his emotions were involved—it was his hormones that were.

He kept his eyes on her face as he walked toward her. He couldn't read her expression at all, but her eyes were nearly hypnotic. Damn it. If it wasn't for those mesmerizing eyes, he might not be having to fight so desperately to keep a clear head.

He knew one thing. He would never consider her plain again, not after having seen her in animated discussion, not after having been the recipient of her radiant smile.

He didn't consider himself given to fancies, but he had a strange sensation of inevitability as he walked up the path toward her. Of something set in motion that could not be stopped.

Impatiently, he shook the impression off. He and Ian's daughter were on different sides of a very important issue, and he couldn't afford to let down his guard. He knew plenty of pretty women who could give him everything she could, women who could assuage that ache that grew even stronger the closer he came to her. But only Kiri had the power to leave Long White Cloud as it was. She had to be persuaded.

"Hello," she said in her low husky voice that burrowed right into him.

His momentary illusion that she was vulnerable vanished at the sight of her cool smile. She looked so poised, so in command of the situation. No woman could be so sure of herself. It had to be a pose.

"Are you ready?" He shifted his backpack and put one foot up on the lower step.

"Ready for what?" A slight wariness came through in her voice, and it made him feel better.

"Ready for the tour of the island I promised."

She hesitated, her eyes shifted from his, and he felt a flicker of triumph. She wasn't as composed as she pretended.

"I appreciate the thought, but it's really not necessary," she said softly. "I walked all over the island yesterday."

"You couldn't possibly have seen it all." He gave her a keen look, suddenly alert that something wasn't quite right. Now that he was close enough to touch her, he saw that her eyes contained dark shadows, her lips seemed on the verge of trembling. Something in the rigidity of her posture looked almost like fear. Of him? Had something happened? It seemed unlikely.

"Did you get a good night's sleep?" he asked abruptly.

"Oh—Oh, yes . . ." There was too much hesitation in her voice, and her lips parted slightly as though she might confide something; then she apparently changed her mind and avoided his eyes. There was something definitely evasive in that downward glance.

His conversation with Rapauru flashed through his mind. Rapauru had denied trying to frighten her, and Rapauru usually didn't lie. But he felt that something was definitely wrong, something she wasn't going to talk about. He would be patient—but he would find out if there was a problem.

"The mornings are beautiful here," he said. "It's a crime to waste one. Want to get started?"

She shoved her hands into the pockets of the robe—he suspected she was clenching her fists. She was carefully studying his expression. "If you have some hidden agenda about convincing me not to sell..."

He held his hands towards her, palms outward. "No hidden agenda. I love this island, and Ian did, too. I think you should see it as we do before you make a final decision. Besides," he said, deliberately donning his boyishly innocent look that more than one woman had told him should get him locked up, "what else do you have to do today?"

Suddenly she smiled. It was as dazzling as the sun breaking through a cloudbank, and a tight band seemed to squeeze his chest. When Kiri MacKay wasn't being prickly and assertive, she was astoundingly beautiful. He wondered why he hadn't thought so before. Startled by the revelation, he appraised her carefully; perhaps feature by feature, she wasn't beautiful in the way he had always measured feminine beauty—soft, rounded, peaches and cream—her looks were more compelling. Words like striking, dramatic, elegant came to his mind. And something about those spectacular green eyes—something vibrant and exciting that made conventional beauty irrelevant.

She glanced down at her feet, still in slippers, and made a self-conscious attempt to tighten the belt of her robe. Apparently she had just realized how informally she was dressed. "Wait until I put on some clothes," she said, vanishing into the house.

He lounged against the pillar of the veranda, hands in pockets, legs crossed at the ankles, and whistled softly, as he waited for her. So much depended on Kiri MacKay. If he could just make her see the island as he saw it. Probably impossible—why should she go against her own self-interest? But she *was* Ian's daughter; there had to be an altruistic impulse in her somewhere. It was worth a try.

"I've been to the crest of the hill," she said, as they set off on one of the many trails that seemed to intersect the island.

He didn't tell her he knew it. That in his mind he could still see her standing on the promontory, her hands on her hips, the wind blowing her hair away from her face. There were a lot of things about Kiri that were beginning to seem unforgettable.

"Ah, but you saw it through the eyes of a visitor," he said lightly. "Did you notice the indentations in the land where the Maori's had their *pa?*"

"*Pa?*"

"Settlement. Fortress. I doubt there's a high point of land in New Zealand without one. This peak is one of the best sites. You can see enemies coming for miles."

He strode ahead, answering her questions over his shoulder. It would have been much more fun to follow her, so that he could watch the gentle sway of her hips, the movement of her shoulders . . . he shook his head ruefully, deciding to keep up a running commentary in order to distract himself from his thoughts.

"You're going through native forest now. Not much of it left. That's a kauri tree. It's bigger than a redwood, and nearly extinct. And those are *pungas.*" He pointed to large, palmlike trees that grew in profusion at the feet of the larger trees. "Plenty of those. That's what gives this place the look of a tropical forest—"

"What's that beautiful sound?"

"The bellbird. And that unbeautiful sound—that shriek—is the weka."

Kiri trailed after him, only half listening to his words. It was the tone of his voice, his obvious pride in what he was showing her, that impressed her. He was conveying more than words, more than hard facts about flora and fauna. His passion for the place came through in every syllable. When he talked about his island, the patina of sophistication fell away, and he was as excited as a cub scout with a new knife.

Suddenly they broke out of the jungle into a clearing, and Kiri stopped abruptly, her eyes widening. It was as though they had taken a giant step back in time.

A small Maori village stood along the shoreline. She had seen parts of such villages replicated in the Auckland museum, and this certainly looked authentic to her. Her gaze went swiftly over the storehouse with the carved wooden entry, the community meeting house, the sparse scattering of other structures, all behind a stockade of *punga* trunks. Dogs barked, the smell of roasting meat drifted tantalizingly toward her.

She turned to say something to Noel, then froze, as a line of young men seemed to spring from nowhere. Spears in hand, faces contorted, they launched into an intricate dance composed mostly of threatening gestures. Not even conscious of moving, she pressed closer to Noel.

He put his arm around her and pulled her against his side. "It's only the Maori welcome."

"I know. Rapauru treated me to it once before. It doesn't improve with familiarity."

As if at an unseen signal, the men dropped their spears and the young man Kiri had seen previously, Neiri's son, stepped forward. In his short flax shirt and woven headband, Rapauru looked so fierce and primitive that Kiri was surprised when he spoke in a cultured even accent.

"Hello, Noel, what brings you here?" His tone was an uneasy mixture of friendliness and belligerence. He ignored Kiri completely.

"Just wondering how you were getting along. I see you've got the stockade up."

"We finished it yesterday. It didn't take long with help." Rapauru gestured toward the other young men who, with several backward glances, were drifting off through the village. "Most of the men can only get over here weekends."

"Rapauru, this is Kiri MacKay."

Kiri put out her hand and Rapauru took it briefly, nodded, then turned back to Noel. He was making his displeasure with her obvious to the point of rudeness. She had no trouble at all envisioning him planting the mask in the middle of her bed.

Rapauru gestured toward a long shed, and his hostile expression changed to one of eager pride. "We're nearly finished with our canoe. Come and see it." The pleasure in his voice was so at variance with his usual sullen anger that Kiri warmed to him in spite of herself.

She stepped up behind the two men and caught her breath as she saw what was in the shed. A Maori war canoe. No matter what her preconceptions were, the actual sight of the canoe surpassed them.

It measured at least forty feet, Kiri estimated. Hollowed from a mammoth log, it had room for over twenty men. The prow and stern pieces soared upward from the horizontal body like strange dark birds in flight. They were ebony black, carved into intricate latticework that looked like lace. It was impossible to look at the canoe and not image it full of chanting, tattooed warriors, paddles rising and falling, sweeping across the sea like some avenging spirit.

Rapauru saw her expression and his features softened. He looked almost friendly. "Another week, and we'll take it out to sea," he said.

"It's beautiful." She ran her hand reverently along the smooth surface. "But I can't actually imagine getting out in the middle of the bay in this."

He gave her a disdainful glance. "These canoes are more seaworthy than anything modern. Our ancestors came to *Te Ika a Maui* in canoes just like this one. Across thousands of miles of open ocean."

Te Ika a Maui? Kiri threw Noel a questioning glance.

"The Fish of Maui," he replied, grinning. "If Rapauru succeeds in turning back time, that name will replace New Zealand on all the maps."

Rapauru scowled. "The Treaty of Waitangi—"

"I know," Noel cut in. "It was unjust. Or it was the fairest treaty ever made with a native population. Take your pick. But let's drop it for now. At least you have your village here on the island."

Rapauru gave Kiri a look that nearly singed her hair. "For now."

"Is your mother here?" she said, determined to ignore his inference. "Mrs. Armi said she'd planned on visiting you today."

"She's down at the other end of the village," he said shortly. "She's going to spend the night here." Without another word, he turned and stalked away.

Noel and Kiri walked from the village, each immersed in private thoughts, not speaking until they crested the hill where Kiri had caught a glimpse of him and the *Island Princess* the day before. Coming out of the forest to this elevated spot was like coming out of a dream into consciousness. Brilliant blue sky stretched away to infinity; the ocean breathed in a soft, rhythmic motion; the island below was an impenetrable mass of green.

"You can see forever," she said, raising one hand to lift her hair to float in the breeze. "It's beautiful."

He smiled, his eyes holding hers in an intimate look. "It is. Beautiful."

She was suddenly, achingly aware of him. From the intent look in his eyes, eyes which seemed to have changed from bright blue to a smoky slate, she suspected he had more than the view in mind. He was standing so close to her, his bronzed arm nearly—not quite—brushing hers. So close she had difficulty in breathing. Even though they weren't physically touching, she was aware of every line of his body. Of heat. Of masculinity.

She inched away, then bit her lip as she glanced up and saw the knowing look in his eyes. He knew how he affected her—he had planned it. He had even said he would try to change her mind about the island. Otherwise, why would a handsome, exciting man like Noel pay attention to her—a plain, angular woman who had never bowled any man over?

If he touched her, if he tried to take advantage of her momentary lapse, she would sock him in the jaw.

Apparently, he had no intention of doing so. He continued in his role of guide, and the sun was low in the west when they finally made their way back to the main house. She was pleasantly tired, but exhilarated, too. She couldn't imagine where the day had gone. They had tramped the island until she thought she knew every rock and tree. When they were hungry, Noel had produced two sandwiches and some soft drinks from his backpack and they had munched contentedly, sitting close together on an outcropping of rock.

They had talked, mostly about Long White Cloud, about Rapauru's dreams, Noel's studies. He volunteered nothing of a personal nature. She didn't know him any better than she had this morning. Not his history, his life away from the island.

Except for one thing. She knew he had a passion for the island, and her suspicion that he would do almost anything to protect it from what he would consider desecration strengthened.

Now they stood together on the veranda. Noel leaned lightly back against the railing and hitched his backpack to the other shoulder. For the first time today he seemed at a loss for words. She couldn't think of a thing to say, either. Something about being near him did strange things to her thought processes.

"I'm really glad you came by," she finally said. "I enjoyed the day." Not quite enough for Noel's purpose, though, and he must realize it. He was a perceptive and intelligent man; he must know that it would take more than a pleasant day to change her mind about something so important. And he wasn't the type to give up.

But even knowing that, she didn't want the day to end. The words were out before she had time to consider them. "Why don't you stay for dinner?"

He grinned. "Are you a good cook? Mrs. Armi planned on shopping in Russell today, and staying overnight—so we'd be on our own."

"I know my way around a kitchen," she protested, although she suspected Noel had meant something a little different.

"Do you?"

His voice was so intimate it made even the simple words sound like a caress. She felt the heat rise to her face. "Dinner is all the invitation includes," she replied.

In one pantherlike stride he moved from the pillar, coming so close that she unconsciously took a step backward. A mistake. She was standing with her back literally to the wall, and Noel loomed above her, one hand propped against the planking above her head, his face only an inch or two from hers.

"Are you sure? You're a lovely woman. And you're attracted to me, too, Kiri. Face it."

It was hard to respond when he was so close. She felt the heat of his skin, his breath on her cheek, all his surging animal vitality. Even if his body hadn't pinned her motionless, his aura of sexual energy would have had the same effect. She struggled for a reply that would take him down a notch, show him his forceful masculinity was wasted on her, but she knew he was right. She was more than attracted to him.

His eyes looking so deeply into hers were nearly black with desire. She felt it, pure and primitive, she was drowning in the desire in his eyes, the heated scent of his body, scorched by the electric current that arched between them.

She made a titanic effort to regain control, forcing every muscle into immobility. When she spoke, she was proud that there was hardly a tremor in her voice. "Aren't you going a little far with your sales pitch?"

Something changed in his eyes, perhaps a flash of anger, but then he laughed and stepped back. "Kiri, you underestimate yourself. Hasn't anyone ever told you that you're enough to drive the common sense right out of a man?"

"Not recently," she said dryly, fighting back an unreasonable sense of loss. Not ever, really. Her most serious affair had ended when she realized she was just a means to an end, a notch on a belt.

"Want to tell me about him?"

"Who?" Damn him. Could he read minds?

"The man who hurt you," he said softly. "The man who made you doubt yourself."

"It's a long list," she snapped. "Beginning with my father."

"So we're back to Daddy. Don't you think it's time you grew up? You're an adult. You're responsible for your own life, your own decisions."

"I agree," she said crisply. "And I choose not to have an affair with you."

"How about just one kiss? We can discuss the affair later."

He inched closer until they touched along the full length of their bodies. She started to reply, but the words caught in her throat; she could only experience. She had never felt delicate or fragile, before, but his tall frame seemed to dwarf her, to reduce her to quivering femininity. Her pulse beat wildly, a sweet, warm sensation traveled through her heated flesh, becoming an exquisite ache between her thighs. When he lowered his head until she felt his breath hot on her cheek, she stopped thinking and opened her lips to his.

The kiss was searing, demanding, sending spasms of sensation throughout her body. She couldn't get close enough to his kiss. She caught his tongue in the velvet of her mouth, welcomed it, invited it, demanded it.

His breath came harsh and ragged, as he put his arm around her waist and pulled her fiercely against his rigid body. His heart thundered against her chest, she felt the ropes of muscle in his abdomen as he molded her to him, and she gasped when she felt his hard, rigid masculinity against her soft flesh.

Even as she fell deeper into the pool of sensuality, she made a desperate effort to regain her sanity. This wasn't what she wanted, this coupling on a porch with a man she didn't trust. No matter what her traitorous body said, she knew this wasn't right for her. Not now. Perhaps not ever.

She wasn't sure whether she actually stiffened or whether she communicated her reluctance on some other level. Whatever it was, he drew back, gave her a crooked smile, and raised his hand to her flushed face.

With one slender finger he gently traced the line of her cheek, then dropped his hand to his side. She leaned back against the wall, conscious of the space between them. The touch had been so quick, so light, she might even have imagined it. But she hadn't. Somehow it was more erotic than the kiss. It was still sending little shivers of sensation along her spine.

She glanced over his shoulder out into the garden, unable to meet his eyes. He would surely read too clearly what was in them.

"I guess I'd better do the sensible thing and go home," he said, his voice a husky whisper. "I—"

She gasped, and he stopped in midsentence. "What's the matter?" he demanded.

"I just saw a man running away from the house!"

He whirled around to follow her gaze. "Where?"

"He disappeared into those bushes."

Without a word, Noel jogged across the garden and plunged into the foliage.

Chapter 5

A few minutes later Noel came running back, panting a little from the exertion, and hiked one foot on the first step up to the veranda, as he faced Kiri.

"Not a trace. Are you sure you saw somebody?"

"Of course I'm sure! He was crouched down as if he didn't want to be seen. I think he came out of the back door."

"Well, I wouldn't worry too much." Noel ran his hand through his hair, his gaze going to the tangle of brush he had just emerged from. "There's nobody there now. No tracks, either. But a lot of people have access to this house. It doesn't necessarily mean whoever ran away was up to anything sinister. Maybe he just stopped by, found no one home, and hurried away."

"Not from the way he was running." Kiri set her jaw stubbornly. "I don't know how to describe it, but he looked furtive. I'm sure he didn't want to be seen."

Noel moved up the steps and put his arms around her shoulders, drawing her close against his chest. This time there was only comfort in his caress.

"It was probably Rapauru. This was his home for a long time, you know, before he moved to his village. I'll bet he's in and out of the house any time he feels like it. Did it look like him?"

She shook her head in frustration. "Oh, I don't know. It could have been Rapauru, but I didn't recognize him. I just caught a glimpse of his back. He was wearing normal clothes, his head was down, and he was running fast—like a forest animal." A little shiver shook her slender frame, and she moved closer into Noel's embrace. "He disappeared before I could get a good look at him."

"Don't worry, Kiri," he said, smoothing his hand gently over her hair. "I'd bet anything it was Rapauru. There's really no reason he shouldn't be here...."

"But why act so sneaky? Why not just walk away? Or say something to us."

Noel chuckled, a rich deep sound that sent a little thrill along her spine. "Maybe he thought we were too involved in what we were doing."

"Be serious, Noel." She was aware that she was shaking, and made a deliberate effort to control herself. It was upsetting that Noel was taking the episode so lightly, but she supposed he couldn't be expected to see it as she did. He didn't know about the horrible mask that she had found on her bed. He didn't know that someone was trying to frighten her.

Or did he? What bothered her was this tiny niggling doubt that surfaced every time she decided to tell Noel about the incident of the mask. She couldn't forget that he had said he would do everything he could to change her mind about selling the island. Maybe even his kiss was designed for his own purposes—perhaps to weaken her, make her doubt herself. If she could just put a little distance between them, she would be able to think a little straighter.

But now, at this moment, his arms were firmly around her. Protecting her, comforting her, inviting her to lean on him. He couldn't be involved in anything underhanded. She would feel it, wouldn't she? And she had to take a chance with someone.

Her mind made up, she pulled back a little and looked up into his face. "I know you think I'm overreacting, but it's not just this. Last night someone tried to scare me away."

Surprise crossed his face, and then his lips tightened. Taking her firmly by the arm, he led her to a bench and seated her, then positioned himself beside her, as he reached for her hand and held it in a firm grasp.

"Now tell me about it."

It was a firm command in the tone of a man unused to having his authority questioned. Even yesterday Kiri would have instinctively bridled. But a lot had happened since yesterday. Now the words came spilling out—the mask on her bed, the fright it had given her. Noel's expression grew ever more stern, although he continued to gently stroke her palm with his thumb.

When she finished he was silent a moment, then spoke slowly as though reluctant to face the fact. "It certainly does sound as if someone is trying to spook you."

"I'm glad you agree." She gave a shaky little laugh, trying for lightness. "I was afraid you might think it was just another Maori welcome!"

"If so, it's a new one on me." He drew back a little so he could look fully into her eyes. "Why didn't you mention this before?"

Her gaze slid away from his, and the silence lengthened. His expression hardened, as he watched her averted face. He understood.

"You thought I might have left it there myself."

"Oh—no, not really," she stammered. Then, when he tightened his grip on her arm, she lifted her chin and looked directly into his blue slate eyes. "I didn't know," she admitted. "I thought you might be one of the possibilities. After all, you don't like my being on White Cloud—"

"But I also know scaring you away wouldn't accomplish anything! Give me credit for a brain or two, if not for pure motives!" Anger blazed across his face. Then he took a deep breath, and shrugged. "Well, perhaps I can't blame you. In your place, with your history, maybe I wouldn't trust anyone, either. Let's go."

"Where?"

"We're at a dead end with your intruder. Let's go take a look at that mask you put back in the study. Maybe that's what he was after."

He pulled her to her feet, and, still keeping a tight hold on her hand, steered her through the door and down the hall.

Mutely, she walked beside him along the long corridor that led to the study. The door was closed, and Noel reached across her to grasp the doorknob and throw it open. She stepped ahead of him into the room.

She gasped and stopped so suddenly that Noel nearly bumped into her. Shock held her motionless; she hardly heard Noel's sharp intake of breath. The room that had seemed to her an oasis of serenity was now a scene of utter chaos. Papers were strewn about as though in the aftermath of a cyclone. Every book had been torn from the shelves and now lay haphazardly all over the room. Drawers from the rolltop desk lay on the carpet, their contents scattered on the floor. The globe was upended, chairs overturned.

The only thing that wasn't out of place was the mask hanging just where she had left it.

Her ribs seemed to squeeze her lungs until she could hardly breathe. She felt the violation in every nerve. Only a few hours ago she had sensed her father's presence here; now the room had been desecrated, his spirit expunged. She moistened her lips with the tip of her tongue and stepped farther into the room.

"What happened?" she whispered, turning to Noel.

His lips were clamped so tightly together that they were outlined with a tiny white line. She felt a rush of sympathy. He must be feeling the desecration as much or more as she was. He had sat in this room with Ian, laughed, talked of plans, dreamed his dreams of the future. To Noel, it must seem the mutilation of a shrine.

"Someone was looking for something," he said harshly. "Probably whoever you saw running away."

"But what was he looking for? Did Ian keep anything of value here?"

Noel's eyes darkened, and his lips curved in a mirthless smile. "Anything of value? Depends on your point of view, I guess."

"What do you mean?"

"I'd guess someone was looking for a will."

"But my father didn't leave a will!"

"That's a matter of opinion. Just because a will hasn't yet been found doesn't mean there isn't one."

"You keep saying that! If there is one, why doesn't the attorney have it?"

"I don't know. But I did know Ian. He was a man who kept his word, and he promised Rapauru his village, and that this little island wouldn't be developed. He planned to make a will, I know he did. He as much as told me he had. He knew there were people who depended on him, an entire island whose future lay in his hands."

"If there was one—do you think whoever was here found it?"

"I doubt it. He wouldn't have been running like that. Besides," he said, giving her a challenging grin, "I've looked here myself."

She stared back at him. "We'd better call the police," she said finally.

"I suppose so." He ran his fingers distractedly through his hair. "Although it won't do much good. The man could be completely off the island by now. Or he could be in Rapauru's village, and we could never identify him."

"Or he could be Rapauru."

"Yes."

"The police could look for prints."

"And find half of Paihia and all of Russell. Everybody came here to see your father." His shoulders slumped and he sighed wearily. "But I'll give them a call."

Since the phone in the study was buried somewhere in the mess, Noel left to use the one in the living room. Unable at that moment to face the trashed study, Kiri trailed along behind him.

The phone was picked up at the first ring, and Noel heard Jack Keller's familiar voice. "Russell Police Station, Sergeant Keller. Can I help you?"

Although Keller had a part-time assistant to answer the phone and do office work, Noel knew he was the only permanent policeman in the little town, and often wound up doing almost everything himself. Quickly, he outlined what had happened.

"Can you get over and take a look?" he finished.

"Trashed Ian's study?" Keller sounded both exasperated and angry. "Who would do a thing like that? I doubt if my coming over would be much use, though. Whoever did it will be long gone by the time I can get a launch in the water, and it's not likely he left any trail. Is the daughter all right?"

Noel glanced at Kiri, taking in her pale face and wide, forlorn eyes. The sight tore at his heart. He wished he had his hands around the neck of the burglar right this minute. "She's all right," he said. "I'll look after her."

"I'll make a note of your report," Keller said, "and get over when I can. Right now, I have to leave for Paihia."

"Paihia?" It was unusual for Keller to leave his territory. Something big must be going on. "Trouble?"

He heard the huge sigh over the phone. "It's Tainui again, stirring up trouble. He's holding a couple of people hostage, up near Cape Reinga. Something about not releasing them until the government promises to return all

Maori lands. All the police in the area are ordered up there, although he'll surely turn them loose just as soon as the TV cameras show up.''

''I'll look after things here,'' Noel said, replacing the phone. He didn't envy Jack Keller his job. In any movement there were always fringe elements, people who tried to use the group for their own aggrandizement. The Maori movement for the return of some tribal lands was an almost entirely peaceful protest, and the members were mainly idealistic young people like Rapauru. There were a very few like Tainui, but they made up in rhetoric what they lacked in numbers.

He had seen the man once, haranguing a meeting, and he'd thought he might be dangerous. The elders of the various Maori tribes apparently thought so, too. The man was almost universally repudiated. But that didn't stop him. He seemed determined to provoke incidents, both to get publicity for his cause and to gather any converts that might be swayed by his baiting of authority.

But Tainui wasn't his problem. He turned to Kiri. ''He'll get over as soon as he can. He agrees there's not much he can do.''

At the flash of concern in her eyes, he tried a reassuring smile. ''I'm sure you're not in any danger. The mask trick sounds like something Rapauru would do—a little bit adolescent. And he probably searched the study—he never had a delicate touch. But you're in no danger from him. He makes noises like a fire-eater sometimes, but I know him. He would never actually hurt anyone.''

''I wish I could be as sure of that as you are,'' she said slowly. ''I think he hates me.''

''No, he doesn't. Not you personally. He's angry, that's all, and disappointed. But if you're afraid, I'll be glad to stay the night.''

Kiri searched his eyes, as the earlier scene on the veranda flashed through her mind. His kiss still burned on her lips.

He had offered to stay then, too, but his motive had been entirely different.

Or so she thought. Maybe his motive hadn't changed at all. Maybe he still wanted to make love to her.

But that flame that had leapt between them had probably been an aberration on both their parts. A momentary passion. The result of propinquity between a healthy man and a woman, controllable when one recognized it for what it was. Now his eyes held only gentle concern.

At her hesitation, Noel raised an eyebrow, the gesture that to Kiri always made him seem so haughtily aristocratic.

"You're not afraid of me?" he asked, his voice as smooth as butter. "I promise to be a complete gentleman."

She certainly didn't want to be alone in the house tonight. Neither Neiri nor Mrs. Armi were likely to return until sometime the next day, and the thought of Noel nearby was extremely seductive.

Too seductive. She wasn't at all sure of his definition of a gentleman, and after what had happened between them, she wasn't at all sure she could trust herself, either. She *was* sure that she didn't want to involve herself in anything sexual with a near stranger.

"I'll be fine," she said, straightening her spine and lifting her chin as though to prove it. "I'm sure you have other things to do than baby-sit me."

"Nothing half as delightful."

It was his confident grin that made up her mind for her. That, and the vivid memory of the sensation that had coursed through her when she had stood on the veranda and he had traced her cheek with the tip of one finger. It might very well be the case of inviting the fox into the henhouse.

Maybe his motives weren't even seduction. Noel believed her father had left a will. He had known immediately what the unknown intruder had been searching for. He had even admitted that, with his unobstructed run of the house, he had searched himself.

Yes, it was much more likely that he had a motive other than alleviating her anxiety about being alone—or even making love to her—when he had offered to stay. He wanted to keep an eye on her. It might have occurred to him that she could search for the will herself, now that she had the idea and some indication that the will might be in the house. If she found it, it would certainly be in her interest to destroy it.

It would certainly be in Noel's interest to stick close as a burr to see that she didn't.

She rose from her chair and gave him a warm smile. "I appreciate the thought. But, really, I'll be all right alone."

"You invited me to dinner, remember?"

"Do you mind if we make it another night? I'm suddenly very tired. I don't think I could eat a thing, and maybe I'm not so sure I can find my way around in the kitchen."

He put a finger under her chin and looked deeply into her eyes. "You're sure you want me to go?"

"I'm sure."

What he saw must have reassured him, because he gave her a sweet smile. "Then I'll let myself out." Raising his hand in a half salute, he turned and strode from the room. She listened until she heard the click of the front door closing, then walked slowly toward it to turn the lock.

She wished she could get some kind of hold on her emotions and not be so constantly ambivalent about everything. It wasn't like her—she almost always knew her own mind. Now that he was gone, she wasn't at all sure that that was what she wanted.

But it was what was best. This attraction she felt for Noel had better be nipped in the bud. It had no real basis—they shared no community of interests, there was no blending of values. Quite the opposite, in fact. Her fierce affinity for him was undoubtedly fueled by her feelings of isolation, her loneliness, her sense of loss of a father she'd never really had. She was vulnerable, and Noel was a handsome man, that was all.

She wasn't exactly afraid to stay alone, either. Still, it would have been nice if both Mrs. Armi and Neiri hadn't picked the same night to be away.

She went to her room, showered, and slipped into a light lacy nightgown. Glancing out the French doors, she saw that the sun was down, and twilight was softening the landscape with long velvet shadow. The stones on the little patio outside her door gleamed in the last light, and she knew the moon would be up soon. At any other time the patio would have looked inviting, and she would have luxuriated in lying back in the lounge chair as the night sounds punctuated the night.

Now, she shivered slightly as she looked out. The patio looked safe and secluded; a rim of greenery screened it, making it seem a serene oasis. Yet that greenery could be easily penetrated.

She walked to the doors and double-checked the locks and made certain that the windows were fastened. Then she picked up a book and propped herself up in bed.

It was several minutes before she realized she hadn't retained a thing she had read. She was reclining in a pool of light, easily discernible to anyone outside. Feeling a little ridiculous, she put out the light and lay in the darkness, waiting for the sleep that mockingly eluded her.

Noel strode quickly along the trail that led from the main house to the little inlet where the *Island Princess* waited for him. At least, with her, he knew where he stood. He wasn't rocked by totally unexpected sensations that threatened to send him into a tailspin. She didn't trigger emotions that he had thought long behind him.

His lips tightened to a thin line and he lengthened his stride. He would like to be out of this green maze before it got really dark. Although there would be a moon tonight, few rays would penetrate the thick cover of the kauri and punga that grew together over his head. He wouldn't have any trouble finding his way—he had come this way often

enough at night—but navigating in the darkness would require attention he preferred to give to going over the incredible thing that had just happened to him.

It was unbelievable. He had been standing there on the
veranda, engaging in civilized conversation, and suddenly
he'd felt such a wild rush of desire that he'd acted completely on impulse. A wild, primitive impulse. An impulse
that came from some deep inner core he hadn't even been
aware of.

It was completely out of character. He wouldn't have believed it, but suddenly he hadn't been able to think of anything but crushing her in his arms, molding those soft lips
against his own until she cried for more, pressing that taut,
slender body against his until there wasn't an atom's space
between them, demanding her response, which he instinctively knew would match his own in intensity.

He swore softly under his breath. He hadn't been thinking, period. The force that had gripped him had nothing to
do with the intellectual process. It was an elemental, wild
desire that was probably fueled by her attitude of reserved
dignity, her careful composure. Some primeval masculine
instinct wanted to shake her control, make her moan her
need for him . . .

He laughed, a harsh laugh that held no humor at all. He
had never expected he would be trapped that way again. His
body had reacted in nearly the same way to Rosamund, all
need and sexual fury. He'd been so immersed in her delightful body that he hadn't given a thought to her manipulative little mind.

It was the mind he should have watched out for. It was the
guiding force behind the luscious body that she used as a
tool to get what she wanted. He winced, as he remembered
what she wanted. For her, he had nearly given up his dreams
and taken over his father's business. For her he had nearly
donned a suit! Become a commuter!

When, in a last lingering moment of clarity, he had finally told her he couldn't live that kind of life and asked her

to share his, she had laughed. She wasn't going to hitch her wagon to a dreamer, a man out to save the world from its excesses. That had been the end of Rosamund. That had been the end of his youth.

After that he had chosen his women carefully, giving no more of himself than necessary. He liked sex—he certainly did. It was being out of control he didn't like. He had found there were many women, lovely, uncomplicated women, who were content with what he could give—pleasure, fun, friendship.

The hurt had gone deep, surfacing at the strangest moments, although he had nearly convinced himself that what he had felt for Rosamund had been a function of hormones, the desperate striving of the individual to continue the species. It was easy to mistake a biological urge for love, especially when you were young and idealistic.

He wouldn't make that mistake again. An individual woman wasn't that important. What was important was a man's work, his need to leave the world in a better state than he'd found it in. He had long ago decided that his passion would be spent in the service of humanity. All of humanity.

He certainly wasn't going to jeopardize that hard-earned equilibrium just because a woman had mesmerizing green eyes, and an unsettling, crackling sexual energy that nearly reached out and grabbed him.

His idea of getting to know Kiri and of convincing her not to sell the island, perhaps turning on the charm full blast, had seemed like a good one at the time. Now it seemed incredibly naive. She wasn't the mercenary woman he had supposed she was, but she was a threat just the same. And not just a threat to the island. He had spent a long time steering clear of involvement, and he meant to continue doing so.

He shouldn't have left her alone, though, no matter what she said. He suspected that she was scared stiff and had only sent him on his way because of what she felt burgeoning between them. He could hardly blame her. He had acted like a jerk, kissing her as though he had a perfect right to. She wouldn't be human if she didn't wonder how far he would try to go.

Still, he didn't think he could leave it like that. She was a resourceful woman, with a mind of her own, and in most situations he had no doubt she could take care of herself. But she was in a strange country, surrounded by people who resented her, with no friends at all. He had glimpsed the shadow of fear in her eyes when she told him about the mask. And the rigidity of her shoulders, her bewildered gasp when she discovered the study had been ransacked, had betrayed her shock and vulnerability.

He didn't for a moment believe she was in any danger, but she was alone in a big house and Rapauru might just take it into his head to step up the harassment. He'd made no secret that he would like to scare her away.

Rapauru's trouble was that he couldn't think beyond the moment, couldn't see that forcing her to leave the island would only result in hardening her determination to sell it. He didn't understand that Long White Cloud would be safe only if she were permanently removed from it....

A cold little chill went up his spine. Maybe Rapauru *could* see that.

Of course, it was remotely possible that Rapauru wasn't even behind the two incidents....

He sat down on a convenient boulder and looked back down the path he had so recently traversed. Darkness was claiming the forest, throwing pools of blackness under the *pungas*, accentuating the eerie cries of the nocturnal birds and animals. If those unfamiliar sounds penetrated the walls of the villa, Kiri might be frightened....

Noel didn't even notice when he stood up and began walking back down the trail. There was no reason to be uneasy, but he just didn't feel right about the break-in. Even though he suspected she wouldn't invite him in, that didn't really present a problem.

Ian had given him a key to the villa long ago. He often took the opportunity to stretch out on a real bed, chat with Neiri, sample Mrs. Armi's breakfasts. He would just let himself in, go to the room where he had slept so many nights—a room only a couple of doors from Kiri's—and leave in the morning before she was awake. It would save explanations.

He walked across the wide expanse of lawn, knowing that the moonlight made him visible to anyone who might be watching. He doubted that anyone was. All the lights were out; Kiri must be asleep.

He inserted his key in the lock. The door protested only slightly, and he stepped cautiously into the foyer. He hoped she didn't wake up; he'd have a hard time explaining what he was doing creeping around the house in the middle of the night.

Gingerly feeling his way, he moved forward a few steps. He wished he could turn on a light. What was the matter with the woman? Ian had always left a night-light shining in the hall.

He nearly laughed at his unreasonable annoyance; Ian expected him. Kiri didn't.

He bumped against a chair, swore softly, then moved along the corridor toward his room. Although the hall was carpeted, his halting progress wasn't completely silent. He was beginning to feel ridiculous, creeping around like a burglar. Why hadn't he informed the obstinate woman that he was going to stay overnight and protect her whether she liked it or not?

He inched his way along the hall. In another minute he would pass her door, and then it would be clear sailing....

Kiri stood silently off to the side of her half-opened door, every muscle rigid with fright. She tried to swallow, but her throat was much too dry. The sound was getting closer, the soft sound of creeping footsteps. In a minute, whoever was skulking down the hall would be just opposite her door.

She held her breath, afraid even the sound of her shallow breathing might betray her presence. Her heart was pounding so frantically she was sure whoever was out there could hear it.

It was fortunate that she hadn't been able to sleep. She had been lying in bed for what had seemed hours, wide-eyed, motionless, trying to sort out the confusing day, aware of every creak and shudder in the empty house.

Suddenly she had heard something else. Her heart hammered wildly against her chest, and her pulse raced, as she recognized the click of the front door opening, the soft whisper of well-oiled hinges, then the thud as the door closed.

It couldn't be Neiri or Mrs. Armi; they wouldn't be home until tomorrow and neither one of them would have crept in without turning on a light.

Paralyzed with fear, she huddled under the covers, cringing at the sound of footsteps as they came hesitatingly down the hall. They were muffled by the carpet, but to ears straining for every sound, they were unmistakable. In another minute they would be right outside her door....

She couldn't just wait helplessly for whatever was going to happen to her. She forced herself out of bed and opened her door a tiny crack, then eased it farther.

The flowerpot filled with begonias was right by her hand. Instinctively she grasped it, held it aloft—

The intruder was right in front of her door, a dark, ominous shadow. She raised the pot and threw it with all the force she could muster against the side of his head. There was a dull, satisfying thud, a surprised grunt—

"What the hell?" The voice sounded very surprised, very angry.

She choked off her scream and turned to switch on a light. Her eyes widened and she stifled a little cry, as she surveyed the man at her feet. Noel was sprawled on the floor staring up at her, rubbing his head, an expression of combined shock and outrage on his aristocratic features.

She stared back, incredulous. Then disappointment flooded her, jarring in its intensity. She had not completely trusted Noel, but she had never expected he would try to hurt her. Yet here was proof of just that.

Another part of her mind wondered how he could manage to look so suave and elegant lying in a heap on the floor.

He started to scramble to his feet, and she reached for another pot and held it above his head. "Don't move."

"Okay." He kept on rubbing his head, as he grinned back up at her. "The view isn't bad from here, anyway."

Even caught in the act, he was as full of arrogance as ever! She glanced down at her gown, suddenly aware of what he was seeing. Everything. Most of her sleepwear was severely tailored, in keeping with what she considered her personality. What had possessed her to put on a filmy shorty nightgown edged with lace? Had her encounter with Noel on the veranda made her feel so feminine that she had subconsciously wanted the feel of silk and lace against her skin?

She edged back into her room and reached for a robe. "All right. Get up. But don't move."

"Which is it?" He scrambled to his feet, his hand still against his head where a lump was already visible.

She tied her robe firmly around her waist as though it were a suit of armor, and faced him with blazing eyes. "Now, suppose you tell me why you broke into my house!"

"Your house again?" He lifted a finely sculpted eyebrow. "I keep telling you not to be premature. The estate isn't settled yet."

She set her lips angrily, and he shrugged, a sheepish grin on his face. "Okay, okay." He held out the key nestled in the palm of his hand. "I was just going to my room—I didn't want to wake you."

"*Your* room?"

"The one I used when Ian was alive."

She took a moment to assimilate his words, then lifted her chin in a cool gesture. "That still doesn't explain why you're here *now*."

"No, it doesn't." He sighed, running his hand through his hair and wincing as he felt the bruise. "I guess I shouldn't have bothered. You seem quite capable of routing intruders. The truth is, I was a little worried about you."

It seemed to cost him something to admit it. Her features softened, but only a trifle. "I think we'd better talk about this."

He started to move forward into her room, but she motioned him down the hall. "We'll talk in the living room," she said firmly.

A few minutes later they faced each other across the kauri coffee table in the living room. A tray between them held a pot of tea, which Kiri had just brought in from the kitchen. She poured the fragrant brew into a delicate china cup and handed it across the table to him, taking great care not to touch his hand. Then she poured some tea for herself, took a sip, and regarded him coolly over the rim of the cup.

She hoped she looked more poised than she felt. She would never have believed such conflicting emotions could exist at the same time in one person. Anger at his duplicity in sneaking into the house, outrage at his assumption that he had every right to be there, warred with her very real joy at seeing him. At the moment, joy was in the ascendancy, but she would be damned if she would admit it.

"So," she said sternly, "start talking."

He gave her a rueful grin. "It's getting harder and harder to be chivalrous. I'll bet damsels of old didn't hit knights over the head when they came to rescue them."

"Maybe they did if they didn't need rescuing." But she smiled. Face-to-face with Noel, it was nearly impossible to suspect him of anything underhanded.

"I'm sorry I scared you," he said.

"I'm sorry I hit you over the head."

They met each other's eyes and simultaneously began to laugh.

"I must say, you take it very well," she said, when she could finally speak.

"I have a very hard head."

"That's just one of the things I didn't know about you," she replied, curling back into her chair. "I have a feeling you're a complicated man."

"Not really. But what would you like to know?"

For nearly an hour they chatted comfortably. Kiri found out about his childhood—happy—his years with her father—exciting and rewarding—what he liked in music—a surprising medley of country-western and classical—books—biography and history—and sports—tennis and rugby. Although he chatted easily, she was left with the feeling that there was something important he hadn't confided. She noticed he didn't mention girlfriends, and not even her roundabout questions broke through his reserve on that topic.

Finally she glanced at the clock and saw with surprise that it was after one o'clock in the morning.

"I think we'd better get on to bed," she said. "I'll see you in the morning," she added quickly.

He rose and cupped her face gently in the palm of his hand. For a dizzying moment she thought he was going to kiss her, but he gave her the sweet smile she had seen once before.

"Good night, Kiri," he said softly.

Later, she lay awake in her bed listening for the sounds Noel made as he moved about in his room. He was only two doors away. Only a few steps away. The knowledge deepened a vague, sweet aching in her body. At night every sound was accentuated; she was aware of his restless pacing, and finally the squeak of the bed when it received his lean body. Then everything was quiet except her own shallow breathing.

She gazed out the expanse of windows into the darkness of the patio. When she had locked the doors earlier, she had suspected the fragile lock wouldn't keep anyone out who was determined to enter, and she'd been chilled with fear.

Now the door appeared a sturdy enough barrier, because Noel was close by.

So much had happened today, she had so many new ideas to assimilate, that she expected to be a long time falling asleep. Instead, she drifted off immediately. Her last thought was how safe she felt with Noel only two doors away.

Chapter 6

When Kiri came into the kitchen the next morning, she found everyone was up ahead of her. Neiri and Mrs. Armi were both seated at the table having their morning tea, and Noel, who was in the process of devouring a plate of scones generously laden with butter and jam, was sitting across from them.

She glanced at her watch, a little embarrassed to see that it was nearly ten a.m. Both Mrs. Armi and Neiri must have returned early this morning, and she had been sleeping so soundly that she hadn't even heard them come in.

Noel looked up and gave her a brilliant smile, revealing white even teeth against his bronzed skin. Even lounging at the table, he gave the impression of quick restless energy, barely suppressed. Of vital masculinity. In spite of her resolution to keep herself under cool control, her heart beat a little faster.

"Good morning, sleepyhead," he said, his rich voice making her resolution even more difficult to keep. "I wondered if we were going to have to burn the house down to get you out of bed.''

''Now, Noel.'' Neiri, her long, dark hair flowing down her back, and wearing a brightly colored cotton dress that reached her ankles, gave him a fond look as she rose and poured a cup of tea for Kiri, then placed it near her own.

''Let the girl sleep if she wants to—she needs it. Sit down, Kiri, and have a scone.''

''I baked them fresh this morning,'' Mrs. Armi offered.

Kiri sat down across from Noel and took a sip of the steaming tea, then picked up a crisp, buttered scone. The smell of freshly baked pastry made her suddenly hungry, and she took a healthy bite.

''They're delicious,'' she murmured, basking for a moment in the quiet domesticity of the scene around her. Everything—the warm kitchen, the steaming tea kettle, the three people seated with her—all combined to give her a feeling of belonging that she had never experienced before. It was silly under the circumstances, but there was no other way to put it—she felt at home.

It was an ambiance she was unfamiliar with, and rather bitterly, she wondered what else she had missed because of Ian. After her father had left them, she and her mother had lived in a series of apartments; her mother said there wasn't any use trying to make them into something they weren't, so they were often sparsely furnished. They didn't seem to have many friends in the house, either, she remembered, as her mother preferred to go out to restaurants when she entertained.

Kiri had often been alone, and after her mother married the stockbroker, she saw even less of her.

Here, halfway around the world from Lois, Kiri allowed herself a thought she had never considered before. Had her mother resented her? Had she somehow held her responsible for Ian's defection? Had her mother been entirely candid in her constant denunciation of Ian? She'd said he hadn't wanted a home; Lois apparently hadn't, either.

She shook off the unwelcome questions, and turned to Neiri. "How was everything in the village?"

Neiri laughed, a gentle, sweet sound that somehow tore at Kiri's heart. "I'm afraid I'm too old for camping out. As I told Rapauru, I wouldn't mind returning to the past, if I could take my electric stove and my indoor plumbing with me."

Noel speared another scone. "*I* wouldn't return to the past unless I could take Martha with me." He put his hand on the woman's shoulder, and she beamed back at him. "No one can cook like she can." He smiled at Kiri. "What would you take with you, Kiri?"

"My blow-dryer," she said, mentioning the first thing that came to mind. The superficial retort came quickly; she never gave anything away. The truth was, she had never given any thought to the subject, and she had no idea why it made her uneasy. She had no desire to return to the past, with or without any treasured possession. Was it because the past was too much with her, stretching its tendrils into everything she did in the present? Ian's betrayal was in the past, but it was certainly springing to life here, as lacerating as it had been at the time. How did one ever get free of the past?

In spite of their kindness to her, she was an outsider here, too, as she had always been wherever she went. How could she feel so at home among Ian's true family, in the house he had so lovingly built, when she knew what he was?

She heard Noel's comment to Neiri, and realized that the conversation had continued while she was deep in remembrance.

"Have you decided yet what you'll do?" he was saying. "I know you'd like to have things resolved, but there's really no hurry. Nothing can actually be decided until the estate is formally settled."

There was a long pause, as Neiri glanced at Kiri's averted face, then back at Noel. "Rapauru really wants me to stay as long as I can. Sometimes I don't think he's as sure of himself as he pretends. Yet I don't want to spend all my time at the village, as he would like me to, and if it's all right with Kiri..."

"Of course it's all right! I hope you'll stay here until—" She broke off in midsentence. Until when? Until she sold the villa out from under her?

Mrs. Armi broke the embarrassed silence. "Noel told us that someone broke into the study. I can't imagine who would do such a horrible thing."

"I know it might have been Rapauru," Neiri said softly, her eyes suddenly misty with unshed tears. "Although it's hard to believe. He loved Ian so. He always called him his real father."

Would the real father please stand up? Kiri thought bitterly. What made a *real* father? Love, attention, protection? Or the chance bestowal of genes?

Her reverie was interrupted by the sound of the door-knocker reverberating down the hall. Mrs. Armi set down her cup, straightened her apron over her ample waist, and hurried out of the kitchen.

She returned almost immediately, followed by a sturdy, bronzed man with a shock of coarse blond hair, a weath-ered face, and shrewd blue eyes that swept quickly around the table. Kiri had the definite impression that the quick glance missed very little. He was wearing a policeman's uniform, and twisted his hat in large, meaty hands.

Noel arose at once, hand outstretched. "Jack! Good to see you. I was afraid you wouldn't be able to make it over." He turned to Kiri. "Kiri, this is Sergeant Jack Keller, Rus-sell's one-man police force."

Kiri acknowledged his greeting. Keller enveloped her hand in his rough palm, and spoke with obvious sincerity.

"My condolences, miss. Everybody will miss Ian."

Another Ian cheerleader, Kiri thought dryly, trying to ig-nore the ache in her heart. Was she the only person in the world who thought the man less than perfect? Even Neiri, who had the best reason of anyone to be bitter, never mentioned his name without a catch in her throat and love in her eyes.

"I didn't think you'd be able to make it, Jack," Noel said. "What happened in Paihia?"

Keller scowled. "Just about what you'd expect. By the time we got up the coast to where Tainui had the hostages, he'd already let them loose. In full view of the TV cameras. Made a big, impassioned speech for the media. Then he skipped out, and of course no one will press charges. It was all a big waste of time."

"Where did he go?"

Keller shrugged. "Who knows? But he'll surface again someplace, worse luck for us. Anyway, I was on my way back from Paihia and decided to stop in here, just in case there was something I could do."

"Will you have a cup of tea?"

At the sound of her low voice, Keller turned to Neiri, his harsh expression melting to affection. "No, but thanks just the same. I'm pretty strapped for time. I'd like to take a look at the study right away, if it's all right with you. A damn shame, doing that to a man like Ian. The only thing that man ever did was good."

"Come along. We haven't touched a thing in the study," said Neiri.

Keller followed Neiri down the hall, and Mrs. Armi began clearing the table, leaving Noel and Kiri to talk alone.

She leaned toward him, thinking how crisp and fresh he looked in the morning. She was close enough to catch the scent of soap and clean skin. He had shaved, his hair was neatly combed, although still a little damp, and he brimmed over with warm, animal vitality.

"How's your head?" she whispered.

He flashed her a disarming grin. "Don't worry. All the Trevorsons have hard heads. It's a family characteristic. You didn't even dent it."

"Oh. Too bad. Next time I'll try harder."

"Next time I'll see you first."

"And then what?"

"Then, I just may kiss you so hard you'll forget about assaulting me. At least, not with a flowerpot."

She understood his innuendo, and her cheeks flushed. Just thinking about him seemed to stir emotions best left undisturbed. She knew her voice was a little shaky, as she changed the subject.

"What are you doing today?"

"The usual." He finished his third scone—at least his third since Kiri had come to the table—and drained his tea. "There's a study plot on the other side of the island I haven't checked for a few weeks." His eyes held hers in an intimate caress. "Want to go with me?"

"Are you still trying to convince me not to sell?"

"Let's put it this way—I'm still hoping. But aside from that, I'd really like you to see what I'm doing. I think it's exciting. We're learning so much about the balance of animal and plant life, and what non-native animals do to that balance. Once we learn that, we'll be in a position to help stabilize—"

Kiri only half listened to his words, all her attention caught by the enthusiasm and intensity with which he explained his work. His eyes sparkled with animation, his entire body radiated a riveting energy, as he talked of his environmental studies. She was amazed at the transformation. She had thought him elegant and sophisticated, and he was certainly all that, but there was another side to him. When he talked about his work, he displayed all the joy and exuberance of someone who had just won a million dollar lottery.

The comparison wasn't completely applicable, though. She knew that money would never kindle this ebullience in Noel; he was dedicated to something much more lasting.

Keller came back, a frown on his square-shaped face. "Whoever it was did a good job of tearing things up, but he sure didn't leave a trail that I can see. Keep your eyes open."

"I'll walk down to the launch with you." Noel rose from the table and followed Keller out the door, calling over his shoulder to Kiri as he went. "Get your hiking shoes on—I'll be right back."

Half an hour later they were walking along the trail that led over the crest to the other side of the island. The morning, as usual, was clear and fragrant with blooming plants. Kiri was beginning to recognize the various birds that called from the enveloping greenery, and the *pungas* and kauris, once so exotic, were now familiar sights.

The trail narrowed and Kiri paused to let Noel walk ahead and lead the way. She enjoyed watching him. He was certainly a splendid specimen. His shoulders moved rhythmically under his light short-sleeved shirt; long, bronzed legs with a dusting of light hair strode confidently up the trail, and, she noticed, her throat tightening just a little, his khaki shorts fit snugly over his lean buttocks. A very sexy man, from whichever direction you viewed him.

"This is the first site." His voice broke into her fantasies that were becoming more graphic by the minute. Kiri glanced guiltily away, as he pushed aside a heavy screen of branches. Some of her fantasies had been so vivid that she hoped Noel did not have ESP.

She looked to where Noel pointed. An area approximately fifty feet square was securely fenced with sturdy wire netting that was over ten feet high. At the very top ran a single strand of wire, which Noel explained was lightly electrified. Nothing that could harm an animal; he just wanted to get their attention, he explained.

"What are you fencing out?" she asked.

"Opossums, mainly," he replied. "They are just one of a lot of invaders that are getting to be a real nuisance. When Europeans first came here, there weren't any mammals except the Maori dogs. No predators. Naturally, everyone had to make it as homelike as possible, and it wasn't long before there were cats, rats, even exotic animals that people kept in private zoos. Lots of whom got loose, of course. But what concerns me now are the opossums. They were brought here from Australia, and they found they loved kauri trees. They are loving them to death, in fact.''

"How does this little enclosure help?"

"I want to see how long it takes a forest to come back if it's given complete protection. See those little guys in there?'' He pointed to a number of young kauris. "They've only been protected for three years, and already they're huge.''

He moved away and pointed to another plot, this one outlined only with stakes. "Here is our control plot. As you see, almost everything is nibbled off to the ground.''

As Noel walked about the plots, checking, making notes, explaining to Kiri, she was struck again by his complete dedication to his work. It obviously meant so much to him.

"What good will it do to save a few kauri trees?" she asked. "You can't fence them all off.''

"No, I'm working on other means, too. Sterilization, trapping, maybe even genetic changes. I'm sure to find something, in time. And when I do, it can be applied to the trees on the mainland, where the kauri is making a last stand....''

"How long will that take?"

"Who knows? Years, maybe. But it's worth doing, no matter how long it takes, if I can save just a little of this natural world for people who come after us.''

It wasn't only his words that impressed Kiri, it was his manner. He was a man driven by a dream, and she could relate to that.

She had her dream, too.

As Noel continued his tour, she only half listened. She was enthralled by his eagerness, his dedication, and she was also more than a little sad. Neither mentioned what her plans would do to Noel's work. Their dreams were on a collision course and there didn't seem to be anything she could do about it.

The sun was high in the sky when she decided she would return to the main house. Noel had more work to do, and she left him alone, welcoming the walk back by herself. She had some thinking to do.

The more she learned about Noel, the more admirable he seemed to be. His arrogance was a facade, based on his single-minded pursuit of his ambitions. Of course he affected her sexually like a bunch of fireworks all going off at once, but when he talked of his work she saw something else. She glimpsed the inner core of the man, understood what drove him.

The same thing that had driven her father.

There were lots of clues. Noel had never married; she had to assume that a close relationship with one individual meant very little to him compared with his work. He was charming, and she knew he would like to make love to her. Or, rather, to have sex with her. But he saved his serious passion for something else—the future.

She remembered things her mother had told her about her father, her tone scathing and accusing. Apparently the first year or so together had been ideal, but she had felt a restlessness in him. Ian had felt he was wasting his life; he wanted to make a difference to humanity. So he had abandoned his wife and child.

Just as Noel would do, if he ever allowed himself to get to the point where he had anyone to abandon. She was surprised at how much the thought hurt. Had she allowed her emotions to get so involved in just a few days?

Apparently she had. Apparently she was in danger. She couldn't be near the man without wanting to make love to him. If she had been the type to make love lightly, enjoy herself, and move on, it wouldn't have mattered. She could have had a pleasurable time with Noel, realizing that it wasn't permanent. But her response to him was much too intense to allow herself that delusion. Once she'd taken that irrevocable step, she would open herself to hurt and pain.

If she stayed here much longer she was very much afraid she wouldn't be able to make the choice. He was overpowering. That kiss on the veranda had taught her how much she could trust her willpower, how her senses reeled with sweet delirium when she was in his arms. She should get away while she still could.

She walked back the way they had come, negotiating the trail with the part of her mind that wasn't involved in her dilemma. She held so much power in her hands—power to destroy the hopes of three people. Yet in a way, she was powerless. She couldn't sacrifice her own dream to theirs. She wasn't cut out for martyrdom. And since she had been on the island, she was beginning to see a completely different Ian from the one her mother had described, and if even half of what her mother had said was true, she couldn't believe he would have wanted her to leave the island empty-handed, no matter what everyone said.

If only he *had* left a will! She would at least have known for sure that he hadn't given her a thought.

Her mind kept spinning from idea to idea like a top that was off balance. Was there any way she could work something out that would give everyone, if not their dream, at least something? She didn't see how. Selling off only part of the island wouldn't be the answer. An influx of people would spell disaster to Noel's studies. And she had to sell the house or she wouldn't realize enough money to make it worthwhile to herself.

She thought of the piece of sculpture she had been working on before she left home—a young girl in the act of leaping into the air. She had caught the essence, she knew. It was the best thing she had done. But it wasn't finished. She needed time, freedom from distraction.

Freedom that the money would give her.

She shook off the thought. Even Rapauru deserved some consideration. If he were behind the various incidents at the villa, she grudgingly understood his anger. His village was as precious to him as her dream of becoming a sculptor was to her. Perhaps, in his way, he felt as lost and orphaned as she did. She had been cut off from a father, he from a rich and ancient culture.

The villa loomed before her, and she went to her room, still deep in thought. She needed to do something; she could no longer just wait passively for whatever was going to happen. If there was anything she could do to help the people she was displacing, she would try to find it.

She went to her dresser and took out a list of names that the lawyer had given her when she had stopped in Auckland. She had told him that she was thinking of selling, and he had given her the name of a developer in Paihia. Of course, there was nothing she could do legally until the estate was actually hers, but she could at least feel the man out.

She glanced at the slip of paper. Klaus Helborn, at an address in Paihia. If he did buy the island, maybe he could be persuaded to let Noel continue with his studies, and Rapauru's village might possibly become a tourist attraction. As for Neiri—maybe she could have a little cottage somewhere near Rapauru's village....

She sighed, knowing that her proposed compromise would probably satisfy no one, even if she managed to bring it off. Not everyone believed half a loaf was better than none, especially if the half loaf lost was close to his heart.

If she couldn't work something out, she might still arrange for a sale to Helborn to take effect later when it was legally possible, and she could get off this island at once. Her own heart was in jeopardy, and she had to get away from Noel while she still could. She didn't at all believe that it was better to have loved and lost than never to have loved at all!

With Kiri, action almost always immediately followed thought. She had noticed a small powerboat at the dock, and knew it was transportation for people on Long White Cloud. Mrs. Armi had used it to get to Russell, so it must be seaworthy.

The thought of the trip didn't worry her. She had grown up on San Francisco Bay and was no stranger to boats. There was no reason at all that she couldn't go to Paihia at once.

She didn't want to explain her actions, but she didn't want anyone to worry, either, so she left a short note for Neiri on a table in the foyer, and hurried down to the pier. A few minutes later the prow of the little boat was cutting cleanly through the water and she was on her way.

The trip didn't take nearly as long in the powerboat as it had taken to sail the distance in the *Island Princess*. The sea was calm, the air balmy. She was never far from another island, although she had to cross several strips of open water where things got a bit choppy. Although the bay was fairly sheltered, they were close to open ocean, and she suspected that the sea could get stormy, but now everything was serene. She passed Russell off to her left, and within an hour the shoreline of Paihia came into view.

She tied up her craft, and walked quickly up the pier to the main thoroughfare, glancing along the row of resort hotels and specialty shops. It would be fun to explore them, if she had the time. If her errand to Klaus Helborn was successful, she might never have the opportunity to wander through them—she could leave at once.

The thought brought a sharp pang of regret, but she continued resolutely down the street to the office building that proclaimed itself Helborn Enterprises. There were shops in other places in the world—and if she sold the island she would have the means to explore them.

She probably should have called first, she decided, as she walked through the plushly carpeted outer lobby and faced a perfectly groomed receptionist behind a gleaming kauri desk. Kiri knew her art, and the original oils that hung on the walls were fantastically expensive. If Helborn commanded such luxury as this, he might not be available to everyone who just drifted in off the street.

She needn't have worried. When she gave her name, the dark-haired receptionist in a couture suit gave her a brittle smile, spoke briefly into an intercom, and a minute later a large, affable man came toward her, hand outstretched, a wide smile on his broad face.

"Kiri MacKay! I heard you'd arrived. Come in, come in."

With quick familiarity, he put his arm around her shoulder and steered her into his office, then settled her in a comfortable chair and retreated behind his desk. Kiri took the opportunity to observe him closely.

Perhaps not as affable as he'd seemed at first glance. His gray suit was perfectly cut, tailor-made, she decided, to accommodate his considerable bulk. Fat had taken over a body that retained only traces of hard muscle. His pale blue eyes were still hard, though—hard, and shrewd, and a little ruthless, she thought, as he observed her across his desk.

"I hoped you would come in," he said. "I would have been over to see you before now, but I knew you were getting the lay of the land, and I thought I'd give you a little time. How do you like the island?"

He obviously knew all about her, and had decided to come straight to the point. "It's beautiful," she replied. "I'm still a little overwhelmed."

"It certainly is beautiful," he answered, twisting a silver pen between pudgy fingers. "Oh, I could bad-mouth it, try to get the price down, but I see you're a sensible young woman. You know what you have, and I'm no haggler. I'd like to make you an offer."

"I'm not sure yet," she said uneasily. "I just wanted to talk to you—"

"I don't beat around the bush. I'm prepared to buy it."

"Just like that?"

"Oh, it's not the first time I've offered to buy Long White Cloud." His full lips curved in a little smile that pushed his cheeks up under his eyes, making them seem smaller, sharper. "Ian would never sell, although I offered him twice what it was worth."

He pulled a slip of paper toward him and scribbled a figure on it. "I'm prepared to offer you this amount, right now. Cash, of course."

He shoved the paper across to her, and leaned back, a complacent smile on his face. Klaus Helborn had spoken the truth; he didn't haggle, and he was confident that he would get what he wanted.

She glanced at the amount and her eyes opened wide. She'd known White Cloud was valuable, but she hadn't realized how valuable. Carefully, she laid the paper back on the desk.

"That's a lot of money," she said slowly. "Before we discuss it, I'd like to know what your plans are for the island if I do sell to you."

She could almost see him salivate. He leaned forward eagerly, hands clasped in front of him.

"A destination resort, the biggest in the area. A luxury hotel for the rich and famous! Tennis courts, pools, golf courses. It would draw from the crowd that now goes to the French Riviera. And all secluded, off the beaten track, so they can have the privacy they require. The island is perfect. It's one of the few places left in the world that would accommodate the type of resort I have in mind."

Her shock must have been visible; he took a quick glance at her expression, and continued quickly. "Of course, if that's not enough, I could go a little higher." He barked into the intercom, giving quick instructions to his secretary, while Kiri tried to get her breath.

"I had no idea your plans would be so—so elaborate," she finally said. "You know there are environmental studies going on there, and a replicated Maori village along the shore—"

He waved a dismissive hand. "There are other islands for that type of thing. Places where do-gooders would be welcome. Long White Cloud is too valuable for anything less than a world-class resort."

She half rose from her chair, knowing she couldn't sell under those conditions. Her idea had been naive. Helborn's plans left no room at all for anyone else. She couldn't possibly turn it over to him to desecrate.

"I really don't think I'm interested, Mr. Helborn. But thank you for your time—"

"You won't find a better offer," he cut in. "And if you've got some idea of selling off part of it, or allowing certain rights to people who are already there, forget it. No one will buy it unless they get it all. It's not economically feasible."

"The government—"

"The government will be glad to get it as a gift," he said dryly.

"Maybe a private party, a party who would want to live there—"

"Don't waste your time."

The secretary, a short blond woman with cool, discreet eyes entered and handed a paper to Helborn. "The offer is typed up, sir."

The woman left as noiselessly as she had come, and Helborn got up and came around his desk to where Kiri was now standing.

"Here," he said brusquely. "Take it along. Think it over."

Absently, Kiri stuffed the offer into her purse. She was already heading for the door. She couldn't possibly sell to this man. His ambitions meant doom to Long White Cloud, and even if she would never see it again, she already loved the little island too much to see it destroyed.

"Think it over," he called again. "You won't get a better offer."

She let the door slam behind her and hurried out into the street.

Noel glanced at the sky. The light would hold for another hour, and there was still work he could do, but somehow his heart wasn't in it. His mind, usually so absorbed with his experiments, returned again and again to Kiri. He didn't understand her.

A beautiful girl who didn't know she was beautiful. A girl who responded to his kiss like a volcano, and then became ice cold. A girl who carried a chip on her shoulder the size of a log. A girl whose bitterness toward her father colored her every action.

And yet, a woman whose vulnerability and underlying sweetness reached deep inside him to release feelings he had thought he'd outgrown. The haunting sadness he occasionally glimpsed in her eyes made him want to cradle her in his arms, protect her from the harshness of the world, against all his better judgment.

He pounded in a stake, then took out his notebook to record his observations. Later, on the boat, he would compare them with last year's, and next year—

He swore softly, and put the notebook back in his pocket. Next year he probably wouldn't be on this island. Kiri had been interested in his projects, had asked all the right questions, but he knew he hadn't convinced her that Long White Cloud should be left as it was.

How could she be so unfeeling, so blind to what a treasure it was? But then, he supposed he was asking too much of her. Few people would ignore their own self-interest for the good of the anonymous many.

Yet he wasn't satisfied with that assessment. He sensed something deep inside her, some sensitivity, some idealism, that was struggling up through the layers of pragmatism. She had been damaged, somehow, but after all, she *was* Ian's daughter.

Sighing, he put his pencil back in his shirt pocket, ran his fingers through his hair, and looked around the enclosure. Recovery of the trees was happening much faster than he had anticipated; there was hope.

He wouldn't give up on Kiri. She had a conscience, and he'd seen how she looked when Neiri talked about leaving the island. Like someone had given her a powerful blow in the stomach.

He would have to be very careful, though, not because of the island, but because of himself. He was much too close to unwelcome emotional involvement. He had thought his experience with Rosamund had taught him a painful lesson. Even now, the scar still throbbed occasionally. If he allowed Kiri close to his heart, he knew the devastation that followed would be worse than before.

Kiri was different than Rosamund. She wasn't manipulative, she wasn't shallow—quite the opposite. But they were alike in one thing—her values and beliefs were diametrically opposed to his.

Frowning, he started back down the trail toward his boat. Tonight he would open a can of beans for supper, and stay away from the main house.

Chapter 7

Kiri was up with the dawn, although sleep had come late and she had tossed fitfully through the night. She had lingered on the veranda until dark the night before, hoping that Noel would stop by, but in the end only she and Mrs. Armi sat down to a quiet dinner. Neiri had gone again to Rapauru's village; Kiri had no idea when she would be back.

She had admitted to feeling a little relieved that the woman was gone. Although Neiri was unfailingly polite, Kiri sensed her deep reserve. Understandable, but it made her uneasy.

Restless, and ambivalent about her visit to Helborn, she had wandered into the little study before retiring for the night. Mrs. Armi had already restored it to order, erasing all signs of the intruder. Kiri wasn't sure what drew her there. Perhaps she had hoped to find some remnant of the spirit of her father that she had sensed there before, some sense of guidance, but the study was only a pleasant, well-ordered room. Even the mask that had frightened her so before, now appeared to be just a dusty old artifact, forgotten by time.

She had taken Helborn's offer out of her purse and studied it thoughtfully. So much money; it made her dizzy. If he wanted the island so badly, maybe others did, too. Perhaps she shouldn't believe his statement that no one would buy only a part of Long White Cloud. It was one option she might explore. Certainly, she wasn't about to accept his offer, containing as it did the destruction of the island as she had come to know it. She had tossed the document into a basket on the rolltop desk, and gone on to bed.

The next morning she wandered into the kitchen, not surprised to find herself alone at such an early hour. She made a quick cup of tea and roamed desolately through the house until she finally admitted to herself what was wrong.

She wanted to see Noel.

There were a lot of reasons she needed to see him. She wanted to tell him about Helborn's offer, and get his advice about other buyers. He, if anyone, would know whether it was reasonable to try to sell off part of Long White Cloud, and leave Rapauru's village intact. He might even be able to suggest who might be interested in buying it.

She knew that was asking a lot. Noel was adamantly opposed to any sale at all. But if he saw she was trying to work things out, trying to accommodate everyone's interests, he might be persuaded to help her.

Yes, there were things she wanted to discuss with Noel. But Kiri was used to being honest with herself. Her need to be with him went far deeper than she wished to admit. She was drawn to him by a force that had little to do with reason.

So the thing to do was to find him. She left the house and walked along the trail toward the inlet where the *Island Princess* was moored, her depression gone, her heart echoing the joyous cries of the bellbirds along the way. She would talk to Noel. Something could be worked out. There was always a way.

Stepping out of the curtain of trees, she glanced eagerly at the little inlet; then her spirits plummeted to the depths of her toes. The *Island Princess* was gone.

For a moment she just stared, her gaze sweeping over the calm sea, unwilling to admit her disappointment. There was no reason to be downcast; Noel didn't have to check in with her every time he left his anchorage. But why hadn't he mentioned that he was going somewhere?

She turned away, and took another trail into the center of the island. She needed physical activity. She might as well take a morning hike before she went back to the villa. As for Noel's departure, maybe it was just as well that he had gone without saying a word. It served to remind her how undependable men were. Here today, gone tomorrow. She knew that. There was absolutely no reason for that stinging sensation behind her eyes, or the tightness in her throat.

She hiked for several hours, welcoming the exertion that made her breathe deeply and brought a sheen of perspiration to her forehead. The island was crisscrossed by trails, and she thought she had found them all, but as the day wore on she stumbled onto one she hadn't seen before. There was something different about it, she thought, as she followed the narrow path through the dense foliage. Perhaps it was less traveled.

It was narrower than most she had hiked, and darker, more mysterious. The spreading branches of the trees met high above her head, reducing sunlight and probably eliminating moonlight and starlight as well. Still, humid air, laden with moisture from the little stream that gurgled beside the path, felt heavy in her lungs.

She knelt to dip her hand into the clear water, pleased with the moss-covered banks and amazed at the bewildering variety of ferns and bracken that grew right into the streambed.

Straightening, she rubbed her arm over her forehead to dry the perspiration, and continued up the path. It was hot in the tunnel-like enclosure; the foliage intercepted the breeze, but it didn't suppress sounds or smells. Everything was bursting with life; she seemed to be in a multilayered world. The forest floor was deeply covered with moss and bracken. The next layer was composed of small bushes, *punga* ferns, immature trees. Looming above everything was the top layer: huge kauri that blocked the sun; *pohutukawa* blazing with blooms; the contrasting light green leaves of *totara*; all combined to make a nearly impenetrable wall of green.

Then there was sound, sound so loud and insistent she felt it beating against her: cicadas in a cacophony of shrill chorus, punctuated at intervals by the *tui* and the strident call of the weka. And the smells—the air was heavy with the scent of blooming trees, of decaying vegetation, of fragrant moss.

She paused again to mop a sheen of perspiration from her face, gazing around her at the wall of green. The closeness of the place was beginning to give her an eerie, almost claustrophobic feeling. It was as though she had taken a step back in time. No doubt this was what the entire country had looked like in the olden days—days before either the Maori or the *pakeha* had put their mark on it.

She hesitated, then started on up the trail, growing increasingly uneasy. Her isolation was so complete it was difficult to believe she was only a mile or so from the villa. She could have been a hundred miles from civilization.

She realized suddenly that it wasn't just the density of the jungle that was causing her increasing apprehension. A shiver flitted down her spine, and the muscles of her abdomen tensed, as some instinct inherited from primeval ancestors surfaced.

She wasn't alone.

She had an uncanny sensation that unseen eyes were watching her. Something or someone unknown was keeping pace with her, hidden out there in the green darkness.

The impression was so strong that she was rocked by a sense of panic. Rationality fled; she could have believed the

forest was haunted by the ghosts of old Maori warriors
gliding unseen by her side. Or some unknown jungle creature...

She stopped, took a deep breath, shoved her hands into
her pockets, and surveyed the scene around her. Kiri
MacKay didn't indulge in fantasy. She kept her imagination under strict control. Only when she worked with clay
or marble did she make something out of nothing!

She knew very well there were no predatory animals here.
As for the ghosts of Maori warriors—that was the most ridiculous fancy yet. If she felt someone was watching her it
was because her subconscious was aware of something her
conscious mind had not noticed—a twig moving where there
was no wind; a footstep barely heard above the sound of
those screeching cicadas.

She didn't intend to wait passively for whoever was out
there to reveal himself. It wasn't her style.

"Whoever you are—come on out!" Her voice seemed to
vanish into the wall of vegetation.

She waited, feeling sillier as the silence stretched on. She
was shouting at phantoms. But there had to be some basis
for her strong sense that someone was spying on her.

"Stop skulking in the bushes! Come on out!"

Again she waited, nearly convinced that either she had
been wrong or that the unknown person had slipped away.

Then, just a few feet ahead of her, a man stepped out into
the trail, powerful arms akimbo, legs apart, black eyes
shooting fire.

Relief mingled with outrage, as she recognized the young
Maori.

"Rapauru! Why are you following me?"

He stared back at her, his face a sullen mask. She wasn't
being pursued by ghost warriors. This was a living, breathing Maori warrior, but one who resented her every bit as
much as any ancient one would have done.

"Following you?" His voice was deep, guttural. "Why
shouldn't I follow you? You're on *my* island." His words

were a definite challenge; they were wonderfully augmented by a greenstone club he held in one hand, and she gave the weapon a nervous glance. His stern, uncompromising features seemed to be carved from the same stone.

In spite of the shiver of fear that ran through her, she stared calmly back. "*Your* island? Just because my father allowed you to stay here and build your village doesn't mean you own anything."

An angry flush turned his dark skin nearly crimson. "Justice says it's mine." He hesitated, and his next words revealed the anxiety that was mixed with his anger. "I want to know, *pakeha*. What do you intend to do with Long White Cloud?"

She read the anguish behind the words, and hesitated, then spoke gently. "I'll eventually sell, but—"

He started to make a threatening gesture with the club, then let his arm fall to his side. "What will become of my village? Of the entire island?"

Although his expression didn't change, she thought she heard a note of pleading in his voice, and she suspected Rapauru wasn't the big bully he pretended to be. He was desperate—a man about to lose something he loved.

"I'll really try to work something out," she replied, her initial outrage giving way to compassion. "Perhaps I can arrange with the new owner to let you stay...."

"The new owner! Have you already arranged a sale?"

"No—nothing like that."

He stared at her for so long that she shifted uneasily. Then a slight smile crossed his face, a smile that held no friendliness at all, and he lifted his hand briefly. "Take care, *pakeha*," he said softly, then slipped back into the trees.

She took a deep breath to steady herself, then started on up the path, more shaken by the encounter than she cared to admit. Rapauru's last words could certainly be interpreted as a threat. She was almost sure now that he had left the mask on her bed, and that it was he who had trashed the

study. What would he do next? Might he even be dangerous if he became more desperate?

Perhaps she should have told him about Helborn's offer,
but it would probably just add fuel to the flame. She didn't
intend to accept it, and there was no reason to rile Rapauru
up even more.

She walked another hundred feet and suddenly came out
into a little clearing. It was in complete contrast to the
claustrophobic tunnel she had just come through. The
branches above her head thinned enough to admit a flood
of sunlight. A tiny waterfall dropped to a limpid pool edged
by moss and what looked like pennyroyal, and the jungle
growth gave way to a carpet of emerald green grass.

She sank down on one of the boulders that protruded
from the clear water. She had an awful lot of things to think
about, and what better place?

Propping her elbows on her knees, she lowered her chin
to her hands, and stared vacantly at the water, not even seeing the trout that darted like flecks of silver under the surface. Things were becoming much more complicated than
she had expected when she first learned she had become an
heiress.

She had no idea how long she sat there—an hour? Two?
Suddenly she heard the soft sound of footsteps close by.
Startled, she glanced up and saw him. Her pulse raced, not
entirely from surprise.

Noel smiled down at her. "Hi. Am I interrupting something? You looked as though you were in another world."

"Hi," she said softly. Her heart was doing strange things
in her chest. "How did you find me?" She inched over on
the boulder, giving him enough space to sit down.

He accepted her unspoken invitation and lowered himself to the rock. She was uncomfortably aware of the
warmth of his shoulder touching hers, and she couldn't help
noticing how his shorts strained across his thighs. It was
getting a little difficult to breathe.

"Easy," he said, apparently unaware of the way he was affecting her. "Not much goes on around here that Rapauru doesn't know about. I went by the village and he told me I'd find you here."

"When did you get back? The *Island Princess* was gone—"

She broke off at the quick smile that danced across Noel's face. "Did you miss me?"

"Of course not! I mean, I just happened to walk by..."

"Of course." His smile broadened. "I didn't have a chance to talk to you, or I'd have mentioned that I'd be gone awhile. I sailed to Paihia late last night to talk over some problems with the Department of Agriculture and Fisheries."

"Last night?" The stretch of open water between Long White Cloud and Paihia leaped into her mind. She had returned from Paihia well before dark, and had been glad to reach a safe harbor. The crossing hadn't been dangerous, but a wind had risen just as she reached the island, and it was chopping up the sea. "Wasn't it a little rough?"

"Not very. Just a brisk wind. The *Princess* and I have been out in some pretty bad storms and she's very seaworthy. It would take a lot to upset her."

"Do you get a lot of bad weather here?"

"Not usually at this time of year. Of course, bad storms can come up at any time, and when they do, they come up fast, but things are usually calm." He smiled at her. "Don't worry about me—I'm used to them."

"I'm not worried about you!"

His smile was so knowing, that she changed the subject quickly. "This seems a strange way of life for someone like you, Noel. Living on a sailboat, working on a remote island. You told me about your family—you're probably wealthy enough to do anything you want."

"This is what I want. My purpose in life."

"But why is it so important to you?"

He gave her a startled look. "Why? I should think that's obvious. Our planet doesn't have infinite resources. The most important thing we can do is preserve what we have. Stop escalating pollution, resist unthinking development—"

She thought of Helborn's offer sitting in the tray in the study, and swallowed. She was going to have to talk to Noel about that, and she dreaded it. "You can't do anything all by yourself."

"You have to do what you can."

"I believe you're an optimist," she said lightly.

He gave her a keen look. "And you're not? It's not cool to be pessimistic, Kiri. I sometimes think we bring on the things we fear."

Her snort was delicate, but definite. "You're saying if I looked at the world through your eyes, I might change my mind?"

"You might."

"I believe we can't look after the entire world. We have to take care of ourselves—no one else will."

His eyes were suddenly tender, and he reached for her hand, enclosing it in his warm, strong grip. "Kiri, has it been that bad?"

His voice was a caress, and she felt suddenly ridiculous. And vulnerable. Of course it hadn't been that bad. She had her art, her work, she was a strong independent woman. She was overreacting to her father's defection and, if she were honest, to the fact that Noel seemed very much like him. Both had the burning idealism that she had learned to distrust.

You were happier if you didn't expect too much.

He reached toward her and twirled a strand of her hair in his slender fingers. "To think I never knew you existed," he said, almost to himself. "Just before he died, when Ian mentioned he had a daughter, he seemed so sad, so regretful. I assumed you just didn't care enough about him to visit.''

A sharp pain sliced through her chest. "It was the other way around.''

Impulsively, he put his arm around her shoulder and pulled her close, cradling her head against his chest. She felt the whisper of his lips on her hair, and heard the husky murmur of his voice. "It must have been tough.''

She could withstand a lot, but sympathetic understanding unnerved her. Her lips quivered, she started to tremble. She knew she should pull away, but it took more willpower than she had. Why did he have to be so compassionate? So caring?

As she rested in his arms, another stronger feeling began to override her desire for comfort. The texture of his shirt rubbed against her cheek, and she felt the hard muscles beneath the thin material. The even rhythmic thud of his heart vibrated all through her body.

She was aware of the exact instant when his gesture of comfort turned into something else. His heartbeat quickened, she heard him catch his breath. His arms tightened convulsively. Her own pulse racing, she pressed nearer to his heat, his vitality. Little tongues of fire seemed to be traveling all along her nerves, through every vein, heating her blood....

She opened her lips to his seeking mouth. There was nothing tentative about his kiss. His mouth took hers with a savagery of need that matched her own. She raised her hand to his face and traced her fingers along his jaw, thrilling to the texture of his skin, then tangled her fingers in the long thick hair at the back of his neck.

But this was what she had to guard against, this mindless surrender to the senses. Slowly, reluctantly, she pulled away. Long White Cloud stood between them. She had come searching for him so she could discuss Helborn's offer and the future of the island, and she had better do it while she still had a modicum of control.

"Noel," she whispered, her voice still husky with need, "there's something I want to talk to you about."

He drew back, took a deep ravaged breath, and managed a smile. "What marvelous timing," he murmured.

She took a deep breath. "I went to see Klaus Helborn yesterday—"

She broke off abruptly, as she felt every muscle in Noel's body stiffen. Startled, she glanced at his face. A muscle jerked in a clenched jaw, white lines outlined tight-set lips, eyes of ice stared at her as though he didn't know her.

"You went to see Helborn? The developer?" His voice had a quiet, deadly tone she'd never heard before. "Yesterday—after you had looked at all my experiments? Why didn't you tell me right away?"

His expression was as cold and closed as any stranger's, and she felt a flash of anger. He wasn't being reasonable. Her visit to Helborn had been motivated by the hope of helping him, and he wasn't giving her a chance to explain that. She had come looking for him today to tell him about Helborn, and to ask his help; he needn't fly off the handle so quickly.

"I really haven't had time to tell you, have I?" she answered, her tone as cool as his. "I'm talking as fast as I can."

"You're pretty fast at everything. Including sneaking around and negotiating with the most rapacious developer in the islands."

"I wasn't sneaking! And the attorney gave me his name. I didn't know anything about Helborn's reputation!"

"Of course you didn't. You haven't a clue about anything that's been going on." He stood up so abruptly that she nearly lost her balance. "Just what did he offer you for this island?"

Her anger intensified. Noel wasn't going to give her a chance to explain, and she wasn't going to beg. "He made me a generous offer," she said coldly.

PLAY THE
CARNIVAL WHEEL

LUCKY

scratch-off game
and get as many as
SIX FREE GIFTS . . .

HOW TO PLAY:

1. With a coin, carefully scratch off the silver area at right. Then check your number against the chart below it to find out which gifts you're eligible to receive.

2. You'll receive brand-new Silhouette Intimate Moments® novels and possibly other gifts—ABSOLUTELY FREE! Send back this card and we'll promptly send you the free books and gifts you qualify for!

3. We're betting you'll want more of these heart-warming romances, so unless you tell us otherwise, every month we'll send you 4 more wonderful novels to read and enjoy. Always delivered right to your home. And always at a discount off the cover price!

4. Your satisfaction is guaranteed! You may return any shipment of books and cancel at any time. The Free Books and Gifts remain yours to keep!

NO COST! NO RISK!
NO OBLIGATION TO BUY!

You'll look like a million dollars when you wear this elegant necklace! It's a generous 20 inches long and each link is double-soldered for strength and durability.

More Good News For Subscribers-Only!

When you join the Silhouette Reader Service™, you'll receive 4 heart-warming romance novels each month delivered to your home. You'll also get additional free gifts from time to time as well as our subscribers-only newsletter. It's your privileged look at upcoming books and profiles of our most popular authors!

If offer card is missing, write to:
Silhouette Reader Service, P.O. Box 609, Fort Erie, Ontario L2A 5X3

He didn't seem to hear her. "You went to see Helborn," he repeated, as though he still couldn't believe it. "The man Ian has been fighting off for years. And I was fool enough to believe you might understand about the island—"

"I do!" she cried, the pain in his voice making her forget her momentary anger. "I didn't agree to sell! He just made an offer. I thought perhaps I could work something out with him, maybe sell off part of the island—"

He shook off the hand that she had placed on his arm, and shoved his fists into his pockets. "I was right about you all along," he muttered. "You have a dollar sign for a heart!"

The warm protective Noel of a few minutes ago had completely disappeared. This man looked at her with mounting scorn. Before she could say another word, he wheeled away and strode from the clearing, vanishing into the forest.

She stared after him, openmouthed, incredulous. How had the moment of closeness deteriorated so quickly? From a kiss to a quarrel. She shouldn't have responded to his attack as vigorously as she had, but he should have given her a chance to explain, too.

In a way, though, she understood his fierce reaction. This island was closer to his heart than any woman could ever be. He was desolate at the loss of his dream—she meant nothing.

With her heart aching for his pain, angry at both him and her, she rose slowly and stared down at the stream, irresolute and dejected. Why did it have to be this way? Men like Noel were unique—strong, dedicated men who put beliefs, or causes above their own welfare. Why did the two of them have to be on this collision course?

A partial solution was the only thing she could think of, and no one was going to like it. Yet she couldn't give up everything, hand the island over to the government; that was probably the only thing that would satisfy Noel.

Although, as she learned more and more about Ian, the estate began to seem less and less important. What would he have wanted her to do?

Sighing, she started back down the trail toward the villa. It would do no good to follow Noel, although every instinct urged her to do just that. He wasn't prepared to listen.

Still lacerated from the unexpected quarrel, she walked across the lawn to the veranda, head down, eyes on her feet. She wasn't even aware that Neiri was waiting for her until the woman called her name.

"Kiri, I'm so glad you're back," the woman called from the veranda. "Mrs. Armi said you must have left early this morning, and she had no idea where you'd gone."

Kiri smiled stiffly. Neiri, in spite of her welcoming words, looked as aloof as ever standing near the doorway in a long flowered dress, her dark hair caught back in a comb of flowers.

"I hope you didn't worry." Immediately, she rather wished she hadn't let the sarcasm come through quite so clearly.

Neiri ignored it, stepping aside so Kiri could come through the door. "I didn't worry—there's nothing to hurt you on the island, but I am glad you're back. We're having visitors tonight—I thought you'd like a little notice before dinner."

"Oh? Who are they?" She felt hot and dusty, and not at all like entertaining, but there probably wasn't any way out of it.

"Some friends of Ian's—and mine. They live in Paihia, but when they heard you were here—Ian's daughter—" she said softly, "they wanted to come by and pay their respects."

Thus forewarned, she scuttled off to her room, took off her grimy clothes, and took a quick shower, wondering what she had brought with her to wear that might be appropriate for dinner with old friends of Ian's. He had been an affluent, cultured man, and his friends probably were, too.

She frowned doubtfully as she contemplated her meager wardrobe. It consisted mostly of shorts, pants, and various shirts, but she had packed one outfit that might do. Usually she dressed for comfort, but occasionally something stirred inside her that demanded drama, and she had been in that mood when she bought this skirt.

A short time later she regarded herself in front of a full-length mirror. She had used more makeup than usual, rimming her eyes with a hint of shadow and mascara, touching her cheeks and lips with soft raspberry gloss. She had to accentuate her features to balance the impact of the sleek royal blue off-the-shoulder blouse and the long slim skirt.

Kiri had always appreciated the bold colors of Mexico, and the skirt incorporated nearly all of them. It blazed with various shades of blue, intense oranges, the riot of bright primary colors subdued only partially by muted earth tones. It should have been a jarring clash of color, but somehow it all came together in harmony. The geometric pattern around the border was reminiscent of Aztec designs, but it wasn't completely authentic; there was something Eastern in the sinuous drape of the soft material, the subtle slit from hem to knee that showed only when she moved.

It was an outfit that only a tall, slender person could bring off, a woman who knew who she was and didn't apologize for it.

When she entered the dining room a little later, she was glad she had made the choice. Ian's friends, a couple in their late fifties, appeared assured and well-groomed, the woman in a expensive-looking cocktail dress of white crepe, the man in a white shirt and tailored shorts.

No surprises there. It was their daughter that caused Kiri to pause in the archway, and wish she could check her makeup one more time.

A swift glance told Kiri the young woman was probably in her mid-twenties, although she could have been younger.

It was hard to tell about soft, curvy women with round an-
gelic faces and fluttery mannerisms. Women who looked as
sweet and fragile as spun sugar candy. Kiri suddenly felt that
she was all elbows.

Neiri came forward quickly, and drew Kiri into the room.
"Kiri, dear, I'd like you to meet Frank and Leda Ellis. Old,
old friends. And their daughter, Felicia. I know you young
people will have a lot in common."

In the general babble of introductions acknowledged and
compliments exchanged, Kiri regarded Felicia warily. She
was the kind of woman who always made Kiri feel all
thumbs, tall and awkward and gangling. But maybe she
wouldn't be too bad; the girl's smile seemed sincere, and her
eyes were interested and alert.

Suddenly the girl's gaze shifted from Kiri's eyes to somewhere over her left shoulder, and her face glowed, her eyes
sparkled. Kiri turned slowly to follow the gaze, knowing
even before she saw him that Noel had arrived.

He moved easily into the gathering, nodded curtly at Kiri,
smiled at the Ellises, and put his hand lightly on Felicia's
shoulder. If the girl batted her lashes any harder, Kiri
thought, they might fall off.

"Noel, I'm so glad you could make it," Neiri said, coming forward and kissing him lightly on the cheek. Her voice
grew softer. "It's hard, with Ian gone, but at least the rest
of us are together."

There was a murmur of agreement, generalized kissing,
and Kiri settled in to endure the evening. The Ellises were
obviously curious about her, and she answered their questions as best she could. The talk often centered on Ian—on
things he had done, fun they had had together—and Kiri
had to admit he sounded like a wonderful man.

She had wondered initially how she and Noel could dis-
guise their disagreement from the others, but she soon saw,
to her chagrin, that she needn't have worried. He skirted
around her, scrupulously polite, but it was Felicia who held
his attention.

Kiri gritted her teeth as she watched them—the girl, all adoration and fluttering femininity, looking up into Noel's appreciative face. Her delicate hand with coral-tipped nails resting lightly on his arm. Noel, elegant in white shirt and tailored shorts that set off his lean figure to perfection, bending his head to hear something she murmured, then chuckling fondly.

She tried to engross herself in the general conversation, but her eyes kept returning to Noel and Felicia. To be fair, Noel was no more attentive to the girl than he would have been to any old friend, but why did he have to stay so close to her?

The angry, sick feeling that engulfed her was something new to Kiri. She didn't recognize it. She certainly didn't care that he found Felicia so engaging; they were old friends after all, and he had made his feelings about Kiri herself painfully clear. It wouldn't be—it couldn't be—that she was jealous.

Noel took a quick look over Felicia's shoulder, glad that Kiri was turned in another direction and couldn't see the look in his eyes. God, she looked beautiful. Like some fabulous Aztec princess—and about as approachable.

He wished he could apologize for the way he'd acted today, but it was impossible with all these people around. He never seemed to get close enough for an intimate conversation; she moved away every time he came within three feet of her.

He had regretted his outburst almost immediately. She had asked, but he hadn't even given her a chance to explain, and the hurt look he'd seen in her eyes as he turned away still burned in his heart. He knew Kiri wasn't the mercenary monster he had accused her of being; it was just that the name of Helborn triggered something in him that made him want to lash out. The man was ruthless.

It was easy enough to keep his mind on Kiri and still make the correct answers to Felicia's chatter. Strange that only a few weeks ago, Felicia had seemed eminently desirable to him—curved in all the right places, gentle, easygoing, fun... Felicia, or any of a dozen girls like her.

He shot Kiri a dark look. Her arrival on Long White Cloud had changed a lot of things. Apparently it had changed his taste in women.

Kiri picked up the look, and her heart sank even farther. He was still angry. Tilting her chin, she moved away to talk to Frank Ellis, only half hearing him as he once again told her how sorry he was about her father, and how happy he was to meet Ian's daughter.

This evening had to end sometime, Kiri thought, and eventually it did. Dinner over, the group lingered an hour or so in conversation, then Noel accompanied the Ellises to their boat. With a quick good-night to Neiri, Kiri fled to her room.

Flinging open the French doors, she rushed out onto her patio and lifted her flushed face to the breeze that came in from the bay. What was happening to her? She wouldn't have believed it of herself; had she really given in to an irrational emotion like jealousy?

She sank down in the lounge chair, reached down to slip off her sandals, then stretched back along the soft cushions. Absentmindedly, she reached over and picked a gardenia from a potted bush a foot or so away, then held it to her nose. The fragrance was so sweet it was nearly cloying. The jealousy faded. Deep longings, half-recognized needs, bittersweet regrets, all stirred within her; she had never felt so restless, or so alone.

She wasn't a fool. She knew that more than the disposition of Long White Cloud stood between them. In spite of the sexual electricity that sparked between them, they were as unlikely to blend together as oil and water.

Of course, the way she felt about Noel was based on more than sexual attraction, although she wasn't discounting that element. The truth was that she had come halfway around the world and found the man who, if the fates had been kind, could have made her happy. A man she could have loved deeply, passionately, forever—if things had been different.

But she wasn't going to let herself go that far; she could still extricate herself.

To do anything but run would be foolhardy, open herself to sure heartbreak. Noel was a good man, a man of depth and conviction and integrity. A man so like the father she was coming to know that it was frightening.

No, Noel wasn't the problem; it was herself. She didn't want an idealistic man, a man who fought for causes. They were always more important than anything else. She hadn't been able to hold her own father. She was adult enough to know that his leaving hadn't been her fault, as she had thought when she was a child. But the residue of that conviction was still there. Intellectually, she knew nothing had been her fault, that at three years old she couldn't have held her mother and father together.

Yet the inner core of her being had rejected that assessment. Her father had loved something much more than he had loved her. She had never put it into words, hardly ever allowed it to surface into her conscious thoughts. But she knew—she wasn't lovable.

The fountain splashed softly in the moonlight, the faint sound blending with the soft, plaintive cry of a morepork owl. Tomorrow she would have to think, plan, decide what to do; tonight she gave herself up to melancholy, and to the aching need of a woman for a man. A particular man.

Out of the corner of her eyes, she was vaguely aware of movement. She turned her head slightly. The night seemed to hold its breath; nothing moved. She was caught in a timeless moment, as she recognized the tall figure that stood in the shadows that edged the patio. She wasn't startled, she wasn't excited; it was as though all time had been inexorably leading to this moment.

''Noel,'' she said softly.

Chapter 8

Noel didn't know how long he had remained in the shadows, just feasting his eyes on her. Returning to the villa from seeing the Ellises aboard their boat, he had at first planned on going to the main door. He couldn't leave until he had apologized to Kiri, and there had been no opportunity when the visitors were there. But something, some primitive instinct or subconscious force, drew him to the side patio, and he halted there in the hedge just as Kiri came out the French doors and sank into the lounge chair.

Seeing her, he grew very still, as though every sense were poised and waiting for the inevitable. He could hardly breathe, as he watched her idly pluck a gardenia, hold it to her face and inhale the sweet fragrance. The moon was a soft full orb in the velvet sky, and the light bathed her face in silver, caressed her bare arms, fondled the V-shaped hollow between her breasts that was partially exposed by the blue silk.

He shouldn't be staring, mesmerized, at that delectable valley. He shouldn't be spying on her, shouldn't be thinking of running his hand along her cheek, down her slender throat, over the velvet skin of her bare shoulder, outlining her breasts that were clearly discernible through the thin material of her blouse. He certainly shouldn't.

His hands clenched convulsively and his throat was tight and dry. Desire rippled through him, leaving him rigid and hard. He fought to regain control; the sensation was definitely unwelcome. Hadn't he learned anything in the years since Rosamund? This woman was trouble in more ways than one.

Why couldn't he feel this gut-wrenching desire for Felicia? He had observed the two young women all evening, compared, wondered. Making a determined effort to be fair, and possibly to exorcise Kiri's hold on him, he had decided that Felicia was probably the prettiest, if one went by traditional standards. And he knew it didn't matter in the slightest.

Kiri had a magnetism that drew him like iron. In the deepest darkness, he knew he could reach out and trace the lines of her features and know immediately it was she. A whiff of her light scent, and he would know her wherever she tried to hide. She was the intense, sensual kind of woman who wrenched a man loose from his moorings, drew him to her side and kept him there, although she obviously didn't recognize that side of herself.

And he had better watch out. He didn't want to lose control of his life, to be set adrift in a sea of emotion. There were things he wanted to do in this world, things he felt were infinitely important, and he wouldn't be deflected by the demands of his body. He wouldn't be sidetracked by a woman who couldn't share his hopes and dreams.

And in this particular case, a woman who would be gone as soon as she had dismantled his hopes and dreams.

She stirred slightly, closed her eyes, and leaned back against the pillow. He was so close he could see the soft rise and fall of her breasts as she breathed. He should leave, go around to the front door, ask Neiri to call her . . . certainly he shouldn't just stand here . . .

He wasn't aware of that first step out of the shadows up onto the patio. He saw her eyes open, heard the soft cadence of her voice . . .

"Noel . . ."

Like a man in a dream he walked slowly toward her, pulled by an invisible thread of steel. His eyes locked with hers. The moonlight fell across her face in a silver beam, lovingly outlining each separate feature. He saw her pupils darken, widen, until her eyes were nearly black. He could drown in those eyes.

Her lips parted slightly; she seemed to be holding her breath, as he drew closer. He wasn't sure what he read in her expression; there was apprehension, even fear—and a desire that matched his own.

The sure knowledge that she wanted him sent a river of fire coursing through his blood. With a groan, he dropped to his knees beside the chair and gathered her in his arms.

She felt light, pliant, infinitely fragile, as he molded her slender body against his chest. Her head tipped backward, spilling dark, soft hair along his arm, and he lowered his head until his lips touched hers.

At first it was just the feather of a kiss, as he tasted the sweetness of her mouth. A tremor ran through his body, as her lips opened a little, inviting, encouraging. Tightening his grip, he deepened the kiss and pulled her even closer, the urgency of his need apparent in every hard line of his body.

He heard her labored breathing so in tune with his own, inhaled the heated scent of her skin. When she pulled away a little, he instinctively tightened his grip, reluctantly left her lips, and buried his face in the fragrance of her hair.

"Noel . . ." It was a faint, soft whisper.

He drew back a few inches and looked at her face. He couldn't have said anything if his life depended on it.

Her voice was more than a little shaky. "You're on your knees—in your shorts. There's plenty of room here."

She moved away a little to demonstrate the availability of room on the narrow lounge chair, and Noel smiled, suddenly aware of hard cold stone on his bare knees. He half rose, slid onto the chair, and stretched out beside her. She was right; there was room. Plenty of it, if one didn't mind touching along the entire length of one's body. Which he certainly didn't.

She put her arms around his neck and drew him to her for another kiss. And another. It seemed centuries later when Noel remembered why he had come here in the first place—an apology.

"I'm sorry, Kiri," he said softly, between kisses delivered all over her face and along her throat and down into the valley between her breasts. "I acted like a spoiled brat today."

"No, you didn't," she whispered, when she could finally reply. "I should have told you I was going to see Helborn before I went—"

"No, it was my fault," he protested. "I wanted to apologize at dinner, but there was always someone around—"

"I noticed that," she said, her voice suddenly tart.

Exultation surged through him, and he chuckled softly, nibbling her ear. "I think you were jealous of Felicia."

"I wasn't!"

He caught a glimpse of her eyes and recognized the doubt and confusion. Sudden tenderness filled him, so exquisitely that he swallowed a lump in his throat. Slowly, he traced her cheek with one finger, watching the emotions play across her face like sunlight flickering on a brook. It didn't make any sense. Kiri was so unsure of herself; she didn't realize how beautiful, how desirable she was. Of course he hadn't realized it himself until he got to know her. Now he wondered how he could have thought anything else. How a mesmerizing woman like Kiri could feel threatened by a woman like Felicia was beyond him, but she obviously did.

He doubted that words would do much to increase her self-esteem. Besides, he had a hard time keeping his mind on what he was saying. Her proximity heated his blood, sent spasms of desire through every muscle, tightened and hardened his manhood to near pain. The world had collapsed around then, leaving only the two of them at the center. All that was left was urgent need, the imperative necessity to bury himself in her soft, pulsing flesh.

He stroked one hand along the length of her body, then eased back up, finding the way beneath the silky material of her blouse. Her skin felt satin-smooth, warm and alive when he cupped her breast in his hand. He heard her gasp, and realized his own hand was trembling.

Her fragility, her defenselessness, tore at his heart. Her innocence, as she clung to him. This wasn't the tough-minded, independent woman he knew. He wanted to show her the way to ecstasy, fly with her to unimaginable heights. He wanted—he wanted to take her right here on the patio! Right now!

His hands explored her soft flesh, his mouth teased and tasted. He felt her fiery response, as she arched against him, pressed ever closer, and it spurred him on. Soon, very soon, there would be no stopping. Every rational thought would be submerged in the age-old instinct of satiating his deepest longing. He had only felt like this once before, with Rosamund, and even that sensation had not been as intense, as desperate. Every sense urged him to take her, to slake the desire that was consuming them both. He was burning, burning, and she was open and seeking, crying for him . . .

Suddenly something at the very center of him went still. He remembered Rosamund—manipulative, self-seeking Rosamund. Rosamund who had turned a young, vulnerable boy into a hard, sophisticated man, a man determined never to let his hormones rule his head.

Not that Kiri was like her—not at all, although he had thought so at first. He knew she was honest, warm, and even though he had accused her of treachery this afternoon, he suspected there wasn't a duplicitous bone in her body. But she was every bit as capable as Rosamund had been of keeping him from his life's work.

It was this deep, unreasoning descent into primitive need that was dangerous. He could lose himself in Kiri—and lose his direction, as he had nearly done with Rosamund. The road back to sanity had been incredibly painful, and it wasn't a road he wanted to travel again. There was no way he could keep this relationship light. When it was over, as it had to be, he would leave Kiri with only a part of himself— and he was a man who wanted to remain whole.

With more willpower than he had ever thought he possessed, he moved slightly away from her. Instinctively, she clung to him, then, feeling his rejection, tensed. Bewildered, she looked into his face, and her own expression changed, became unsure. He felt as though a hot band of iron was squeezing his heart, as he saw her uncertainty. Then the cool mask dropped over her face, and she struggled to a sitting position.

"Kiri, I'm sorry. I never meant to go this far...."

She flinched. "There's no reason to be sorry. You didn't exactly force me."

Her tone was cool and even. He couldn't believe that only a few seconds before she had been wrapped around him as tightly as a vine around a pillar. She rose from the chair, taking considerable time to straighten her skirt and adjust her blouse, then lifted her chin, somehow managing to avoid his eyes.

"It's late... I'd better be going in."

"Kiri, I—" He didn't know what to say. In pulling himself out of the vortex of passion, he had thought only of his own safety, his own need to remain autonomous. He hadn't thought how it would seem to her. He sensed a deep hurt under Kiri's cool facade, and it astounded him. There was nothing wrong with Kiri—*he* was the problem.

He moved toward her, and she drew back quickly. Another minute, and she would disappear inside the French doors and any opportunity to explain would be over.

"Kiri, please, we have to talk."

"There's nothing to talk about. We nearly made a mistake, that's all, but we recovered in time. Probably something to do with the moon." Her smile was a little crooked, but her voice was even and controlled. She was definitely moving toward the doors. Not sure of what he should do, he raised his arm, then let it fall to his side.

"I'll see you tomorrow," he called, as the doors slid shut behind her. A cold hard rock seemed to form in his stomach, as he watched her go. He had hurt her, but wouldn't he have hurt her more if he hadn't been able to stop?

Safely inside, Kiri stood with her back to the wall until she could breathe normally. It took a while. Every nerve, every muscle, every cell, ached with loss, but at least she had made a dignified exit.

She had made a fool of herself, but she supposed she should be grateful that the lesson had been learned. In spite of all her resolve to stay clear of Noel, she had fallen into his arms like a ripe apple. At that moment, she had wanted desperately to make love to him, and hadn't given a thought to the consequences. It was totally uncharacteristic of her, and just went to show the hold Noel already had over her.

He, at least, had shown a little sense. He had rejected her easy availability, as she had always known he would. It hurt—God, how it hurt—but it was better now than after she had given him her heart, before she began to believe in the illusion of happiness.

She had to leave Long White Cloud, and she had to leave fast.

She awoke the next morning to the sound of a light tapping. Struggling into a robe, she opened the door and Neiri stepped quickly into the room.

"I'm sorry I woke you. I could have left a note, I guess, but—"

"Come on in." Kiri, still half-asleep, glanced at her watch and rubbed her eyes. As early as it was, Neiri was completely dressed in neat white trousers and a flowered blouse, her hair pulled back and tied with a red silk scarf, a purse slung over her shoulder. "Is something wrong?"

"Oh, no, nothing is wrong." Neiri spoke quickly, and Kiri, always sensitive to nuances, caught a hint of anxiety in her voice. Neiri also seemed to be looking everywhere but straight at her.

"I just wanted to tell you that I'm taking the launch into Paihia," Neiri continued. "I didn't want you to wonder where it was, in case you wanted to leave the island."

Kiri studied her face thoughtfully. Neiri had never used the launch before; Rapauru had always taken her anywhere she wanted to go. "Of course it's all right," she said slowly. "I hadn't planned on using it today."

"I'll be back this afternoon. And Kiri—" Neiri hesitated, then spoke quickly, "Why don't you stay around the house today? You haven't even glanced at your father's books. He had a very good library."

Kiri frowned. Her daily routine was pretty well set. Long morning and afternoon walks around the island, home for dinner. Was Neiri trying to warn her about something by suggesting that she confine herself to the house? She'd never shown the slightest interest in Kiri's daily activities before. Anyway, it wasn't a bad idea. In strolling around the island she was likely to run into Noel, and she wasn't ready for that. A lazy day of reading might take her mind off her more pressing problems.

"That might be just the thing to do," she said easily. "Have a nice trip."

"I'll be back this afternoon." Neiri's tense shoulders sagged, with relief, Kiri suspected. She was definitely uneasy about something. She wished she could question her, but Neiri would reveal only what she wished to reveal. Their relationship was neutral at best. If the woman's agitation had anything to do with Rapauru, her loyalty to her son was such that Kiri would never know it.

The morning dragged slowly on, as Kiri tried to find some activity to drive away her depression. The more she tried to forget last night's scene with Noel, the more vividly it played itself over in her mind. She needed the release of physical activity, and Neiri's vague warning would never have stopped her from her usual tour of the island, but the thought that Noel was out there did. What could she say to him, after the way she had practically thrown herself at him the night before?

Perhaps reading wasn't a bad idea. Or, if not reading, at least cataloging the books, determining which should be kept, which sold or given away.

She opened the door to the study, and paused on the threshold, her eyes traveling around the small room. Nothing was obviously out of place, but something prickled along the back of her neck. She could have sworn someone had been in here.

Well, why not? Mrs. Armi dusted, Neiri might come in for a dozen different reasons. She walked toward the rolltop desk, glanced at the in-tray.

She stood very still, and her heart missed a beat. The offer from Helborn was missing.

Not yet overly concerned, she leafed quickly through the papers on the desk. Frowning, she shoved them aside and looked again at the in-tray. No question about it. The offer from Helborn which she had placed there the day before was gone.

More annoyed than worried, she caught her lower lip between her teeth, and gazed out the window toward the entangled greenery that screened the island. There was really no question in her mind as to what had happened to it. Rapauru. Again.

She hadn't the slightest idea as to why he would want to steal the offer; it was of no value to him, and he couldn't possibly be naive enough to think that stealing an offer would stop a sale. But whatever his motive, she was tired of him coming and going in her house whenever he felt like it, taking whatever he wished. It was time she put a stop to it.

A few minutes later she stepped out the door and started down the well-traveled trail to Rapauru's village. Neiri's warning—if that was what it was—flashed through her mind, but she ignored it. She wasn't the kind of person who let vague worries deter her from what she needed to do. She had been as understanding of Rapauru's problems as anyone could be; now it was time for a showdown.

Her steps slowed as she neared the village, and she hesitated before moving out into the clearing, glancing quickly around. Rapauru believed in authenticity; there were likely to be guards around, or at least the ubiquitous dogs. But nothing moved, there was no unusual noise, so she squared her shoulders and stepped out of the curtain of green into the settlement.

She saw at once that there was much more activity than there had been the last time she had come here. Over two dozen people, mostly young men in the abbreviated Maori costume, moved purposefully around the village; one or two glanced at her, but then went on about their business, whatever it was. She stood still for several minutes, observing the busy scene, and no one challenged her.

There were more dwellings, too, than there had been when she had originally seen the settlement. The new structures were mostly tents, their vibrant colors looking out of place among the thatched cottages. Rapauru's village was obviously expanding and at the expense of authenticity. She bit her lip, her gaze roving over the little settlement. It was odd that Rapauru was permitting such growth, when he must realize he might not even be able to keep what he had.

A footstep crackled on the scattering of shells behind her, and she spun around. She might have known her arrival wouldn't go unnoticed for long. Rapauru stood behind her, his face a dark, sullen mask, legs apart, muscular arms folded across his chest in obvious challenge.

She lifted her chin, and met his eyes squarely. She was in the right here, and she wasn't going to let him intimidate her again.

"I want to talk to you, Rapauru."

He shrugged, with no change of expression. "*Pakehas* are good at talk. That's about all they're good at."

Her lips tightened; his insolence angered her, even as it made her uneasy. Rapauru always blustered, but now she sensed something in him—some tightly leashed violence that in spite of all his posturing she hadn't felt before; she put her hands on her hips and surveyed him coldly.

"Don't think you've gotten away with anything. I know you put the mask in my bedroom, trying to scare me away. And trashed Ian's study. And now you have Klaus Helborn's offer to buy White Cloud. I want it back."

A rush of blood turned his dark face nearly purple. His chest seemed to swell, sparks of anger shot from his eyes, as he spat out the words.

"Helborn's offer! You lied to me, *pakeha!* You said you hadn't made any plans to sell. All the time you had the offer right on your desk!"

"I hadn't made definite plans! Not then, and not to him. You had no right to take it from the study!"

"I had every right! You went behind our backs, you sneaked around and got an offer. If you didn't mean to sell, why did you keep it? No more lies, *pakeha!*"

He had somehow inched closer; he was looming over her, his face contorted in fury. Out of the corner of her eye she saw that other men had inched closer, too. A chill went down her back. She was standing in a circle of bare chests, bronzed legs, scowling faces. She tried to remind herself that these men were only playing warrior, that they all had jobs and families somewhere else, that they were just acting out a fantasy. Nonetheless, her throat felt dry, and she swallowed nervously. For the first time since entering the village, she was afraid.

"I don't lie," she said, managing to control her voice. "When I sell the island, I'll try to figure out some way your village can remain, but I can't promise anything."

"Promises of a *pakeha*," Rapauru snorted. "Feathers in the wind."

"Rapauru, why did you want the offer? What good can it possibly do you?"

She felt a sudden movement in the crowd around her, like wheat rippling in the wind. Rapauru's gaze left hers and fastened on something behind her. She turned slowly.

She was face-to-face with a man she had never seen before. As tall as Rapauru, he was much thinner and less impressive physically, although the feathered cape he had thrown over his shoulders gave him an air of authority and command. It was hard to guess his age—he had brown, unlined skin, and the posture of a man in his prime. Probably in his early thirties. Definitely a Maori, although, she thought, her heart sinking, he was the type you might find in any group. A fanatic.

Even before he spoke she was sure of it, and she shivered as though blasted by a cold wind. His expression was cold, contemptuous, while his black eyes burned with fire like an ancient prophet. His voice had the cutting edge of a razor.

"You want to know why we need the offer?" He turned to the crowd, and spoke with the practiced tone of an experienced orator. "The *pakeha* wants to know why we need the offer. So we can prove to the world in black and white the perfidy of the woman. She comes from far away to take our land, land that belongs to all of us. There is only one way to handle this theft. We reclaim what is ours."

There was a murmur of agreement from the crowd. Suddenly, Kiri realized who the man was. Tainui.

It all added up. Tainui, the agitator who had disappeared from the mainland. The extremist who wanted to return all New Zealand to the Maoris was here on Long White Cloud. And he had followers right here. One look at Rapauru's entranced expression told her that.

She flashed back to Neiri's uneasiness that morning, when she had asked her to stay in the villa today. She must have known Tainui was here. Was that why she had left?

Tainui's impassioned speech had turned into a harangue, and she only half listened, intent on seeing the impression he made on the assembled men. There was nothing new about his words; they were depressingly familiar. Violence, terror, push back the imposter. Words that had inflamed men over the centuries, sent them to their deaths. Was Tainui actually prepared to go that far?

A glance around the circle showed that his message was getting through to some of them, although most of the men shuffled their feet and looked a little uneasy. Tainui, ever the showman, must have sensed that he had gone a little too far, for he toned down his rhetoric a little.

"Long White Cloud is ours," he said simply. "Ours long before the *pakeha,* who took it from us with trickery and death. We will reclaim it."

He paused, and Kiri spoke quickly. "Just how do you plan to do that, Tainui?"

He smiled, a shrewd, cunning smile. "So you recognize me? Soon everyone will. Why, we will reclaim the island through moral strength, of course." His eyes mocked her. "We will take our cause to the world, ask for justice."

"And you, Tainui? What's in it for you?"

His eyes narrowed to tiny slits, and she caught a glimpse of pure hatred. She felt a force emanating from him, and knew she was very close to danger. Then the muscles in his shoulders almost imperceptibly relaxed, and he broadened his mocking smile.

"What's in it for me? Justice for my people, of course."

He reached over and put his hand on her shoulder. It might have appeared a casual gesture, but she felt his fingers digging deep into her flesh. She felt a chill right through to the bone. He gestured toward the murmuring group of men, said something in a language she didn't understand, and they dispersed quickly, leaving only Rapauru who, seemingly unable to decide what to do, shifted his weight from one foot to the other.

"We'll talk inside," Tainui said, shoving her toward the carved doorway of a hut a few feet away.

She absolutely did not want to go into that hut with Tainui. Her muscles were stiff with fear, and she glanced beseechingly at Rapauru. He might not be her friend, but she didn't sense in him the pure evil that surrounded Tainui like a dark aura. Tainui was no Maori patriot, she would bet on it. He had his own agenda of seeking personal power.

She dug in her heels and tried to pull away. Tainui merely increased the pressure on her shoulder until she winced with pain, and moved her inexorably toward the hut. Rapauru was going to be no help at all. She could read his expression perfectly—confusion, bewilderment, but no intention at all of challenging Tainui.

Panic made breathing difficult. She didn't know what would happen if Tainui got her out of sight of the others. Surely he wasn't crazy enough to actually harm her—was he? When he had been talking to the men she'd had the definite impression that he had been honing his image, almost giving a speech for the media. Harming her wouldn't go over so well on television, would it? Where were the cameras when you needed them?

But he had already taken two hostages, and although he had released them, she sensed he was unpredictable. He seemed strung tight as a wire, and who knew when he might step over the line of rational behavior? Maybe he'd decided to be a martyr, go down in history instead of only making the front pages.

"We can talk out here." The squeak that came from her mouth didn't sound much like her own voice.

"No," he said, his voice revealing cruel amusement. "We need privacy for what I have to say. We can't talk out here."

"Of course you can."

The voice, quiet, calm, full of a deadly anger, came from somewhere to the side of them. Tainui jerked her around and her legs almost folded under her. Standing a few feet away, a coiled mass of energy ready to spring, his steel-blue gaze sweeping over Tainui like a laser, was Noel.

Startled, Tainui grunted, released his grip, and she jerked free and scurried across to Noel. His eyes never left Tainui, as he put an arm around her and positioned her a little behind him. Then he swung around to Rapauru.

"What's going on here?"

Rapauru looked first at Tainui, then at Noel, obviously a man caught between two fires of equal intensity.

"Is that how you treat Ian's daughter?" Noel demanded.

Rapauru hesitated, and Tainui, snorting with disgust, moved quickly away and disappeared among the village huts. Rapauru, frowning, watched him go, then turned back to Noel, his expression a mixture of embarrassment and bravado.

"This isn't anything for you to mix into, Noel. She came to our village, picked a fight. Tainui wouldn't hurt her, but she needs to be taught a lesson."

"I'll do any teaching that needs to be done," Noel said dryly, his eyes still on Rapauru. The Maori shrugged, lowered his eyes and strode away after Tainui.

"Let's get out of here." Noel grasped her hand and they hurried back along the trail, not speaking until they came to a little outcropping of rock. She was out of breath when Noel seated her gently, then knelt beside her, taking both her hands in his. "Are you all right?"

"I'm fine," she managed. "A little shaken up, but fine. How did you happen to arrive just in time, like the cavalry?"

"You weren't at home when I stopped by this morning—neither was Neiri. Mrs. Armi didn't know where you were, but I guessed you might have come here."

He squeezed her hands, then rose and sat beside her on the boulder. "That was quite a little scene I stumbled onto. What happened back there?"

So Noel had come by the house early this morning. He wanted to see her. The knowledge warmed her heart, but she kept her voice under control. "I'm not entirely sure what was going on. That was Tainui, you know."

"I recognized him—I've seen pictures. But what's he doing in Rapauru's village?"

She sighed, and leaned her head back against his shoulder. "Stirring up trouble, for one thing. He's a real firebrand. I'm a little concerned about Rapauru."

He arched his eyebrow in obvious surprise. "Concerned about Rapauru? After the way he's treated you, done everything he can to frighten you away?"

"I know. But in some ways I'm not sure I blame him. He's never really tried to harm me—just a lot of bluff and bluster. In some ways, I respect him, sympathize with him, although I know he's a hothead. But Tainui is something else."

"He certainly is," Noel said briskly. "I can't help but think there'll be trouble with him on the island."

"Should we notify the police?"

"There's nothing they can do. He has a perfect right to be here—no one has filed any charges against him. But I'll call Jack when we get back and let him know where he is— they'll want to keep an eye on him, at least."

"I think there's been a big change in the village," she said slowly. "It was obvious that Tainui was the man in charge. It's possible that Rapauru is getting in over his head, that Tainui is using him for his own purposes. Can you talk to Rapauru?"

Noel sighed. "We were never that close, although I believe he respects me. He loved Ian, but perhaps he tolerated me only because Ian liked me. That's why I reminded him that you're Ian's daughter...."

They were both silent, so many unspoken words between them. Idly, he caressed her shoulder, and his touch was warm, comforting. When he finally spoke, it was obvious his thoughts were still on the village.

"I think you have Rapauru pegged—he's impulsive, a hothead, but he's never done anything violent that I know of. But he's a follower, in spite of all his posturing about being a Maori chief. Tainui is undoubtedly using him for his own purposes."

He kicked idly at a rock. "I just wish I knew what those purposes were."

Chapter 9

"Are you sure you'll be all right alone?" Noel held her lightly by the shoulders and gazed down into her upturned face. He was frowning slightly, a look of concern in his clear blue eyes. "I don't believe for a minute Tainui or any of his gang will come here, but you must be a little shook up. That was an ugly scene."

Her throat tightened, though she tried to smile; Noel was right. She was still shaken up from the encounter at the village, and was relieved to be back on the veranda of the villa. She drew a deep breath and held his eyes, struck again by the cool elegance of his features as he bent above her, although she now knew the man himself was anything but cool. Those firm lips had turned to flame under hers, and his eyes, now searching and intent, had blazed with passion. Remembrance of last night's emotions flooded through her, and she trembled. For one moment, before she gained control of herself, she wanted nothing more than to move closer into his embrace and accept the protection he was offering, as a child would have run to safety.

But she wasn't a child. She had been on her own for a long time, and while Noel might offer one kind of safety, he certainly presented a danger of another kind. She couldn't forget her willingness—no, she had to be honest—her eagerness to make love to him last night, nor could she forget his rejection. Even now, just thinking of it, she flushed with embarrassment.

"I won't really be alone," she answered softly. "Mrs. Armi is here, but thanks for the offer. Anyway, one rescue a day is enough," she said, trying for lightness. "Not that I really believe I was in any physical danger. From what I've heard of him, Tainui strikes me as a man with one eye on the media, and actually harming me wouldn't go over too well on the six o'clock news."

"I'm sure you're right—he was just posturing for the crowd. But he's unpredictable. If you're sure you don't want me to stay, please promise you won't go wandering around the island. The situation at the village seemed pretty tense. I had no idea all those strange men were camped there, and I wonder whether Rapauru agreed. If you truly don't mind staying alone, I think I'll go back and have a talk with him."

"Please—don't worry." She glanced around the spacious veranda; down at the lawn, spotted with the vibrant color of blooming flowers, the sound of a far-off splash of the fountain could be heard. This place had seemed an oasis of serenity in a troubled world; now she realized that it was not isolated from all the problems of civilization. There was no escape from them even on this idyllic isle.

She moved away from Noel a fraction of an inch and gave him a warm smile. Noel wasn't everything she had thought he was, either. He was much more complex. Certainly there were problems between them, but right now he was her ally—her only one. "Don't worry about me," she repeated softly. "Neiri planned on returning this afternoon, and it's nearly one o'clock now. I'll find plenty to do inside."

He held her eyes as though trying to see inside her heart, then lifted his hand and brushed a finger gently over her lips, then along her throat. The tenderness in the gesture nearly broke down her resolve, but she didn't move as she stared back helplessly. Before she realized his intention, he lowered his head to give her a light kiss on the cheek, then turned, took the steps two at a time, and vanished into the bush.

She riveted her eyes to the spot where he had disappeared as though he might miraculously emerge again, then sighed, and turned back into the house, completely ambivalent about her encounter with Rapauru. Her determination to confront the young Maori with the theft of the offer from Helborn hadn't accomplished anything, but at least she knew more about the situation at the village. And what she knew was disconcerting. If Tainui actually staged a demonstration or provoked some kind of incident, it would make selling the island more difficult, and from what she had seen and heard of him, he certainly didn't seem to be the type who was interested in negotiating.

Her thoughts were interrupted by the jangling of the phone; she heard Mrs. Armi's footsteps padding down the hall, and a moment later her raised voice.

"Telephone, Kiri."

She picked up the phone, vaguely wondering who could be calling her here. Helborn, to press his offer? Or perhaps Mr. Marston, the lawyer, and if so, she hoped the news was good. She wanted to leave this place as soon as possible.

But it was neither of them. Across the miles, crackling only a little, came her mother's crisp voice. Her heart sank, and she took a deep breath. She wasn't ready to cope with Lois.

"Kiri, dear, whatever is going on?" The melodious, high-pitched voice allowed no hiding. "I thought I'd have heard from you by now."

Kiri closed her eyes. She could almost see her mother sitting by the pool in her Woodside home, her skin a golden brown, her hair expensively streaked with blond. With her marriage to the stockbroker, Lois had finally achieved everything she wanted.

"I told you I'd call as soon as anything was settled, Mother. So far, there's nothing to tell you."

"Nothing? What's the island like? Is that all there is in the estate?"

"That seems to be all of it—and the island? Well, it's very beautiful, and—"

"Have you looked into selling yet? There's no problem, is there?" Her mother's tone sharpened. "You will get the money, won't you?"

"There's no real problem," she said slowly. None that her mother would recognize, anyway. "Things take time, especially without a will. There are some people living here who have sort of a right—"

"A legal right?"

"Not exactly... but I did inherit only because Ian didn't leave a will, and everyone here seems to think—"

Her mother cut her off before she could continue, the exasperation clear in her voice. "Kiri, there are times when you seem too much like your father. This dreamy altruism. Genes will tell, I guess. Certainly he wasn't around long enough for it to be anything else."

Kiri could tell by the inflection in her mother's voice that she was winding up for a real tirade on Ian's shortcomings. She cut in quickly. "Mother, did Ian ever try to see me after he left? Any word at all? Any letters?"

The pause was so long that Kiri wondered if they were still connected. When Lois's voice finally came, she heard the wariness. "You never asked anything like that before, Kiri."

"Well," she stumbled along, "I always assumed he never tried to see me. You always said he just abandoned us—"

"He certainly did! Oh, I won't say there wasn't a letter or two, but what's that over twenty years? I don't know why you're digging up things so far in the past. What about now? Have you found a buyer?"

Kiri wasn't sure why she had asked the question, either. It had just sprung out of her subconscious. Now she half listened to her mother's barrage of questions, answering as briefly as she could. When Lois finally rang off, Kiri drifted into the living room, her mind still on the one-sided conversation. Lois had hastily glossed over the matter of letters, but apparently her father had written once or twice.

She felt vaguely depressed. Her mother hadn't asked how she was, or how she was feeling, but it shouldn't bother her. Her mother rarely did—she wasn't demonstrative.

For a couple of hours she wandered from room to room, unable to settle down, resolutely trying to keep her mind off her childhood. Her mother was right; the past was past. Besides, it hadn't really been all that bad. No one had beat her, or even been seriously unkind. It was more that she had been invisible, except for those times when her mother had been feeling particularly bitter and had needed a listener. Then she was very visible, a living reminder of Ian's betrayal.

She picked up an intricately carved piece of greenstone and rubbed it softly, marveling at the artistry of those ancient craftsmen. A dozen faces, all contorted in smiles or grimaces looked back at her. She knew by now they weren't representations of gods or spirits. They were ancestors, lovingly detailed, a means of keeping track of a family's history.

She shivered slightly, thinking how ancient the artifact was, how it represented a culture that went far back in time, with traditions still alive and vital. What a contrast to her own home in California. The apartment sleekly modern in a beehive complex, with contemporary furniture, all the conveniences, but she would have a hard time describing anything about it. Nothing in it really touched her. All her energy had been poured into the one little bedroom that she had turned into a studio.

She had lived there for over five years, and she felt more at home here, after one week, than she ever had in that efficiency apartment. The thought alarmed her. She couldn't afford to become sentimental about Long White Cloud.

It was late in the afternoon when she heard the pulsing sound of a motor, and, peering out a window, saw Neiri coming up the path from the pier. At her side was a tall, dignified Maori man. No ancient Maori costume for him, Kiri saw, smiling slightly. He wore a pair of khaki shorts and an olive green knit shirt, but with his stiffly erect posture, his cap of snow-white hair, his slow, deliberate stride, he looked more like a Maori chief than anyone Kiri had yet seen.

As they came closer, she was able to discern his features. She had never before seen on a living person the facial tattooing that covered his broad face, but on him it didn't appear exotic at all—it seemed to belong there. She knew at once who he was—Neiri's oft-mentioned brother. The resemblance was striking.

Neiri quickly made the introductions, then hastened away with her brother along the hall, but Kiri managed to stop her before she was out of sight. Neiri had a little explaining to do. There had been more than enough mystery around her to suit Kiri. She had apparently made a special trip to bring her brother to the island. Had she suddenly decided to leave Long White Cloud? Or did his presence have something to do with whatever was going on at the replicated village?

"Neiri," she called, "did you know that Tainui is in Rapauru's village?"

The woman's back stiffened, then she turned slowly. "Did he come here to the villa?"

"No—I went to the village. I wanted to see Rapauru about—about something, and Tainui made quite a scene. I wondered if you knew he was there, and if that was the reason you warned me about leaving the house."

"Warned you?" The startled look that had been in Neiri's eyes when she'd turned was replaced by cool amusement. "If it was a warning, apparently you didn't pay any attention." Suddenly her eyes softened. "You're all right, aren't you, Kiri? Nothing happened?"

Unconsciously, Kiri fingered her shoulder where she could still feel the grip of Tainui's strong hand. There would probably be a bruise.

"I'm fine," she said crisply. "But it looked to me as though there were a lot more men living there than when I first saw the village. And what is an agitator like Tainui doing on the island?"

"It's nothing to do with you," Neiri said. "Don't mix in." She shot a look at her brother, then relented slightly. "We'll talk later, Kiri, but Tahu is anxious to see his nephew. It's been awhile since he and Rapauru had a visit. We'll see you this evening."

With the poise and presence that made their hasty exit seem almost like a processional, Neiri and her brother walked on through the villa. A few minutes later Kiri, watching from the kitchen window, saw the couple disappear into the jungle. She wished she was in Neiri's confidence, but she had already learned that the woman, with all the exquisite politeness in the world, never told her anything she didn't want her to know.

At least Neiri's return released her from the house. If Rapauru's mother and uncle were going to the village, Kiri had nothing to fear from anyone there. They would keep Rapauru and Tainui both under control. She desperately needed to get some air, stretch her legs, start her blood pounding through her veins. She always had one cure for depression or anxiety—fast, purposeful walking. Exercising her body seemed to work wonders for her mind.

To think was to act; she slipped on walking shoes and struck out along a forest trail. She wouldn't go near the village, nor would she visit the *Island Princess*, but there wasn't any reason why she couldn't go to the promontory and look out over the island. If she didn't do something, she knew she would be in for a sleepless night.

An hour later she arrived at the outcropping of rock from which she could get a panoramic view of the island. For a few moments she just stood there, head back, eyes closed, savoring the breeze that swept across the open water to ruffle her hair and slick her shirt back against her slender body. Here at the top of her world everything—her mother, the dilemma of the protesting Maoris, even the moral problem of the will, seemed petty in the face of such grandeur.

But even the grandeur of nature palls before the intensity of human emotions. She opened her eyes, her gaze drawn irresistibly to the little cove where the *Island Princess* was moored. The vessel was still there, but though she swept the deck with her binoculars she saw no sign of Noel. Not that she would have gone down to the boat even if she had seen him. Not at all. But she couldn't help wondering—was he below deck, or somewhere on the island?

At least he wasn't away on the mainland. The thought was comforting.

Turning slowly in a circle, she surveyed the entire shoreline of Long White Cloud. Rapauru's village was hidden by foliage, but she knew where it was located. Long stretches of sandy beaches edged the east side, and to the west were secluded coves, rocky headlands, beaches of black sand. It was just as well she had decided to leave Long White Cloud as soon as she could conclude her business. The feeling enveloping her was as unusual as it was unwelcome. This was *her* island; she felt at home. If only she had come while Ian was still alive. Would he have welcomed her? Or even acknowledged her? Now she would never know.

She caught sight of two dark moving specks in the ocean, and watched them curiously. They weren't sailboats, or power launches, and they appeared too large to be an animal. She slipped her binoculars from her pants pocket and swept them over the ocean, catching the two objects in the lenses.

Her breath caught in her throat at the power and majesty of the sight. Maori war canoes, two of them, propelled over the water by the rise and fall of dozens of paddles. She knew that almost every Maori tribe had its own canoe, but aside from the one Rapauru was building, she had never seen one complete and operational.

She watched as the vessels drew closer, curious about their destination. Perhaps they were in training for the races that were to take place in Auckland in a couple of weeks. Then her pulse raced and she narrowed her eyes in sudden understanding. The canoes were headed for Rapauru's village.

Without making a conscious decision, she ran lightly down the path that connected with the one to the village. This might be the answer to the puzzle about all the strange men on the island, men who did not appear to her to be Rapauru's usual followers. Had they come by canoe at night? Anyway, it would be exciting to see those canoes up close.

For just a second she hesitated. Tainui was still at the village, as far as she knew. Then she thrust out her chin and increased her pace. This island would soon be hers, and she wasn't about to let Tainui frighten her. Giving in to his kind always made them more dangerous. Besides, Neiri and her brother Tahu were there, and even though Rapauru might be volatile, the two older people were more than competent to restrain him.

Out of breath from her fast pace, she paused in the hedge of trees that screened the village and peered out from beneath the branching limb of a *totara*. The scene before her was bustling with activity. Several knots of men stood on the beach, gesticulating and talking among themselves. Close by stood about ten warriors, all clad in the scanty Maori skirt, brandishing spears, stomping rhythmically. At least she knew what they were doing—performing the Maori welcome to visitors. From one of the canoes came an answering sound—the low, eerie call of a conch shell.

She felt as though she had been transported several centuries back into the past, and she actually shook her head to rid herself of the feeling that time had run backward. This scene didn't belong in the modern world. It was too incongruous. These were modern men who had jobs, families, men whose livelihoods depended not on raiding neighbors but on getting to work on time at a farm, a mill, an office. What strange ancestral pull had brought them here, half-naked in hollowed-out canoes, brandishing spears, blowing conch shells?

She watched closely as the canoes reached the beach and strong hands pulled them up onto the sand. Each vessel was fully loaded with men, about thirty per canoe, she estimated, and at the prow of the nearest one stood a man who was obviously in charge.

She blinked with surprise as she recognized him, and eased back into the bushes, almost afraid that the fierce hawklike eyes surveying the clearing could see her even through the screen of trees.

Tainui.

A cold feeling settled in her stomach. He must have left the village soon after she and Noel had gone. Perhaps these canoes had been waiting for him on one of the nearby islands. She watched as he jumped ashore and raised his hands above his head, palms up, in a wide, all-embracing gesture. Immediately he was surrounded by a group of men, one of whom was Rapauru. Then Tainui began to speak, and although she was too far away to hear his words she could tell from the movement of the crowd that he had appreciative listeners.

Well, not all were appreciative. Neiri and her brother stood under a tree several feet away, obviously not a part of Tainui's audience. And another man, a non-Maori by the looks of him, thin, sharp nose in a narrow face, casually dressed, stood by the canoes, camera ready. He looked somewhat bored, Kiri thought, as he spoke a few words into a recorder, then aimed his camera at Tainui.

So Tainui had brought his own reporter-photographer. He must have something really interesting planned, she thought, shifting uneasily. Something sure to make the papers.

"He's good, I'll give him that."

Startled, she turned toward the voice. Noel was leaning against a tree a few feet away, regarding her with cool, grave eyes. Before she could reply, he moved toward her and slipped his arm around her waist, edging her around the clearing toward a clump of trees almost directly behind Tainui.

"What are you doing here?" he whispered. "I thought we agreed you would stay at the house."

"We didn't agree on any such thing," she protested. "For that matter, what are you doing here? Did you talk to Rapauru? What's going on?"

"Shh." They were now so close to Tainui that she could see the perspiration beaded on his forehead, and distinctly hear every word he said, as he threw back his head and waved his arms like an old-time preacher.

"Are we men or boys? Free or slaves?" His voice thundered across the rapt group. "This land was stolen from our ancestors. Now sheep graze where warriors hunted, we live in shacks while the *pakeha* lives in mansions." His voice went on and on. He said nothing new as far as Kiri was concerned, but some of the crowd seemed to be eating it up.

"Now," Tainui said, shifting his feathered cape to one shoulder and raising his clenched fist, "now is the time for action. Long White Cloud is ours, but we will never claim it by asking. The woman from America will sell it to the highest bidder. You all saw the offer, saw what she will receive for our inheritance. We have no choice. We must march on the villa, occupy it, and see what the *pakeha* make of that."

Kiri gasped, and Noel tightened his grip. Tainui certainly did intend to provoke an incident. Should she do something, challenge him, speak to the group herself? It didn't seem like a very wise idea, considering the way he had worked everyone up with his oratory.

"Are you with me?" he demanded.

There was a chorus of yells. The shouts broke off abruptly as Tahu stepped up beside Tainui.

"I am not with you," he said quietly.

There was a buzzing from the crowd, and Kiri held her breath, as Tainui's face flushed an angry red. Yet his composure was only slightly shaken; he stared haughtily at the older man and drew himself up like a hawk over a plump pheasant.

"Who are you, old man? Your time is over. It is for younger, braver men to guide our people."

"Maybe. But not stupider men."

Tainui's eyes shot fire. "We have had enough of your leadership, and those cowards like you. These are times for action. This is the time to right injustice."

Tahu straightened up to his full six feet and stared at Tainui, then turned to the crowd. His voice, when he spoke, was soft and affectionate, like a father speaking to his son.

"Tainui is good at empty speeches, meaningless slogans. You all know me, know I am an elder of the tribe. For centuries elders have made the decisions, and why? Because they are wiser than firebrands like this outsider. There may be injustices—I do not deny it—but we will resolve them legally."

Kiri watched as the two men debated, each playing to the crowd in his own way. She was seeing two different worlds in conflict, she thought—the ancient Maori way of Tahu, where elders were revered, listened to, and the new way of activism, exemplified by Tainui.

She glanced at Neiri; the woman had gone to stand by Rapauru who was doing his best to ignore her, but not having much luck. Her hand was lightly on his arm, but Kiri suspected it might feel like steel to her son. So this was the reason for Neiri's quick trip. She had known that Tainui was bent on stirring things up, and had gone for her brother.

Again, Tainui raised his arms. "Now is the time to decide. Are you with me or not?" His fierce eyes ranged over the crowd, noting each hesitation, each averted face.

Rapauru was the first to make a definite decision. He worked his way through the crowd until he stood in front of Tainui and his uncle.

"Occupying the villa seems a little drastic right now, Tainui," he said slowly. "Not that you don't have a point," he added quickly, as Tainui glared at him. "But, well, it is a little extreme. The house was Ian's, and he was always more than fair to us. Besides, the authorities are bound to take some action—"

There was a murmur of agreement from the crowd, and they seemed not so much to walk away as to melt away. Tainui stared after them, then wheeled around, and with a sharp gesture to the reporter, disappeared into one of the little huts.

Kiri slowly let out her breath; she felt as though she'd been holding it for ages. When she glanced at Noel, she saw that his expression was thoughtful.

"Tainui's gone," she whispered. "Should we let Neiri know that we were here and heard it all?"

He pursed his lips, considering. "I don't think so," he finally said. "This was Maori business, and I doubt they'd welcome *pakeha* interference. Let's just get out of here."

They edged back into the forest, and then, finding the trail, strode silently along side by side. Perhaps the same idea was in both their minds; in any event, Kiri wasn't surprised when they came up to the little cove where the *Island Princess* floated at anchor.

Noel untied the rubber dinghy and rowed them swiftly to the boat. He clambered quickly up the ladder, then reached down to give her a hand. In a few minutes they were seated side by side in the miniscule cabin, and Noel had put a tall drink in her hand, murmuring something about settling her nerves.

Relaxing on the narrow seat, she took her time looking around the cabin. Although tiny, it looked surprisingly livable. A well-equipped galley, a chart table, two upholstered seats that could double as bunks on each side of an oak table. Through the brass portholes she could hear the slap of waves against the hull, the quarreling of seagulls. Everything was as neat, as ordered, as Noel himself. What was there about him that made breathing so difficult, that made her so excruciatingly aware that he was only inches away? The knowledge that under that cool facade a volcano smoldered? But she had better not let her mind travel that avenue.

"So," she finally said, when she had taken an appreciative sip of her drink, "what do you think will happen next? Will Tainui give up?"

"I doubt it," Noel replied, apparently unaware that he was stroking her hand softly, or that each fingertip sent little currents of excitement all along her arm. "Not unless he finds a better cause somewhere else, and I doubt he will. This one seems made to order. Ancient Maori land, undeveloped all these years, their artifacts still scattered around, inherited by a foreigner. I suspect he'll play it for all it's worth."

Frowning, she turned to search his face. Put that way, even she might think Tainui had a point, if she didn't know the historical background of the island. "What would happen if he could somehow get the land back? You'd be able to keep on with your studies, wouldn't you?"

He grinned, and raised one sharply chiseled eyebrow. "Are you asking me which side I'm on? But to answer your question—I don't know what would happen if the Maori reclaimed the land. They would probably kick me off as quickly as Helborn would. But it's a moot question. The island isn't going to be returned to the Maori, at least not by this tactic. They can cause trouble, frighten prospective buyers, but in the end the question of ownership would be decided legally."

"It doesn't seem fair that they could cause all that trouble with so little basis for it. Is there a possibility that eventually they might get it through the legal system?"

"Very doubtful. Ian researched the title thoroughly before he bought the island. Everything is in order from the first Maori chief who sold it to the first European. Ian believed Rapauru had a moral right to build his village, but that was all."

"Speaking of Rapauru," she said, her mouth tightening, "he as much as admitted he put that mask on my bed and searched Ian's study for the will."

"I'm not surprised." Noel rubbed his chin thoughtfully. "He's desperate to find some way to remain on the island. Trying to scare you away didn't work, and he obviously didn't find a will. I wonder what he'll come up with next."

"At least he stood up to Tainui."

"Because his mother and uncle were there, I imagine. And because he doesn't like his own village being taken over by an outsider like Tainui. It doesn't mean he doesn't have something else in mind. Are you frightened?" He put his hand under her chin and tipped her face up to his so he could look into her eyes.

"No, not of Rapauru," she said slowly, meeting his gaze. "I don't really know why. It may sound silly, but I just don't feel any great animosity in him, in spite of everything he's done. But Tainui—he's another matter."

He removed his hand and squeezed her shoulder, then picked up his drink. "Yes, I think he is. I hadn't wanted to involve the authorities in this, but I think perhaps we should. Want to sail to Paihia tomorrow? We'll stop in at the police station and then play tourists for a while. I think we need the break."

Her heart did a flip-flop in her chest. An entire day with Noel, free from the anxieties of Long White Cloud. It sounded perfect.

"I'd love to."

"Well, then," he said, setting his empty glass on the table, "perhaps we should get you back to the villa. I'd like to get an early start in the morning, and you'll need your rest—you've had quite a day."

She nodded reluctantly. The thought of going back to the villa, where everyone seemed to wander in and out at will, wasn't at all appealing. It was crazy, but part of her wanted to stay here, crowded close to him on that little bunk. What would Noel do if she told him she wanted to stay, wanted everything that implied? The thought of being wrapped in his arms throughout the night was so seductive that it nearly overpowered her rational knowledge that that was the last thing she should do. Why not? Other women didn't make a federal case out of simply making love with an attractive man.

She knew, though, that wasn't the real problem. He would reject her, of course, as he had before. She wasn't even appealing enough for a brief affair—not to Noel, who could have beautiful women like Felicia just by putting out his hand.

He hesitated, then reached out and brushed a strand of hair back from her face. "I'll sail you back—it's getting dark out and the trails can be treacherous at night."

"Can you see to sail?"

"I have lights, and there'll be a moon soon. There's more visibility on water than there is under the trees." He turned and swung himself up out through the hatch. Kiri watched his bare, muscular legs disappear, and then slowly followed.

As Noel turned the winch that hoisted the anchor, he cast a surreptitious glance over his shoulder at Kiri. She was standing at the railing gazing down at the water, apparently absorbed in its depths. Yet she wasn't as cool as she tried to appear. He had seen the flash of desire in her eyes, and it had been all he could do to keep from crushing her against his body, easing her backward onto the narrow bunk.

God, how he wanted her. Not just for a light, pleasurable interval, either. She had gotten into his blood, worked her way so deep inside of him that he was actually frightened. Yet, possessing her body as he wanted to do, wildly, passionately, was only part of it. He was caught by the elusive mystery of her personality, by her uneasy mixture of cool, independent woman and frightened vulnerable child. Alternately, she brought out a desire to protect her, and a pride in her autonomy.

He hadn't meant to ask her to go to Paihia with him, although he had intended to sail there himself and talk to the authorities—the situation on the island was becoming much too volatile for comfort—but the thought of being away from her had been suddenly unbearable, and the words had just slipped out. How was he going to manage an entire day with her without making a complete fool of himself?

Chapter 10

Kiri perched on the narrow seat and rested her hand lightly on the rope railing that encircled the deck of the *Island Princess,* twisting around to see Long White Cloud vanishing behind her in a soft mist. As the island disappeared, her spirits revived proportionately, happiness fizzing up inside her like seltzer water. For the space of a day she intended to leave her troubles behind on the island.

Noel's presence had more than a little to do with the elation that threatened to bubble over and disrupt her serene facade. She glanced at him through narrowed eyes, hoping he wasn't aware of the intensity of her gaze. She never tired of looking at him. This morning he wore a white knit T-shirt that left his smoothly muscled arms bare, and brief white shorts; the white against his bronze skin dazzled her.

Thankfully, he kept his eyes on the horizon, as she drank in every detail—sun-bleached hair blowing in the fresh breeze, long legs wide apart as he adjusted to each movement of the boat. She still thought he was incredibly handsome in an elegant, patrician sort of way, but now that she knew him better she noticed tiny imperfections: his nose was a little too straight and uncompromising, his mouth a little too wide for his square jaw. Still, he reminded her of one of the Greek heroes; not Hercules, all muscle and brawn. On second thought, Noel was more like Mercury, the messenger of the gods; he was like a laser beam, swift, lean, built for speed and endurance.

The first time she had seen him, she had realized he was an extremely handsome man, but now she knew he was much, much more. An intelligent, compassionate man, with a charm that could entice the fish from the sea. Strange that he was content to spend his life on an isolated island involved in wildlife studies. She wondered if there was more to it than that. Had he been hurt somehow?

At one time she might have thought him lazy, or at least unambitious, but now she knew that wasn't the case. He had ambition, burning ambition. It just wasn't directed at the usual goals.

He turned with a companionable grin, and she smiled back, raising her hand to let the wind ruffle through her hair. The canvas sail snapped rhythmically above her head and made sounds like dozens of tiny firecrackers; the bow of the *Island Princess* cleaved the water into two translucent waves crested with fine spray, which floated back to cool her skin and dampen her lips.

"Do you want to take a turn?" Noel gave her a lazy smile and without waiting for her reply, reached for her hand and drew her across the lurching deck until she stood beside him. Positioning her hands on the wheel, he moved behind her and locked his arms around her waist, as she hesitantly took over the helm.

She leaned lightly back against him, ostensibly for balance, luxuriating in the feel of the boat responding to her touch and to the long, lean length of his body. Excitement surged through her, as she turned the wheel and the vessel followed her command, skimming across the water like a great white seabird. The light material of Noel's shirt hardly presented a barrier as she rested her head against his hard chest. She felt the flexing of each muscle as he moved to accommodate to the roll of the boat. He shifted until his hands rested lightly on her hips, and she sucked in her breath, acutely aware of his nearly naked body pressed closely along her back, her thighs.

His warmth flowed through her light cotton shirt and brief shorts, permeating to the center of her being, in sharp contrast to the brisk breeze cooling the front of her body. She sighed with contentment, tilting her head back and half closing her eyes. She refused to think, to worry, to enumerate all the reasons she shouldn't be doing this, and gave herself over to pure feeling. *God's in his heaven, all's right with the world.* If there was ever a time when that old saying was true, this was the time. For this one moment, this tiny speck of time out of all eternity, everything was perfect.

But of course it couldn't last. Noel put his hand over hers and made a slight correction in course, and she realized they were coming into Paihia harbor.

"Head for that pier over there," he said, releasing her hand and moving so that a rush of cool air flowed between them. "I'll drop the sail."

Now all was brisk activity; they docked, tied up the boat, and walked to Noel's car, a vintage cream-colored convertible, which he had parked near the pier. Driving from the waterfront into the main part of town, a cluster of buildings that perched on the hill overlooking the bay, they pulled up in front of a gray, two-story building. To Kiri, it looked like just about any police station in the world.

Noel was well-known here, too, she realized, as introductions were made and they were seated in a small office with a man Noel had introduced as Jeff Doyle—a lanky, unassuming person in a wrinkled gray suit and surprisingly sharp, pale blue eyes.

Kiri guessed he was a man who wasted neither time nor words judging by the way he took a newspaper from the top of his steel-gray desk and tossed it toward them. "Is this what you wanted to talk about?"

Kiri glanced at the paper; it was a small item, but there was a picture of Tainui with raised arms exhorting the crowd, and a short article about his demands for the return of the island.

Noel glanced over the item, then handed it back to Doyle. "That's it, all right. Tainui didn't waste any time."

"What's your assessment of the situation, Trevorson?"

"Guarded, but I think things have simmered down for now—he ran into some opposition from some of the cooler heads. I don't think we've heard the last of him, though."

"What about backing? Will he get support from the others?"

"Not from the few Maori who live on the island or come over for weekends, but I didn't know some of the men who were with him. He may have recruited them from almost anyplace, and I have no idea what they will do."

Doyle turned to Kiri. "You seem to be in the thick of things, Miss MacKay. Like a lightning rod, I'd say. Up to now, Tainui hasn't broken any law on Long White Cloud, so our hands are tied. We'll keep an eye on him, but that may not help much if things really heat up. Have you thought about leaving the island until this situation blows over?"

"You actually think I might be in danger?"

"Oh, probably not. There's been a lot of rhetoric from Tainui, but so far he hasn't hurt anyone. I'll admit, though, things seem to be escalating. It might be wise for you to stay in a hotel for a while, just until things cool down."

"Just when might that be? I might never get back. Tainui might take my leaving as an indication that he has won, and who knows what he'll do?"

She glanced at Noel's profile, but his expression was unreadable. Did he agree with Doyle that she should leave? Well, she wouldn't do it. It was ironic that only yesterday she had been anxious to escape Long White Cloud; now she couldn't possibly think of going, chased away by a bully like Tainui. She had a right to be on the island and no one was going to frighten her away.

"You better think about it. It would take us a long while to get over there if anything did happen," Doyle said slowly.

"I'm there," Noel reminded him. "I'm not going anyplace until this situation is defused. I'll take care of her."

Doyle searched his face, his eyes cool and assessing. Then he grinned. "Yes, I expect you will. Can't say I blame you." He rose from his desk and extended his hand to Kiri, then to Noel. "Thanks for coming over and filling us in. I'd appreciate your letting us know if anything else develops. And I shouldn't worry too much, if I were you."

Easy for him to say, Kiri thought a little sourly, as they left the building and climbed back into Noel's convertible. His expression was thoughtful as he slid behind the wheel, and she decided not to question him just now. She concentrated on the spectacle all around her, as they drove past opulent high-rise hotels that soon gave way to neat little residences all covered with flowering vines and shrubs.

What a fascinating, exotic-looking place. She felt very much like a child let out of school for the day; eventually she would have to go back to her problems, but for the moment she was free.

Noel turned to her with a sudden grin, apparently deciding to shelve the problem of Long White Cloud for now just as she had done. "What would you like to do for the rest of the day? Shop? There are some nice boutiques, and you've been away from civilization for days."

Smiling, she shook her head. The day was too beautiful to spend even a minute inside. "I can't think of a thing I need."

"I didn't know that had anything to do with it. I thought shopping was the female equivalent of the male passion for fishing."

"Not for me, I'm afraid. And I hadn't noticed you hanging out with a fishing pole in your hand."

"So we're both oddballs. I have an idea, though. With everything that's happened, I suspect you've gotten a rather poor impression of my country. Would you like to play tourist for the rest of the day?"

"I *am* a tourist," she said, matching his playful tone.

"So you are. Well, I'm going to show you some sights no tourist should miss."

"Is this a ploy to keep me away from the island and out of trouble? I thought for a minute you were going to go along with Doyle and try to get me stashed away in some hotel."

"This is a ploy to keep us both away from the island. I doubt our problems will worsen if we forget about them for a while."

"Lead on."

They drove north, keeping close to the shoreline and passing dozens of secluded inlets and bays, then stopped for a delicious lunch in a wayside tearoom. It was late afternoon when they reached the very tip of New Zealand, Cape Reinga, and Noel pointed out the lone *pohutukawa* tree at the tip of an outcropping of rock. It looked lonely and forlorn, she thought, starkly silhouetted against the endless ocean.

He held her close, shielding her from the cold wind that blew from the spot where the deep green Tasman Sea met the blue of the Pacific Ocean.

"That tree is big in Maori mythology," he told her, continuing the role of tour guide he had adopted at the beginning of their trip. "When a Maori dies, his spirit travels up the coast, rests for a while in Spirits Bay, leaps off the tree and then continues its journey to its old ancestral homeland."

"Where is that?"

"*Hawaiki,* so their legends say."

"Thousands of miles away," she said softly. "Do they still believe that?"

"Hard to say. They'd never admit it—"

"You know a lot about Maori legends, don't you?"

He pulled her a little closer and her pulse raced, suspecting he was motivated by more than a desire to keep her from the chill wind. She was almost sure of it when his voice cracked a little as he replied.

"It's a fascinating culture," he said. "But I don't romanticize it—they're like everyone else—good, bad, or a little of both. No noble savages, no modern villains. I just think it's time that all of us, Maori and *pakeha,* work together to preserve what we have."

"What you have is very beautiful," she murmured.

"Beautiful," he agreed, tightening his grip around her waist. She heard the slight tremor in his voice and it went straight to her heart. She acted totally on impulse. Twisting slightly in his arms, she moved until she faced him, then reached up to take his face between her two hands. Standing on tiptoe, she stretched up and touched his lips with her own warm mouth. For a long, agonizing moment they clung together, a moment of bittersweet rapture.

This speck of land at the top of the world was somehow symbolic of the problems between them—an unimaginable expanse of open sea separated this country from California, separated her world from his, her values from his, her self-interest from his.

As though aware of her thoughts on some subliminal level, he dropped his arms, took her hand, and together they walked slowly and silently back to the automobile. That moment, so brief, so intense, had affected her more than she cared to acknowledge, and judging by the grim set of his mouth, she suspected the same might be true for Noel.

Noel kept his eyes on the road, and Kiri took in the familiar lines of his profile as they retraced their route down the coast. She hadn't planned to say anything, but she blurted out what was on her mind.

"Noel, why haven't you married?"

The words were out of her mouth before she had time to consider that they might be impertinent—or even worse, that they might convey an interest she wasn't ready to acknowledge.

She thought his fingers tightened on the wheel, but his expression revealed nothing.

"I was waiting for you?" He grinned and elevated one eyebrow. Although her pulse quickened, she knew he was merely being evasive, and she refused to be diverted. She knew enough about him now, had seen the passion with which he pursued a goal close to his heart, to suspect that light, superficial involvement with women wasn't really like him.

"I doubt you were waiting for me," she replied. "Did someone break your heart and cause you to swear off women?" She smiled to show him she was teasing, but she waited tensely for his answer.

"Who said I swore off? Some of my best friends are women."

"That's what I mean! Were you ever serious about anyone?"

She thought he was going to make another light quip, but instead he was silent. Finally he glanced at her. "I was serious, once, a long time ago. So was Rosamund. The problem was, we were both serious about different things."

"Were you in love?" she asked softly.

"I thought so." He set his lips and kept his gaze firmly on the road ahead.

Getting information was like pulling teeth, but she thought she detected a hint of pain underlining his terse replies. He wasn't usually a taciturn man, but he certainly couldn't be called a blabbermouth about past love affairs. "What happened?"

"You are nosey, aren't you?" His smile took the sting out of the words. "I don't mind talking about it. We wanted completely different things. She wanted what most women want, I suppose—money, a glittering social life—"

"That's a terribly cynical thing to say," she interrupted. "You think that's what most women want—money, glamour?"

Now he did glance at her, his eyes dark and unreadable. "Don't you want money? Why else are you selling White Cloud?"

"Yes—but that's different! It's not just the money. I could concentrate on my art—"

She broke off and settled back against the seat, gazing out the window at the swiftly moving landscape. It was different, wasn't it? Finally she turned back to Noel.

"What did you want that she couldn't accept?"

"Oh, I wasn't much different than I am now," he said, turning the wheel to negotiate a looping bend in the road. "I wanted to do something that would matter, something bigger than my own self-interest . . . I don't want to sound self-righteous, but I wanted to build something for the future. . . ."

Kiri bit her lip, taken aback at the flash of pain his words evoked. There was nothing wrong with that goal; in fact, it was admirable. The problem was, as she knew too well, it didn't leave any room for a woman.

"So, have you completely dissected me, Miss MacKay?" His tone was light, but his eyes were unsmiling. "Then it's my turn."

"Your turn?" She knew what he meant, but she was sparring for time.

"Yes, my turn. You seem to think I should be married. You almost implied there was something wrong with me. So what about you? Haven't you ever been in love?"

He was right—she had opened this conversation, and she owed him a reply. "I thought so, once. But I was wrong. I recovered, and after that, I just never found any man I wanted to marry."

"What did he do, this fellow who ruined you for any other man?" He grinned, throwing her own words back at her.

"He just decided he'd rather have someone else." Even now, it hurt to remember how Tom's betrayal had shattered her, how deeply angry she had been at him and her best friend. Then, after the anger had come a deep hopelessness, a realization that no man could be trusted. Her father hadn't loved her, Tom hadn't loved her. She was unlovable.

"That seems unbelievable," Noel said softly. "It must have hurt..."

She wasn't going to let his instant compassion get to her. "It did, for a while," she replied. "But it's been over a long time."

"Is something like that ever really over?" he mused. "Sometimes it colors your whole life until you come to grips with it. Want to talk about it?"

She shrugged her refusal. Noel was the last person on earth she could talk to about her feelings toward men. How could she say, *I would like to love you—in fact, I think I'm almost in love with you now, but I can never let myself be so vulnerable again. I know you would break my heart, and I can't chance it.*

They chatted lightly for the remainder of the drive to Paihia. Noel was witty, charming, kept the conversation impersonal, and Kiri was grateful. She felt as shaky as though she had skirted a moment of danger every bit as frightening as what awaited her on Long White Cloud. She had never had the impulse to confide in a man before, but something about Noel made her want to spill everything out—her fears and insecurities, as well as her warmth and passion. She especially longed to talk to him about the enigma that was her father. She felt intuitively that it might assuage some of the deep hurt that still racked her when she thought of that long-ago abandonment.

Maybe, with his help, she could even open her heart to love.

Impatient with herself, she shook her head, oblivious to Noel's curious glance. She might as well accept the fact that her character and attitudes had been formed too long ago to allow change now. There was a giant aching void where her heart should be; there always would be. She was ready to admit that she was falling in love with Noel, but there was no reason he had to know it, too.

She was unnaturally silent, Noel thought, as they docked at Russell and walked up the wooden pier toward the Duke of Marlborough Hotel. What could he do to bring back the animation to her expression, the joy to her smile? Although darkness had long since fallen, the lanterns were lit along the quay, and he could see every emotion that flickered across her mobile face. Right now, he saw wariness and a faint, haunting sorrow that touched him profoundly.

The massive double doors swung open and a hostess flashed them a warm smile, then led them along a hall lushly carpeted in crimson. The spacious, formal dining room provided a glimpse of a bygone era, Noel thought, his eyes roving over the familiar dazzling white linen, silver candlesticks, dark, ornately carved furniture.

Except for a couple whispering together in a far corner and three businessmen totally concentrating on their food, the room was empty. He greeted the woman who brought their menus. Tall, slender, in her mid-thirties, she was dressed in Victorian style with a long swishing skirt and white ruffled blouse—although the bodice was cut much lower than Queen Victoria would have approved, he suspected. In this, the proprietor had added a more modern touch.

The thought of the proprietor reminded him. "Is Sam back yet, Julie?"

"Not yet. We're expecting him any day. He did call, though." She glanced at Kiri. "He was sure upset about your father—said he would get back as fast as he could."

Kiri murmured something and Noel glanced at her face. Her every thought danced across her face like sun on water. How well did she know herself? She wasn't at all the tough, no-nonsense woman she prided herself on being, the one he had first thought she was. There was a hurt, lost child behind that facade. A damaged child, one whom he suspected might never be able to love unless she resolved her feelings about her father.

For the first time in his life he was angry with Ian. How could the man have neglected her so? Noel would never treat a child of his in such a callous manner.

He stiffened, sobered by the thought that had flashed unbidden into his mind. A child of his—it had never occurred to him to want a child. The world was poised on the edge of disaster, there was too many people already—it was no place to bring up a child. Not a helpless child, a child who would have to battle for scarce resources. A boy, possibly, with those deep emerald eyes of Kiri's, that same defiant set of the chin...

Almost angrily, he pushed the thought away. "How about the lobster, Kiri? It's the specialty of Russell."

She agreed, and they observed each other across the expanse of white linen. She was thinner than she had been when he'd first met her. Her translucent skin showed a trace of sunlight, but there were hollows under her cheekbones, and her brilliant eyes dominated her narrow face even more dramatically than before. He would have to see that she ate better, rested...

Although he realized lack of food wasn't the problem. She was under incredible stress, and he was contributing to it with his campaign against the sale of the island. But he couldn't change that—he still wished he could convince her not to sell Long White Cloud.

He also wished he could be more sure of his motives in opposing the sale. At first there had been no question, but as he got to know her, his motives became less pure. Was it solely because he wanted the island to remain in its pristine state—or partly because he wanted Kiri to remain?

His lips twisted in a rueful grin. Talk about fantasy time!

His ruminations were interrupted by a burst of laughter from the entryway, and he raised his head to see Julie escorting two men to a table. They saw him at the same time, and immediately changed direction.

"Noel! Old Buddy! I thought you'd be long gone by now."

Noel rose and stretched out his hand. The taller of the two men grasped it with both of his, the other threw one arm around Noel's shoulder, then pounded him with his free hand.

Noel pounded back, but he was ambivalent about their presence. He was glad to see his friends, but he admitted to himself he didn't want to share Kiri. He glanced across at her as the two men stood expectantly, their eyes on the woman.

"Hi, Jim. Arnie. This is a surprise." He hesitated, then smiled at Kiri. "Kiri, these two wild men are friends of mine. Jim Jackson, Arnie Foss. This is Kiri MacKay, boys." Again he hesitated slightly. "Ian's daughter."

Jim, the skinny, tall one with keen gray eyes and dark, flyaway hair, inclined his head. "Delighted to meet you, Kiri. Sorry about the circumstances. We'll miss Ian."

Arnie, shorter, sturdier, but with the same keen interest in his eyes, murmured agreement.

"Thank you. I guess you knew him pretty well."

"We all worked with him off and on, though not as much as Noel, here." Jim indicated Noel with an affectionate gesture. "Noel was the one he was grooming to take over. The two of them went all over the world together." His eyes darkened with memory. "We'll miss Ian, but it's good to know his mission will live on."

Jim glanced away from Kiri and back to Noel, revealing large white teeth in a broad grin. "I thought you'd be in Kenya by now, old hoss, but I can see what the attraction is here."

"Kenya?" Kiri's voice revealed her surprise. "You never mentioned anything about going to Kenya."

Jim grimaced. "Did I let the cat out of the bag. I didn't know it was a secret."

"It's no secret," Noel said equably, though a glance at Kiri's startled expression made him wish it had been. "It was only for a short trip. It just never came up, I guess."

"Well, I'm not surprised you kept mum," Jackson continued. "You never were one to toot your own horn. You're with a celebrity here, Miss MacKay."

"I'd hardly say that." Noel raise his eyebrows and smiled. "It's only a meeting with the government of Kenya about what can be done to preserve their wildlife. I'm only one of many so-called experts."

"Buddy, you're the primary expert," Jackson contradicted. "The meeting wouldn't even be held without you. But I thought you'd be there by now."

"The meeting isn't until next month. I'd planned to go a little early, collect some data, but some things came up on the island—" He glanced at Kiri, knowing the reason he was still on Long White Cloud was apparent in his expression.

"Where do you go from there? Aren't you speaking in Brazil to that South American conference on rain forests?"

The man was an absolute blabbermouth, Noel thought, observing the consternation on Kiri's face. It was true he had been neglecting a few things since Kiri's arrival, but Long White Cloud was worth it. Somewhere along the line he'd begun to think that Kiri was, too.

"Won't you join us?" Noel asked, his voice conveying absolutely no sincerity at all.

Jackson grinned, glancing from Noel to Kiri's set expression. "I think I'm in enough trouble already. It was nice meeting you, Kiri. I hope I didn't spill the beans. I'd supposed you knew you were with one of the world's foremost ecologists." His tone was light, but there was an undertone of sincerity that couldn't be missed.

The two men moved away, and Noel tried to catch Kiri's eyes. "Don't pay any attention to Jim. He's an old friend, but he tends to exaggerate."

"He obviously respects you."

"Well, we've worked together a lot. All over the world..."
Why was this conversation making him uneasy?

"I don't know why I jumped to the conclusion you spent all your time on the island. You must travel a lot."

"Enough," he said quietly. "Ian was getting a little tired of it. I was taking over a lot of his projects, and they're scattered all over the world. The health of the planet has to be addressed worldwide, you know. What happens one place affects everyplace else."

"I know..."

There was a shadow in her eyes, and he hoped they could drop the subject, but Kiri gave him an assessing glance. "There's a lot more to you than a man who spends his time trapping opossums on a remote island, isn't there?"

"Isn't trapping opossums enough for one man?" He tried to get a smile out of her, but when she remained serious, he twisted his fork in his hand, his consummate poise for once deserting him. Why was he so reluctant for her to know that he was one of the foremost scientists in his field? It was a cause for pride, not the opposite. But there had been something measuring in her glance, a definite withdrawal when she heard of his prominence, and it bothered him.

"So you're Ian's scientific heir, the young prince who will take up the king's mantle," she murmured.

"That's one way of putting it, I suppose," he said slowly. "Although I'd put it another way. I'm carrying on his work, seeing that his vision doesn't die."

"And that means a lot to you?"

"A lot," he agreed.

"Perhaps that's what Rosamund couldn't accept. Maybe it wasn't about money, but the fact that your primary allegiance wasn't—would never be—with her."

A cold, ominous feeling seeped through him, lodging like a rock in his chest. So this was where everything was leading. She saw him as an extension of her father, a man whom she believed had cared nothing for her. A man who had abandoned her to continue his precious work. It was at that moment that he became aware of something that had been hiding in his subconscious for days, saw clearly the self-knowledge he had been fighting.

He was in love with this woman.

And he had a real dilemma. There was no way he could accept her view of Ian, but he could understand her conflict. He tried to remember everything Ian had said about Kiri. It was little enough, but he swore there had been regret, love in his voice. At the time, it had served only to fuel Noel's resentment of Kiri—why hadn't she come to see her father?

Now he could see it from Kiri's point of view. If Ian had loved her, she had never known it. But perhaps Ian had wanted it that way. He said that when he left California he had closed out that chapter of his life, closed out Kiri. Had he regretted it? Noel thought so, but his opinion would never be enough to erase the scars—for that she would need proof. Impossible, when her father was dead.

His mouth tightened and he felt a sheen of perspiration on his forehead. How had things gotten so out of hand? He didn't want commitment, he didn't want involvement, certainly not with a woman like Kiri whom he knew could wrench him inside out. It would only lead to pain, it was the death knell to his plans. After the fiasco with Rosamund, he had arranged his life as he wanted it, and women—a woman—couldn't be allowed to interfere with his serious purpose.

He sighed inwardly. All that had been before he met Kiri, before he had been blindsided by the passion that colored every moment they were together. Before he had come to understand the force of her intellect, the depth of her courage. He was fast approaching the point where he couldn't bear to be away from her. And from the look on her face, the look of wary reserve, he suspected he might be in for another disappointment. One that would hurt far more than losing Rosamund ever had.

It was a moment before he understood how far his thinking had gone, and when he did he took a quick breath. He was actually thinking of her as a permanent part of his life. He who had always considered himself a practical man! But he could stop now. It would hurt when she left the island, but it wouldn't be gut-wrenching pain. He would cut his losses on Long White Cloud—and with Kiri. There were other places in the world.

They continued the meal, the comfortable silence replaced by one of mutual wariness and withdrawal. He suspected she was as relieved as he when they finally left Russell and stood once more on the dock at Long White Cloud.

Chapter 11

"Mr. Marston?" Kiri held the phone a little closer to her ear so she could hear the faraway voice. She had discovered that telephone quality on the island was a bit irregular, depending on what was happening to the cable that lay on the ocean floor between Long White Cloud and the mainland. Strong tides or boats with extra long keels had been known to disrupt it entirely, according to Mrs. Armi.

But after some initial static, the lawyer's voice came through clearly.

"Yes, Miss MacKay. What can I do for you?"

She pictured him at his desk—a dry, gray man, a little abrupt and impatient—and spoke firmly. "I'm sorry to take you out of a meeting—your secretary said it was important—but I hadn't heard from you for quite awhile and I wondered if there was any news."

"Everything is going through the usual channels," he said, his voice faintly disapproving, as though she were questioning the law itself. "I told you I wasn't sure how long it would take—the system is crowded, as you know—"

"Can't you make a guess? Give me an idea? I'd like to know how much longer I'll be here."

"Make a guess?" He sounded slightly shocked, and if Kiri hadn't been so depressed, she would have smiled. "I wish I could tell you that, Miss MacKay, but without a will, it could take considerable time. You could always go back to California, and return when the necessary papers are ready."

Not with the present state of her bank account, she couldn't. Besides, she didn't want to leave the island until something was settled, and it would be difficult to do until the estate was legally hers.

"Some of the people here think my father did make a will," she said. "Is it possible you overlooked it, or—"

"Miss MacKay! You are speaking to a reputable firm. I have handled Ian's legal matters for years. It's true I wasn't always his confidant—" here a note of petulance came into the voice "—but I assure you I would have known if he had made a will. As a matter of fact, I kept urging him to do so, but he seemed to think he was immortal." No doubt about it now—heavy disapproval—but she couldn't drop it.

"Is it possible he made one and left it someplace—in the house, or a safe-deposit box?"

"I have opened his safe-deposit box, as I told you when you were here. Ian wasn't evasive—he would have told me if there was another. As for leaving the will in the house—I searched it soon after his death. Why do you think he might have left a will?" His voice sharpened. "Has something happened?"

"Oh, no. But there are some people on the island—people I think he would have wanted to provide for."

"I know very little about his private life. There's a woman, isn't there? And her boy? Don't let them play on your sympathies. When a propertied person dies, people are often prone to think they deserve more than they get."

"Yes . . . well, please let me know when there are any further developments." She replaced the phone, not wanting to speak another minute to the lawyer. How could he refer so coldly to Neiri as "a woman" and Rapauru as "her boy"? Along with Noel, they were Ian's family. It hurt to admit it, but it was true.

She still couldn't think of a way to resolve all the conflicting interests other than just leaving the island to them, and she wasn't ready to do that. She knew, though, that her thinking had changed in the last few days. The money wasn't nearly as important to her as it had once been. If she could come out with a reasonable amount, and safeguard the others' interests, she was going to do it. The question was, how?

She walked slowly down the hall, hearing her own footsteps echoing behind her. She was completely alone in the house, and after Tainui's actions the day before, she felt somewhat uneasy about it. When she returned from Paihia last night with Noel, she had half expected that Neiri would have gone back to the mainland with her brother but it had been Mrs. Armi who had gone with him. A visit to her daughter, Neiri had told Kiri this morning, a daughter who desperately needed help with a new baby.

It was probably true. It was also possible that she sensed trouble and was leaving a sinking ship.

Then, this morning, after cooking Kiri a quick breakfast over her protests, Neiri had left for the village. It hadn't been necessary to inform Neiri that she and Noel had witnessed the entire scene with Rapauru and Tainui. She had merely shown her the newspaper article and asked her about it.

Neiri, though, added very little to what Kiri already knew. Tainui was still at the village, though most of his men had left. She was obviously upset and Kiri understood her desire to be with Rapauru, but just now she would have appreciated a little company.

Noel had not stayed last night; Kiri hadn't asked him to, either. The atmosphere between the two had been so strained by the time they returned to the island that Kiri had been glad he hadn't even suggested coming in for a night-cap. She knew why her spirits were down today, but it didn't help. When she had learned of his prominence, she had been confirmed in her belief that Noel was unattainable in any permanent way, and that it would be emotional suicide to let her guard down.

She had no idea why Noel had changed from the companionable man she had spent the day with to one so morose she could hardly get a word out of him, but she had felt miserable and uncomfortable. That was why she had called the lawyer this morning, hoping that the estate would soon be settled. She wasn't sure how much more of this she could handle.

There were things she could do, though, even though the estate still wasn't legally hers. She could never accept Helborn's offer, but she should feel out someone else. Noel was the logical person to ask about it, and the next time she saw him she would get some names. If he knew how hard she was trying to straighten things out, how determined she was to be fair to everyone, he couldn't help but cooperate.

Noel. She drew her finger across her lips, lips that still remembered his kiss at the top of the world. Perhaps she was looking too deeply for a reason he had suddenly become so reserved and withdrawn. Perhaps it was simply that he was bored with her. She wasn't sparkling and witty like Felicia, and Noel had certainly liked that young lady well enough. But what did it matter? She would soon be leaving Long White Cloud, and Noel, and it couldn't be soon enough.

There had been no activity at the villa for the last hour, and Noel was beginning to think he might as well have stayed in his bunk and caught up on his sleep. Not that he could have slept, he reminded himself. He had spent what was left of the night dreaming of Kiri, asleep or awake; sometimes he wasn't actually sure which was which. Discordant images flashed through his brain—Kiri being swept away in a flood, calling out to him; Kiri with her long legs wrapped tightly around him, pulling him ever closer; Kiri regarding him with cool level eyes, eyes that suddenly changed to green fire as she moved to kiss him. Whether he had been asleep or awake, the dreams were enough to get him out of bed at dawn and into a cold shower.

A cold shower was better than a broken heart, he reminded himself. Kiri wasn't for him; she had armored herself in bitterness, and although he saw some evidence that her opinion of Ian was changing, it wasn't likely to do him any good. If Kiri did come to the conclusion that her father was a kind, honorable man, it would only make her doubt herself more. Why hadn't this paragon of virtue wanted her? He doubted that she had reasoned it all out that way, but deep in her subconscious, which doesn't lend itself to logic, it would hurt all the more.

From his sheltered spot, he watched Neiri leave the house, and edged back a little farther into the screen of foliage. Sometimes it seemed to him all he did these days was lurk around the villa, but he didn't want to go in and see her, and he didn't want to let her out of his sight.

Earlier this morning he had gone to Rapauru's village and found Tainui still very much in evidence, although most of his followers seemed to have left. He felt deep sadness as he thought of his visit. Once he would have strode in like a welcome friend. Now he wasn't sure how Rapauru would receive him. He would have liked to talk privately to the man; he sensed something was troubling Rapauru more than he was saying, but Tainui was always nearby.

The village had been uncharacteristically quiet, too. Men moved about at various tasks, but there was none of the joking and horseplay that he was used to witnessing. He had a feeling that everyone was waiting for something.

The whole situation made him deeply uneasy. He had promised Jeff Doyle that he would look after Kiri, and that was exactly what he intended to do, even if he had to hang around here all day.

Neiri was probably going to see her son. He hoped so; what was needed now was a calm head, and God knew that Rapauru, although Noel liked the man, wasn't noted for having an even temper.

With Neiri gone, Kiri would be alone in the house. He wondered if he should go on in instead of skulking around in the bushes, but on second thought, decided to stay put. This was a good vantage point if anything *was* going to happen.

He settled back on a boulder and unwrapped a sandwich. When this crisis was over, he would leave at once for Kenya. And then Brazil. Keep as busy as he could, and let Kiri do what she would with the island.

The sound of a body crashing through the brush jolted him out of his reverie. He sprang to his feet, his eyes on the green lawn that surrounded the villa, just as Rapauru lunged out of the trees and ran for the door.

Damn! Had he misjudged the man? He had been certain that Rapauru posed no physical danger to Kiri, but he was sure running like a man with a mission. If that mission was to hurt Kiri, he'd kill him!

When Rapauru leapt up onto the veranda, Noel was two strides behind him.

The door swung open before Noel had a chance to say a word to the Maori. Kiri stood in the doorway staring at the two men, her eyes round saucers of surprise. She hesitated, as though unsure whether to dart back inside, and Noel had to stop himself from taking her in his arms. She looked so fragile, with no makeup, her dark hair flying around her face. There were purple shadows under her eyes, too, and a flood of tenderness engulfed him. Apparently she hadn't slept any better than he had.

But he had to hand it to her—she was no shrinking violet. She regained control of herself instantly.

''Are you two in a race of some kind?'' she inquired politely.

For once Rapauru didn't give an angry retort. In fact, Noel saw, he looked almost scared. Ignoring Kiri, he put his hand on the man's shoulder. "What's the matter, Rap? You were crashing through that brush like a thirsty elephant headed for a river."

"I thought you might be here."

"Well, I am," Noel drawled, "but why the hurry? When I saw you this morning you didn't seem too eager to talk to me."

"How could I, with Tainui there?" Rapauru clenched and unclenched his large fists. "He didn't leave us alone two minutes."

"So you noticed that, too."

"Come on in the house," Kiri said, stepping back into the foyer, her eyes going from one man to the other. "It sounds like you have some talking to do. Where's Neiri? Didn't she go to the village?"

"She's out looking for Noel," Rapauru said, stepping inside and glancing back over his shoulder at the encircling trees, then glaring accusingly at Noel. "You weren't at your boat, so Ma went to the other side of the island to see if you were on one of your study plots."

Noel frowned, his eyes on Rapauru's face. This was apparently serious, if both Neiri and Rapauru were desperate to locate him. He had a deep, sinking feeling that he was about to find out why, and that he wasn't going to like it.

"We don't have much time," Rapauru said. He nodded briefly at Kiri. "You'd better call the police, although they won't be able to get here in time. It's Tainui."

"Who else?" Noel said dryly. "Shouldn't you choose your friends from a better class of people, Rap?"

"He's no friend of mine," the Maori exploded. "Came over here to my island, took over just like he had a right to. Keeps telling me I'm an Uncle Tom, whatever that is."

As Kiri waited to find out what she was to tell the police, he paced back and forth, occasionally casting quick glances out the window. "But now he's really done it."

"Done what?"

"He's coming over here to set fire to the villa."

Kiri gasped; Noel saw the blood drain from her face, as he turned and grabbed Rapauru hard by the shoulder, spinning him around until they were face-to-face. "He's what? The man must be crazy!"

"Maybe he is. Most everybody seems to think so now, although they sure didn't seem to think so before. But he's got three or four men still with him, and crazy or not, they're on their way. I got here first because I knew a short-cut."

Noel's mouth set in a hard, thin line as he released his grip on Rapauru and sprang to the window. He knew the short-cut, too. It didn't give them much time.

He drew in his breath sharply, as he saw the line of men walk out of the trees. Five of them. It didn't give them any time at all.

He whirled around to Kiri. "We'll meet them outside, try to talk to them. Call the police, then go to your room. If things get bad, you can always get out the patio door."

He didn't wait to see if she obeyed; it was too late, anyway. The police would be no help at all. The villa would be aflame before they launched their boat.

A moment later when he and Rapauru faced the approaching men he wasn't at all surprised to find she was standing right beside him.

His eyes never left the ominous group that **stro**de toward them across the lawn, but he put out an arm and drew Kiri close beside him. One part of his brain registered that she was trembling slightly, and he was filled with rage. These men would pay for this.

Silently, he watched them come closer. Out of the corner of his eyes he saw that Rapauru had assumed a warrior stance, legs apart, fists clenched, face contorted. A good man in a fight, but with two against five, they'd better try talking first.

At a signal from Tainui, the men with him halted, and he stepped out in front of them. The sunlight glinted off the shells around his neck, turned his brown skin a tawny gold. Noel kept his face expressionless as he coldly surveyed the Maori. Tainui was still in his feathered cloak, and his appearance gave Noel an unreal feeling, as though he were confronting a ghost from the distant past.

But Tainui was all too real. His eyes burned with a zeal that was familiar to Noel, who had seen the same look in the faces of terrorists in the Middle East just before they threw a bomb for the glory of Allah.

Had he misjudged Tainui? Was he more than a self-seeking publicity hound? Did he really believe in his cause? If so, he was doubly dangerous.

"Step aside," Tainui said brusquely, moving up onto the first step of the veranda. He was only a couple of feet away now, and from his expression Noel knew that talking was not going to do him much good. Tainui was beyond logic. His mouth was set in a hard line, his chin jutted forward, and he looked as though any random move would trigger the violence that seemed to reflect in his eyes.

"Step aside," he repeated. "We have no quarrel with you."

"If you plan to burn the villa down, you have a quarrel with me," Noel said quietly. Maybe he could keep him talking long enough to think of some strategy.

Tainui reached beneath the folds of his cloak and, with a gesture like that of a magician pulling a rabbit from a hat, produced an unlit torch. Noel's throat constricted, and he clenched his hands, but he didn't move away.

"This villa is on Maori land," Tainui proclaimed. There was a murmur of agreement from the men behind him. "Out of the way, *pakeha*. I will remove every trace of the foreigner."

"You can't burn it—think, Tainui! So far you haven't done anything you can be jailed for. If you torch the villa, things will change—you'll be hunted down, arrested."

"Every leader has faced jail," Tainui retorted. He took a butane cigarette lighter from under his cloak and, even as tense as the situation was, Noel recognized the incongruity.

He glanced sideways at Kiri. Her face was pale, but her expression was calm, resolute. She wouldn't panic.

"Don't do it, Tainui." Rapauru spoke for the first time, and Noel shot a glance at the young Maori. His forehead was beaded with perspiration, and Noel felt a flash of sympathy. Rapauru was caught in the middle. This was one of his own people threatening to burn down the house that had been home to him.

Tainui cast him a scornful look. "What do you plan to do about it, boy? Go back and tend to your play village."

Rapauru's face flushed a deeper hue. "What do I plan to do about it?" he growled. "I plan to stop you."

Tainui laughed. "You and the *pakeha*? There are five of us, boy. And I'm through talking."

For Noel, events started to unfold in slow motion, as Tainui put the light to the torch, waited for the blaze, then held it high above his head, ready to throw. He knew a moment of near panic. The roof of the villa would go like tinder when that flame hit dry wood. He tensed, pulled himself into a crouch, ready to spring—

Rapauru was before him. Like an adder striking, he hurled himself at Tainui, knocking him backward off the steps. The torch fell from his hand and sputtered in the grass a few feet away. Noel saw the men behind him surge forward, and he leapt down the stairs and placed himself between them and their embattled leader.

"Cool it!" he shouted. "Get back! This isn't a toy gun in my pocket!"

Would it work? The men stared at the sharp object in his shorts pocket, and indecision crossed their faces. They didn't really believe he had a gun—but they weren't sure. He pressed his advantage.

"One of you could die finding out," he taunted.

First one man dropped his eyes and then, as Noel's gaze swung around the group, the others looked away, too, refusing to meet his eyes. Finally one shuffled backward.

"Ah, let's get out of here," he muttered. "It never did seem like such a good idea. If I know Tainui, we'd have been the ones to take the rap."

Mutters of agreement, and Noel stood watching, hands on his hips, as the four men turned and slunk away into the bushes. He let out the breath he hadn't realized he'd been holding, and absently wiped the sweat from his face. That would be the end of them. They could never face Tainui again, and they had apparently been his only loyal followers. He turned back to the fight behind him—Rapauru might need help.

He narrowed his eyes, watching closely, as the two men surged back and forth in front of him. They seemed evenly matched at first, but it was soon apparent that Rapauru was winning. He fought like an enraged tiger, huge hams of fists slamming into Tainui like battering rams.

For several agonizing minutes, Tainui gave as good as he got. Blood gushed out beneath Rapauru's eye, and an occasional grunt told Noel that a blow had hit home.

But there was now no question of the outcome. Tainui retreated inch by inch, as Rapauru seemed to gain strength. Noel winced as a particularly hard blow snapped Tainui's head backward. Perhaps he should intervene, but this was Maori against Maori. Rapauru was fighting for the right to set the goals for his own village, and Noel suspected he wouldn't welcome interference.

The torch that Tainui had lit still smoldered on the green grass. Out of the corner of his eye Noel saw Kiri slip down the stairs and extinguish it; then, carefully skirting the combatants, she moved over beside him.

Tainui was retreating even faster beneath Rapauru's punishing fists. Finally he turned, put his hand over his bleeding nose, and ran for the cover of the forest. Rapauru did not pursue him; he put his hands on his hips and watched as the man disappeared.

Noel tightened his arm around Kiri's waist, and looked at Rapauru, as the man stolidly gazed after his retreating enemy. He appeared to be carved of stone, all brawn and muscle. Noel could almost imagine him as some old-time chieftain, routing an invader. Whatever Rapauru's conflict in the beginning, he had come through.

"Good job, Rap," he said tersely.

The Maori smiled; the stone statue reverted to a man. "Glad I had you at my back."

Kiri moved out of Noel's encircling arm and started up the stairs, calling over her shoulder. "If you two gladiators will come inside, I'll put something on those cuts, Rapauru."

Kiri worked quickly, cleansing Rapauru's cuts, applying bandages in strategic places, as she listened to the two men discuss the situation. Rapauru leaned back in a comfortable chair, obviously enjoying the attention, while Noel sat across from him, elbows on knees, chin in his hands, watching the procedure with enigmatic blue eyes.

These two were more than a little proud of themselves, she thought. Well, they had reason to be, but she was getting a little tired of all that mutual congratulating.

"What if he comes back?" she demanded, pressing just a little on the cut under Rapauru's eye.

He winced. "I doubt he'll be back—not after that loss of face. Deserted by his own men, running from a fight."

She hesitated, then decided to bring it out in the open. "I was scared to death when he raised that torch. And I wasn't sure what you would do, Rapauru. Noel couldn't have handled them all. I know you resent me, and Tainui is your own blood, so I'm doubly grateful—"

He scowled. "True, I'm not thrilled you're here. I'll still get you off the island if I can. But he was going to burn down the villa—Ian's villa." Rapauru clenched his jaw at the enormity of the outrage. "I couldn't let him do that to Ian—not after everything he did for me."

So she was still an outsider, an object of resentment. But Rapauru did have loyalties, and he obviously revered Ian, even though it had been her father's thoughtlessness that had left them all in this situation. She glanced at Noel.

"It was lucky you had a gun. I didn't know you carried one."

He grinned, reached in his pocket, and pulled out a flashlight. "I don't. But the bluff worked. Either that, or they were just looking for an excuse to get out of a sticky situation. I don't think they were ever fully committed, but Tainui is a hard man to say no to."

"How can you be so sure he won't be back?" Remembering the fanatical sheen in his eyes, Kiri couldn't suppress a tiny shiver as she bathed one of the minor cuts on Rapauru's broad face.

The Maori scooted the chair back and rose to his feet, pushing away her hand. "I'm sure. But it won't hurt to go back and see that he does. Coming, Noel?"

Noel shook his head. "I'll stay here and watch out for a while. I agree it's doubtful he'll come back, but I'd just as soon be positive."

Rapauru shrugged, and headed for the door. A few seconds later they heard it slam behind him.

Kiri sank down in the chair Rapauru had just vacated, slipped off her shoes and tucked her feet up under her, then looked across at Noel.

"Whew, am I glad that's over! I don't mind telling you, my legs were getting a little shaky. If it is over," she said slowly. "If Tainui doesn't come back here, what do you think he'll do?"

"Hard to say." Noel put his hands behind his head and stretched his long legs out in front of him. "He's lost a lot of credibility. There's bound to be talk among the Maori, and most of them don't go for violent solutions to problems. He'll probably leave the island, lie low awhile, then start up someplace else.''

She rose and padded barefoot to a window, putting her hand on the sill as she looked out into the yard. So they were back where they were before Tainui's arrival. One island, four competing claims. Although Rapauru had softened toward her, she didn't deceive herself that he liked her. Yet he had acted heroically, saving the villa. It made it harder than ever to think of dispossessing him.

Noel came up behind her and put his hand on her shoulder. ''You handled yourself very well, Kiri.''

She turned, a grin lighting her face. ''What did you think I'd do, faint?''

''Okay, okay, I get your point. How about a little lunch? I was just having a sandwich, and had to throw it down when it looked like it was time for the cavalry to rush in.''

''If you'll fix it.'' Her eyes challenged him.

In the end, they both fixed lunch, a light omelet and a green salad. For the rest of the afternoon they talked sporadically, stretched out on lawn chairs in a sheltered corner of the yard, neither wanting to talk about what was on their minds. Would Tainui really come back? Perhaps sneak in after dark and finish the job? He was like a wounded wild animal, Kiri thought, doubly dangerous. She knew Noel wouldn't leave until they had some word from Rapauru or Neiri.

Suddenly Kiri remembered that in the excitement she had completely forgotten to call the police.

''Hadn't we better do it now?''

Noel nodded. ''I think so. At least they can keep an eye out for Tainui if he leaves the island.''

He was a few minutes on the phone. Then there seemed to be nothing to do but wait.

It was dusk when Neiri came hurrying across the expanse of green. Waiting for news, Kiri took a deep breath, her shoulders tense with apprehension. Then she caught a look at Neiri's face and relaxed. The woman was smiling; the crisis must be over.

It was. Tainui had left the island in his war canoe, Neiri reported, along with all his men, most of whom were obviously disgruntled. Perhaps Tainui's days as a leader were numbered.

Insisting on fixing dinner for them, Neiri bustled around the kitchen, then all three sat down at the dining-room table. Kiri felt as though a huge weight had been lifted from her shoulders. It was a companionable, friendly meal and Kiri felt like a fool because she had a hard time keeping the tears out of her eyes as she relaxed and let the warmth generated by the little gathering seep through her. Perhaps it was a reaction to her earlier panic that made her respond so emotionally, but she felt as though for the first time in her life she was really part of a family.

It was all over too soon. She and Noel helped Neiri clear away, and then the woman insisted on going back to the village to be with Rapauru.

Left alone with Noel, Kiri paced restlessly, almost equally afraid that he would stay with her or that he would go back to his boat. Even though there was no longer any danger from Tainui, she couldn't face being alone in this empty house, jumping at every sound, not tonight. Her nerves were frazzled, and she knew she didn't want to face the night alone. Yet what if he stayed? That possibility was equally frightening.

"You're going to wear a hole in the floor," he said gently. "It's all over. You've nothing to be afraid of anymore."

Oh, didn't she? What about the fact that just looking at him turned her to jelly? But she probably didn't have to be afraid that she would succumb to passion; her own senses might be reeling under the impact of his presence, but he certainly seemed to be immune to her. He had spent the entire afternoon without so much as trying to kiss her.

She felt the light touch of his hand on her arm. Such a light touch, and yet it held her securely. She stood quite motionless, every atom, every cell, alert and waiting. At some level she was aware of the call of a night bird through the open window, and the haunting scent of daphne wafted in on the breeze, but the full force of her attention was focused on the man beside her.

Slowly, not even breathing, she turned her head to meet his eyes. Her gaze caught his, locked, held.

Chapter 12

His grip tightened on her arm, his fingers pressing into her tender flesh, while he continued to hold her gaze. Electric-blue eyes, charged with desire, held her as motionless as a statue. For an incredible instant, every atom of her being was concentrated in a laser-sharp beam of answering desire. Her body slackened, trembled, ached with the need to merge with this man, to assuage her loneliness in the comfort of his arms, to enfold him in complete intimacy.

But she couldn't allow it. It wasn't right, not for her, not now. She knew well enough that there was a physical affinity between her and Noel that was as easy to light as Tainui's torch. But there was more to a relationship than physical attraction, however fiery and all-consuming. There was caring, shared values, common goals. Maybe it was impossible to achieve such a relationship; certainly her own experience tended to point that way. But it was the only kind that didn't guarantee pain and misery.

From what she had learned of Noel's values, seen of his character, their relationship would be about as permanent as a dragonfly skimming over a summer pond. Not that his values weren't admirable; they were. But they didn't leave room for anything else, certainly not a personal relationship.

With a supreme effort of will, she tore her gaze away and let her arm fall to her side, moving away from his touch. The instant feeling of loneliness, of numbing cold where his warm fingers had touched her flesh, struck deep in her heart, but she managed to keep her voice even.

"Noel—I think we should talk."

He went very still. Then a curtain seemed to drop over the warmth in his eyes, his lips tightened, a pulse pounded in his temple, as he struggled for control.

Finally he gave her a faint ironic smile. "I thought we'd been talking all afternoon."

"Not really talking," she insisted. "We kept skirting around everything except the explosive situation here on the island. There's so much about you I don't know. I know your feelings about Ian, I know how you feel about Long White Cloud, but—" She swallowed, then lifted her eyes to his face. She had to know, and she'd always been direct. "How do you feel about me?"

Surprise showed in his eyes, then his lips curved in a provocative smile, a smile that sent shivers all the way down to her toes, as he arched an elegant eyebrow. The man was too sexy to live!

"I was about to show you, but you insisted you wanted to talk."

"Please . . . I'm serious."

"Seriously, you are the most incredibly desirable woman I've ever met. Does that answer your question?"

"Not really. Oh, I know you'd like to make love with me," she said hastily, blocking out his protest. "We do seem to have a physical affinity for each other—"

"Physical?" He gave her a long look that singed her flesh. "I'm not sure you can divide a person—physical, mental, spiritual, whatever segments you come up with. There's something between us, and I can't categorize it. Something I felt when I first saw you."

"When you first saw me, you thought I was a money-grubbing, selfish person," she said slowly.

"That, too." He brushed a lock of hair back from his forehead and grinned. "But I saw something else, right from the moment you walked toward me on the dock at Paihia. As for your being selfish—I haven't thought that for a long time. You're generous, compassionate, giving—"

"How can you say that, when you know what I planned for the island?"

"Planned? Past tense?"

"It's something I need to talk to you about."

He reached out and gently brushed a lock of her dark hair away from her cheek. The soft brush of his hand against her skin sent little shivers all through her body; she hoped desperately he hadn't noticed, but knew he had from the way his eyes turned dark and smoky.

"Later." His finger traced a path of fire down her smooth cheek. "All that can wait. You asked what I think of you. I think," he said softly, his voice as intimately caressing as his touch, "I think that you are a proud and honorable lady. A warm, loving woman, struggling to get free from your shell."

Her elemental response to his touch confused her, made it imperative to assert her independence before she lost all semblance of will.

"And you think you're the man who can free me?" She meant it as a challenge, but her voice sounded shaky, even to herself. Typical masculine logic! She didn't want to make love, so he thought there was something wrong with her. He was wrong in his assessment; her distrust of men wasn't enclosed in a shell, it was a reasonable, logical defense against what could happen if she allowed herself to love.

But might it be worth the pain of the ultimate betrayal? Right now every atom of her body longed for Noel. She had told him she knew very little about him, but that wasn't really true. She knew he was kind, dedicated, loyal to his dreams and his visions. She suspected that making love with him would open a realm that would remain forever closed if she didn't take the chance.

Whatever happened between them, whatever decision she made, she couldn't allow wishful thinking to blind her to one unalterable fact—the future didn't include the two of them together. But why not take this opportunity—the one opportunity that might be given to her—to see what loving could really be like?

Noel's voice broke through her thoughts, and she realized he was replying to her challenge. She jerked herself back to the moment.

"Free you?" He sounded infinitely sad. "No, I can't free you. I don't think one can ever free another human being. You'll do that yourself one day. I'd give a lot to be with you when it happens."

At some deep level of her unconscious, she made her decision. She moved a fraction of an inch closer and placed her hand lightly on his arm. His muscles flexed beneath her touch, sending tiny shocks of awareness all along her nerves. Her breath came faster, and she elevated her chin and met his eyes. She wanted Noel to stay with her tonight, wanted to make love with him, no matter what the consequences to her future emotional equilibrium.

It was important, too, that she take the initiative in letting him know. She didn't want to be seduced, to allow him to think she was led into intimacy against her better judgment. This was a clear and conscious decision. She was a woman, and she would claim her lover.

Even though he would only be a temporary lover. She would have the memory all her life.

She would be brave enough to accept this wild, singing moment and worry about future heartache later. It was better to have one crystal moment than nothing at all.

There would be tears aplenty later; all her experience assured her of that, but perhaps they would be bearable if she had this golden moment in time to look back on.

Noel must have read her decision in her eyes. Slowly, deliberately, as though gathering a delicate treasure, he put his arms around her and drew her to him. As though in a dream, she closed her eyes, tilted her face upward and opened her lips slightly to invite his kiss. He claimed her mouth, first tenderly, exploring gently, then with a searing intensity that raged through her blood like wildfire.

Gasping, she gave herself over to the torrents of sensation flooding through her as he pressed himself firmly against her and ran one hand down her back, over the swell of her hips, molding her to the demand of his aroused body.

Still cradling her against him, he drew his head back so that he could look into her eyes; his own were smoky with desire.

His voice came ragged and breathless through the white-hot haze that enveloped her.

"Darling, are you sure? Do you want me?"

"Yes, yes…" She forced herself to meet his eyes proudly. Of course she wasn't sure. She still retained enough rationality to know that making love with Noel was going to have a cataclysmic effect on her life. She'd face that when it came. *Now* she wanted him, beyond any question, and if she was wrong in taking what life offered her, she would handle that later.

With a low groan, he picked her up in his arms and carried her down the hall. She let her head fall back against his shoulder, aware of his strength, the warmth of his skin through his knit shirt, the heated aroma of his skin. Now she would only feel, luxuriate in his masculine force. No judging, no fear, no regret. All that could come, if it must come, later.

Noel toed open the door to her room and deposited her gently on the flowered bedspread. His breath caught in his throat as he saw her stretched out on the pink and green satin material like some exotic flower, her dark hair spread like a fan of silk beneath her head. She looked back up at him through a screen of impossibly long lashes, her green eyes dark and shadowed with mystery. She was so beautiful it hurt; hurt like nothing he'd ever felt before.

And she was brave, with a gallantry that touched his heart. He guessed what it must have cost her to offer herself so proudly, and knowing she needed the feeling that she was in control of her own response, he had let her lead the way. She was a gift; an incredible shining gift he would cherish forever.

"My God, you're beautiful," he half choked out the words. "The most beautiful woman I've ever seen."

"I love your saying that—even if it's not true," she whispered back. Her eyes, green emeralds smoldering with an inner fire, fastened on his.

"Oh, Kiri, Kiri," he groaned, "why can't you realize what an amazingly beautiful woman you are? Why can't you accept that you're infinitely desirable?"

"I feel that way—now," she replied.

He wanted to tell her he loved her, but he doubted she could accept it. He would go slowly. He would show her, he vowed, make her understand in every cell of her body just how lovable and desirable she was. He would exorcise all those disabling doubts...

Leaning over the bed, he began to unbutton her sleeveless shirt, his fingers quick and competent, then raised her slightly to slip it off her shoulders. Next he removed her lacy bra, caressing each breast as he freed it, thrilling to the way they quivered under his hands as each nipple sprang erect.

Stroking the soft flesh of her ribcage, he moved down to unfasten the band of her slacks and draw them down over the soft curve of her hips, along her long, silky legs, then dropped them to the floor. Then, as she shuddered beneath his caress, his hands reversed their path, stroking up over her smooth skin, lingering on the delicate flesh of her thighs, until finally he leaned over her and gently kissed the pulse he could see beating in the hollow of her throat.

He felt her stiffen. Instantly he stopped, although his body throbbed and sent urgent messages to his brain demanding that he continue.

"What is it, love? Is something the matter?" he whispered, gently running his lips along her cheek, nuzzling her ear.

"Oh—I—I'm not prepared—I never expected anything like this." Her voice was so low he could barely hear her. "I'm not on the Pill." Her eyes were wide with shock and embarrassment.

He chuckled softly. "Well, I am prepared. You don't think I'd ever do anything to hurt you, do you?" His voice was suddenly intense, serious.

She smiled shyly, tentatively, and his heart did a flip-flop. Such a lovely, complicated woman. She had been so strong when she had initiated the lovemaking, but now she was endearingly vulnerable. He'd never expected she would travel with birth control, although he knew many women did, not wanting to chance a problem as a result of brief encounter. But it was unlikely that an intense, private person like Kiri would expect to find a lover on a brief trip.

Not that he believed she was a virgin. She'd told him about the man who had hurt her—the one besides Ian, he thought, his face suddenly grim. Both of those men had something to answer for.

Something flickered in her eyes and he knew what she was thinking—that he was very well prepared for a casual encounter himself.

"I got them when we were in Paihia," he whispered.

"You must have expected . . ."

"Not at all." He flashed her a grin. "I'm a sailor, but I take care not to have a child in every port."

At the look on her face he wished he hadn't joked about it, and added quickly, "I don't have a girl in every port, either."

He slipped out of his clothes, leaving them where they fell, and stretched out beside her on the bed. Propping himself up on one elbow, he looked down at her, drinking her in with his eyes. She was glorious. Dressed, she looked elegant, almost too slender for his taste. She might seem even a little intimidating to some people. Though never to him. He had seen behind her prickly facade to the lovely, vulnerable woman there.

Now, lying naked beside him, she resembled a fragile, but completely womanly, goddess—Diana of the Chase, perhaps, with long svelte legs, slender body, clear ivory skin. Her small breasts were firm and taut; he cupped one in his hand, thrilling at the springy texture, then circled the dark areola, the rigid nipple, with his thumb. How could he have ever thought that she was too slender!

Passion, hot and wild as a brushfire, swept through his veins, demanding that he possess her now, this instant. Clenching his jaw, he fought it back. He had to hang on to his control; he wanted to take her slowly, tenderly, make the sensation last, be sure that she attained the heights he longed to bring her to.

It wasn't easy. Elemental, primitive need burned like a hot coal in the pit of his stomach; his arousal was so hard it was part exquisite pain. Still deep in a kiss, he ran his hand along the delicate curve of her hip, found the tangle of dark curly hair at the juncture of her thighs and then caressed the sweet moist center of her womanhood...

At his touch she gasped and arched underneath him like a tightly strung bowstring. One questing hand traveled the same path along his abdomen that his hand had taken on her. He winced with nearly unbearable pleasure, unable to move, as her fingers closed on soft velvet, then moved down to fasten on hardness and rigidity.

He choked, waves of sensation dashing against the rock of his control, and he guided her hand to where he felt the most exquisite pleasure.

"Noel," her voice was soft, panting, "Please...now..."

Fiercely, exultantly, he kissed her, then raised himself above her, her moans and clutching hands stripping him of all vestige of control. She was his, he was hers, and she demanded all of him. He plunged into her sweet molten heat, exulting in her wild response.

Now there was nothing in the entire world except the two of them swept along in the elemental force of life.

He heard her moans, felt her nails digging into his back as her head thrashed wildly on the bed, and it spurred him on. Just as he was hers, she was his—his woman, his lover, his mate. The experience transcended his body and he felt a mystical sense of union, as all feeling, all sensation, coalesced into one powerful point.

He felt her tense, and for a shattering instant become almost still, as she approached the precipice. He thrust one more time, wildly, deeply, wanting to give her his very soul.

Her long quivering cry, her arched back, her arms holding him in a viselike grip, sent him over the edge with her. As spasm after spasm rocked her, he held her as though he would never let go, until finally, replete and exhausted, he let his head rest on the moist warmth of her shoulder.

Eventually her shallow breathing penetrated his drugged satisfaction, and he rolled over on his side, holding her so that they still maintained the contact.

"Am I too heavy?" In spite of her response, she still seemed fragile to him, delicate; he felt as though he might crush her.

"You're just right..."

He raised himself on one elbow, still holding her hips tight against his with his other hand. Her face in the half-light was so breathtakingly dear that even breathing was painful.

"I wanted it to last," he said softly. "I wanted it to be perfect for you. But, my God, woman, I had no idea—"

"Neither did I," she whispered.

He placed a gentle kiss on her moist cheek. In the years since Rosamund, he had not been celibate; in fact, there had been a number of lovely women who had been happy to accept what he offered—enjoyment, fun, good healthy sex. Not once, not even with Rosamund, had he suspected such a normal, natural act could shake him to the core.

"I meant to have a little more control," he said ruefully. "I'm not sure what happened—I'm really not a barbarian."

She gave a low, throaty laugh, quintessentially feminine, he thought. "Aren't you?" she whispered. "I certainly have no complaints. Besides, we have the rest of the night to make it last, don't we?" she teased, as her hand, soft, seeking, found and caressed his fevered skin. He gasped, as he felt himself stirring beneath her fingers.

"You'll pay for that," he growled, lightly nipping her on the shoulder.

"All night long," she whispered.

This time they did make it last, exploring every sensation, every possible nuance of feeling. It was near morning when Kiri finally fell asleep. Noel cradled her in his arms for a long time, his mind as active as his body had been a short time before.

His thoughts were disquieting ones. Although he had fought the knowledge, he had suspected for some time that he was falling in love with her. This glorious mating confirmed him in his belief. Yet he knew they were no nearer to a happy solution than they had been before their soul-shattering coupling.

It did no good to admit that this woman meant life to him. He knew, too, that he wasn't like her father, a man who could love and abandon, completely forget his responsibility. Although he still couldn't believe that of Ian, he had to admit it was beginning to look as though the man had done just that—to everyone. But whatever Ian's shortcomings, Noel knew absolutely that without Kiri, all his dreams, his plans, would be colorless and dull, drained of vitality and purpose.

Even with Rosamund, whom he had been sure he loved, he had never felt this certainty, this knowledge that life meant nothing without her. When the time had come for a choice, he had been able to walk away from Rosamund.

He could never walk away from Kiri. He was as tightly bound to her as a vine around a *totara* tree. Yet he knew, knew with a desperate cold certainty, that she was not bound to him in the same way. Nothing she had said or done during their night of passion and abandon had changed the fact that she was afraid of love, afraid to trust. Oh, she could risk her body, but not her heart. Unless he could change that, erase her doubts, awaken her to her own self-worth, there was no chance for them at all.

A cold feeling of desolation gripped him, and instinctively he tightened his grip on the woman sleeping beside him. She moaned, twisted slightly in her sleep, but didn't awaken. He continued to hold her, his eyes staring blindly into the darkness.

He knew he had been right when he told her that no one else could free her to love. She had to do that for herself. But could she? Had the wounds gone too deep?

Only half-awake, Kiri reached out instinctively. When her hand met emptiness, she opened her eyes and jerked herself erect, as memories flooded back. A glance at the large, rumpled bed confirmed that she was alone. The pillow beside her still bore the imprint of his head, but Noel was nowhere to be seen.

It was late, too. Midmorning sunlight lay in bars across the floor, and through the bank of windows she saw that the hedge cast a short shadow on the stones of the patio.

She lay still for a moment, savoring the memory of last night. Gingerly, she raised a finger to her lips; they were still slightly sore and swollen from last night's kisses. She ran her hand slowly over her breasts, her rib cage, the softness of her abdomen, with a feeling that approached awe. She had been right to risk. Her body still bore the imprint of his kisses, smelled of his scent, and of love.

They might have rushed to completion the first time, but, she thought, a soft inward smile on her face, they had indeed made up for it.

Fully awake now, she closed her eyes and lovingly went over every detail of the night before. She wanted to fix it firmly in her mind and heart. The memory might have to last a long time.

Thinking of how she had instigated the lovemaking, she smiled with inward satisfaction and triumph. She suspected Noel was accustomed to taking the initiative himself, but he had understood her need to lead. It had been important to her that she didn't see herself as a wavering girl, swept off her feet by passion. Proudly and fervently, she had reached for what she wanted—a precious memory.

She smiled, too, recalling their first wild coupling. She had sensed he wanted to go slow, to take her gently to the heights, but she couldn't wait—she was already at the top. She had met him at the crest, not needing or wanting the slow buildup. She had been eager, passionate, aching for fulfillment. Later she had luxuriated in the sweet teasing, the long slow journey to satisfaction, but that first time she had responded to Noel with a ferocity she hadn't dreamed she was capable of.

And now she faced the morning after, the time for accounting. She was almost glad that she had time to marshal her defenses before she saw Noel again. Not that she loved him any less; she suspected she would always love him, but that didn't change the way things were between them.

The French doors slid open and Noel stepped in from the patio. He wore only a pair of brief white shorts and scuffed thongs. Her heart rate quickened, as she took in his tall bronzed body, a body that was now so familiar to her. He looked fresh from the shower, skin glistening, thick hair that always reminded her of ripe dark wheat combed back from his forehead, his firm jaw freshly shaved.

"Hi, Sleeping Beauty." He strode to the bed and leaned over to give her a warm kiss. He smelled like fresh mint and sunshine. "If you don't get out of there pretty soon, I swear I'm going to join you."

She stretched lazily, raising her arms above her head, not missing the glint of interest in Noel's eyes as the sheet slid down to expose her firm breasts. She smiled softly. "Is that a promise?"

"Is that an invitation?" As he moved toward her, a devilish smile on his face, she hastily drew the sheet up over her shoulders.

"It really is time I got up. It must be late. Is anyone around?"

"Neiri slipped in for a while this morning, but she didn't stay long. Just picked up a few things and hurried on back to Rapauru." He sat down on the bed beside her.

The thought of the Maori woman brought a slight frown to Kiri's face, replacing for a moment her awareness of Noel.

"I feel so guilty about Neiri," she sighed. "I'm sure I'm the reason she spends so much time at the village—and the reason she comes back so often, too. She must feel caught between wanting to live in her old home, and feeling uncomfortable because I'm here."

"Don't feel guilty about anything." He took her face between his two hands and looked deeply into her eyes. "It's a useless emotion." Releasing her, he smiled. "Just get out of bed and try some of the breakfast I made for you."

"Coffee?" she asked hopefully.

He grinned. "And you've been drinking that morning tea with such appreciation! But yes, there's coffee—and don't worry. Your secret is safe with me."

"Turn your head." She slid her long legs over the side of the bed, and, holding the sheet with one hand, reached for a robe. Last night with Noel she had been completely without embarrassment. She had even gloried in the way his eyes drank her in, but this morning she felt unaccountably shy.

Was it because she knew the night had been a one-time thing, and that this morning they were back on the old uneasy footing?

If they were back on the old footing, Noel didn't seem to realize it. Ignoring her words, he put his hands on her shoulders and gently lowered her back onto the bed. Sliding alongside her, he held her tightly against his nearly nude body, moving his head to nibble her ear, trail little kisses along her cheek.

His breath quickened, his muscles tensed. She had thought it would be hours before the sweet delirium could rise again, but as she fell back against the pillows she moaned softly and pulled him to her.

An hour later they did make it as far as the kitchen where Noel's breakfast, scones with jam and cold scrambled eggs, awaited them. The electric coffeepot was still plugged in. The coffee, at least, was still hot, and Kiri poured them both a steaming cupful.

"What happens today?" she asked, taking a long, appreciative swallow of the fragrant liquid. "Will the police be here?"

"No." Noel made short work of his scone, then elaborated on his reply. "Doyle called while you were still getting your beauty sleep—and it certainly worked, by the way." His words were measured and serious; only his eyes danced. "You're absolutely ravishing."

"And you're ravenous," she laughed, as Noel reached for her hand and kissed first her palm and then transferred his attention to her wrist.

She managed to retrieve her hand, which appeared to be going the way of the scone to judge by his spirited attack, "Be serious. What did the authorities say? What about Tainui?"

"Past history," he replied. "At least as far as we're concerned. He was spotted up north near Spirits Bay, in with another tribe."

"Will they arrest him?"

"Probably not." Noel frowned. "They're keeping an eye on him, but things are pretty touchy, and he didn't actually set the fire. I told Doyle about Rapauru fighting him off, and I guess they think that's enough—let the Maori handle it. Unless you want to press charges? If you do, we'll sail into Paihia this afternoon."

She shuddered, and shook her head. She never wanted to see or hear of Tainui again, and if she had seen the last of him that was all she wanted.

"I thought you'd feel that way." He gave her a warm smile. "I have to leave for a while—will you be all right here by yourself?"

Her heart seemed to stop, then beat more rapidly. She had known Noel would leave her sometime, but she hadn't suspected it would be today! Nevertheless, she managed to return his smile. "Of course."

"Good." He stood up, drank the last of the coffee, then crossed to the sink and rinsed out the cup. "I have a few things I need to take care of on the boat—some reports, a couple of items I've let slide over the last few days. Then I should check on my study plots, but it shouldn't take long— I'll be back as soon as I can."

She swallowed, knowing her instant of panic had been ridiculous. Of course he wasn't just going to sail away without a word, float off like a dandelion blown by the wind! He wasn't that irresponsible; when he left, there would at least be a goodbye.

He came toward her and pulled her to her feet, then gave her a long, enthusiastic kiss. Pulling away, he gently massaged the back of her neck. "Get some rest," he murmured. "I'll be back in time for dinner."

She watched him go out the door, then wandered back to her own room, wondering how she would fill the day. If she had been home, there would have been no problem. Free time was scarce, highly prized, and every available minute was devoted to working in her tiny studio.

Unconsciously, her fingers curved as though they were forming soft clay into forms and shapes that existed only in her mind. She should have brought some materials with her, or else picked some up in Paihia, but she had never expected that she would have to stay on the island this long.

Perhaps she could make a sketch or two, preparatory to working the idea out in clay. The thought didn't appeal to her though. She had always preferred to work directly with the soft mud, the idea taking form as she worked the pliable clay.

She threw open the French doors and stepped out onto the patio, throwing back her head to catch the breeze on her hot cheeks. The air felt cooler, brisker, than it had before, but her mind wasn't on the weather. Who was she fooling? She couldn't concentrate on anything, not even her sculpting, which could usually consume her to the exclusion of everything else, while she still felt the imprint of Noel's caresses on every inch of her flesh.

But now was the perfect time to think things through, away from his distracting presence. Last night had been shattering in its impact. It had rocked her to her very foundations, mocked her naive idea that she could keep things under control and guide her destiny by her mind alone.

It now seemed naive to think, as she had done, that she could make love with Noel just once and then leave him alone. While there was still time, she had better give some clear hard thought to the ramifications of what had happened between them.

Chapter 13

Noel swung aboard the *Island Princess* and hurried below deck, without so much as a glance around him. Gulls called, bellbirds sang from the shore, but he was oblivious to everything but the remembered feel, taste, feminine fragrance of Kiri. God, how he loved that woman.

The irony of the situation didn't escape him, either. He, who ever since Rosamund, had fashioned his life to escape entanglements, was as securely hooked as any callow high school boy in the throes of first love. Worse, he was in love with a woman who had convinced herself she was unlovable, and so was afraid to open her heart to the risks of love.

How could he convince her that she was what he knew her to be: intelligent, loyal, courageous, heartbreakingly beautiful, warm and loving—a woman any man would give his soul to possess?

Well, this man, anyway.

He crossed the tiny space to the chart table, picked up the hefty pile of overdue letters and reports, and shuffled through them quickly. The group in Kenya wanted a synopsis of his planned talk for the international wildlife federation so they could get started on advance publicity; the New Zealand government wanted information on his latest count of opossums, and the rate of recovery on his protected plots; the Friends of the Rain Forests wanted to discuss strategy on how to save thousands of presently little-known jungle medicinal plants before they were forever lost.

All necessary and important. And impossible to concentrate on.

He shoved the papers back in a haphazard stack and bolted up the ladder to the deck. Running his fingers through his hair, he stood a moment at the rail, then shoved his hands in his pockets and paced back and forth across the deck. Damn Ian for dying! He had a hunch that only the knowledge that her father had loved her would free Kiri to trust love, and although in his heart Noel was almost sure Ian had loved his daughter, he had to agree with Kiri that he had had a strange way of showing it.

He stopped his pacing for a moment, aware of something nudging the periphery of his consciousness. With a sailor's instinct for weather, he noted it, cataloged it, dismissed it. A slight change in the direction of the wind.

Obviously he wasn't in the mood for paperwork. He would check his study plots. The walk across the island would give him the opportunity to stretch his muscles and work off some excess energy.

He dropped down into the cabin to pick up some tools and was starting back up the ladder when he heard his call letters on the ship-to-shore radio.

Grimacing at the delay, he answered the operator and was patched in to his waiting telephone call. He wasn't in the mood to talk to anyone.

"Don't you ever stay home, boy?" The deep voice, familiar even over the distortion of the ship-to-shore phone, boomed out at him. "I've been trying to get a hold of you for hours."

"Sam!" Recognizing the voice of the proprietor of the Duke of Marlborough Hotel, Noel's frown changed to a grin. "You old pirate! When did you get back from Australia?"

"Just last night. Would have come sooner, but I didn't hear about Ian until a few days ago." Although the man's voice sounded scratchy and a little garbled in the transmission, Noel caught a hint of concern in his tone. "I've been trying to locate you ever since I got back."

Noel's groin tightened at the thought of where he had been while Sam was trying to call him, and he smiled to himself, but his reply was brisk. "What's up?"

"I have to see you. Right away."

Noel frowned slightly. He and Sam were casual friends and he'd downed many a pint with Sam and Ian, but he couldn't think of anything so important that he would need to sail immediately to Russell. Certainly not now, with Kiri waiting for him...

"What's the matter, Sam?"

"I don't want to talk about it over the phone. How soon can you get here?"

Noel's frown deepened. Why the hurry? Sam had been gone for months, and now he had to see him immediately? Of course, he understood why he would want to discuss whatever was on his mind in person. Radio-phone calls were open to anyone who might want to listen in—and many wanted the diversion.

"It's important?"

"It's important," Sam said firmly.

"I suppose I can come right over," Noel said slowly. "An hour, two."

"Good. See you then. Over and out." Before Noel could ask further questions, the conversation was abruptly over.

Still puzzled, he weighed anchor and hoisted a sail, then turned the bow of the *Princess* out into the bay. The sea was somewhat choppy after the tranquility of the little cove and the canvas snapped in the wind. Not for the first time, Noel

was grateful that the main part of Long White Cloud, lying
as it did on the outer rim of the islands, sheltered his harbor from the open ocean.

He debated briefly whether to swing by the pier at the villa
and tell Kiri where he was going—maybe even take her
along—then decided against it. It would take up time, and
Sam's summons had sounded urgent. Besides, he had already told her he would be gone until late in the afternoon.
He had plenty of time to get to Russell and back before she
even knew he had left the island.

The radio squawked behind him, and he gave half his attention to the weather report. Nothing unusual. A possible
storm brewing in the South Pacific Ocean, but nothing to be
concerned about. The disturbance was miles away, and
moving in a direction that would keep it far from the coast.
The Bay of Islands had been hit by some pretty good gales,
but storms rarely came ashore at this time of year.

Kiri leaned back in the lounge chair, eyes closed, her hair
spilling darkness over her bare shoulders, as she trailed one
languid hand over the cool stone of the patio. After Noel
had gone, she had changed to a gauzy, off-the-shoulder
blouse and trim cotton slacks, and she felt comfortably cool
in the rising breeze. Everything around her was so reassur-
ingly familiar: the buzz of cicadas in he encroaching forest,
the splash of water from the fountain, the fragrance of roses
mixed with the tang of salt floating on the stiff breeze.

Familiar and soon to be lost.

She tried to shake off the desolation that seeped right into
her bones, but it was hopeless. She had finally come to a
decision about the island, and it left her feeling as bereft and
miserable as she had ever felt in her life. She couldn't deny
that it was the right decision, though. Right for everyone.

She was thankful that Noel had left her alone for a while;
she needed space after the emotional storm of the night before. It had given her time to think, to realize fully where her

actions were taking her. And they were taking her right into dangerous territory.

After last night's delirious lovemaking, there could be no question about her feelings. She had been dry tinder, lighted by his touch to flame. She didn't delude herself that it had been only physical, either. She admitted that she loved Noel, loved him with an intensity that she had never suspected she was capable of.

That very intensity would be her undoing if she allowed it to be.

Perhaps she could have handled a light, playful love. A love no one took too seriously. Then, when the inevitable occurred, she would have been able to pick up the pieces, accede another round to experience, and go on with her life. But what she felt for Noel was anything but light, and if she allowed him fully into her life, his eventual loss would be devastating.

She rose abruptly from the chair, paced a few steps, then sank back down. The problem was that Noel was so eminently worthy of love. He was warm, compassionate, intelligent, and there was no question about his character. He was so like her father—the real father she had been getting to know through listening to the talk of his friends, the comments of Neiri and Rapauru. She was seeing a man she had never known—charming, intelligent, driven by an altruistic desire to save the world.

One had to admire such a man.

But one mustn't marry him.

She dropped her head in her hands, and a long sigh shook her slender frame. For her, any permanent relationship with Noel would spell disaster. She knew what it was like to be second best. If she married at all, she had to come first with her husband. Noel's work would always come before her needs. Like Ian, he would always see higher priorities, oblivious to the wreckage left behind.

Unable to sit still, she jumped up from the lounge chair and walked through the house to the veranda, her mind still on Ian. Perhaps she could understand his treatment of her. She had been far from the center of his life, and from the evasiveness of her mother's answers when she had asked about him, she wondered if Lois may have thrown up roadblocks Kiri had never suspected.

But he had been totally irresponsible as far as his own family was concerned. She had to admit it—Neiri, Rapauru, even Noel, were far more his family than she was. It wasn't blood ties that made a family. It was love, concern, interdependence. And there, Ian MacKay, world-renowned author, revered conservationist, savior of the environment, had failed miserably. He had left the woman who loved him destitute, cheated his sons-in-love of their rightful inheritance.

The shrill ring of the phone tore her from her thoughts. Glad of something to break her mood, she ran down the hall and picked up the receiver.

"Miss MacKay?" The masculine voice, confident, assured, slightly abrasive, swept along the line. "Helborn here."

Her muscles tensed, and she took a quick inward breath. Helborn, the developer. The man who wished to change this treasure of an island into a glittering resort. In the confusion of Tainui's abortive attempt to take over the island she had nearly forgotten about the developer. But naturally, he wouldn't give up.

"Yes, Mr. Helborn," she replied, her voice as cool as lettuce. "This is Kiri MacKay."

"Hear you've been having quite a time for yourself over there," he said heartily. "Lots of trouble."

"How do you mean?"

"It's in all the papers, Tainui's move to take over the island, kick out the *pakeha*. Maoris acting up like that won't make the place easy to sell, you know. Bound to scare off buyers. Have you given any more thought to my offer?"

"I told you before, Mr Helborn. I really can't sell to you."

"Have you got a better offer?" His voice cracked sharply over the wire, and Kiri was reminded of a voracious shark circling ever closer. Instead of intimidating her, it made her angry.

"Yes, I have, Mr. Helborn. A much better offer."

"Who?" If he shouted any louder, he wouldn't need a phone, Kiri thought. "I'll top it, whatever it is."

"I don't think you could," she said sweetly. "I'm giving it away."

Silence stretched on for so long that Kiri wondered if he was still on the line. Then he said softly, as though the words didn't quite fit. "You're giving it away?"

"Giving it away," she repeated firmly. "To the New Zealand government."

She hung up in the midst of his sputtering response, not wishing to argue uselessly. She was absolutely certain that she had made the right decision. Everyone was positive that Ian had wanted the island to revert to the government, and she honored commitment, even the commitment of a parent who had forsaken her. It was the right thing to do.

Besides that, it would solve everything. She would stipulate that Long White Cloud be kept just as it was. Neiri would keep her home, Rapauru his village—and Noel could continue his studies. Best of all, the island would be safe from people like Helborn.

It was even best for her, she thought, wincing slightly. Now she didn't have to stay here, falling ever more deeply in love with Noel, moving inexorably toward heartbreak. She could leave immediately, and get on with her life.

So she wouldn't have the money the sale would have brought her—so what. She had known for a long time that the money was only a symbol of the love Ian hadn't given her. But it was too late for that now—she didn't need it. As Noel had told her when they first met, it was time she grew up. She would have to go on with her work without the money. It shouldn't be too difficult, she thought, with a wry twist to her mouth. Burying herself in her work might blunt the sharp pain of losing Noel.

A sudden gust of wind rattled the windows, and she glanced outside, surprised by the change in the weather. Even from inside the house she could hear the moan of the wind in the tops of the trees, and the usually clear sky was mottled with clouds.

With her head down and shoulders slumped, she went back to the phone. She supposed she should call her mother and tell her what she had decided to do, and alert her that she would be home in a day or two. There was no reason now to stay any longer. She would stop over in Auckland and give the necessary instructions to Mr. Marston, and catch a flight home.

The only difficult part would be telling Noel. He did feel something for her, she knew, even if it was only the excitement of sex. Still, she was doing what he wanted, wasn't she, what he had urged her to do? As for what had happened between them, they had both known it was only a temporary thing. He certainly hadn't said that he loved her.

The thought brought a quick wince of pain, and she hurriedly brought her thoughts back to Lois. She half smiled, as she thought of her mother's reaction when she heard the news. Lois would be certain that her daughter had lost her mind, and she wouldn't hesitate to tell her so. Sighing deeply, she reached for the phone. She had better get it over with.

She put the phone to her ear, and frowned slightly. No dial tone. Strange that it would be dead. She had talked to Helborn just a few minutes before. Impatiently, she jiggled the dial tone button. Nothing.

Puzzled, she replaced the phone in the cradle. Something must have disrupted the underground cable. Neiri had told her phone service was erratic, so there was probably nothing to worry about. Still, she was here alone . . .

She glanced at her watch, surprised that it was already midafternoon. Noel should be coming back soon. He certainly couldn't be working on his study plots this late. More likely he was at the boat, so immersed in his reports that he had forgotten the time.

Suddenly it was impossible to stay in the house a moment longer. If the lights went off, too—well, she wouldn't think about it. It wasn't far to Noel's boat. As much as she dreaded the coming encounter, she certainly didn't want to be alone just now. The sky was overcast, and there was a strange waiting quality to the air, but she probably had some time before a downpour started. Time to get to the boat, if she hurried.

The way was so familiar she didn't even need to keep her mind on the trail, and once she entered the depths of the forest she didn't even feel the brisk wind, although she heard it moaning in the treetops.

She had put on a light jacket, just in case, and she clutched it tightly across her chest as she increased her pace. There was no reason to run. Still, she was panting when she came out of the forest to the shore of the little inlet.

She stopped dead-still, staring incredulously. The harbor was empty; only a lone sea gull bobbed unconcernedly on the light swell, somehow accentuating the fact that the *Island Princess* was gone.

A wave of disappointment swept over her, and, suddenly weak, she sank down on a fallen log. She hadn't realized how much she had counted on his being here. He had *said* he would be here. A couple of hours on the study plots, some paperwork on the boat, and then he would be back, he had said.

She stood up and brushed the sand from her slacks with a defiant gesture. So much for what he said. So much for what any man said.

"Thanks for coming over on such short notice," Sam called, tossing the bowline to Noel who stood on the deck of the *Island Princess* ready to cast off. "I didn't like having that on my mind. Sure you won't change your mind and stay awhile?''

Noel caught the line and coiled it tightly, then gave the man standing on the dock a half salute. ''Better be getting back, Sam. But thanks for everything.''

He turned the wheel and headed the boat toward open water. He had already stayed in Russell much longer than he had expected to. But Sam was a talker, and he liked to tell things in his own way—slowly.

Noel's heart beat a little faster as he thought over what Sam had told him, and he patted the package in his pocket to reassure himself that it was still there.

He had tried to call the villa before leaving the hotel, but hadn't been too surprised that the phone was out. It often was, and his call certainly was no emergency. Still, he didn't like to think of Kiri alone with no way to get in touch with anyone. Neiri was probably still with Rapauru; he had seen her there this morning when he had passed the village on the way to Russell.

Out in the harbor now, he noticed that the water was choppier than when he had arrived. He lifted his eyes to the horizon. A little farther out white flecks of foam crowned the waves for an instant before they broke loose to spin into the air like rows of nimble dancers. Frowning, he reached behind and turned up the radio.

The storm that they had been forecasting all day wasn't moving much. It was still well offshore, although the winds were getting a little higher. He thought briefly of turning back, then shrugged, dismissing the thought.

It wasn't likely it would hit anytime soon. This wasn't the season for it. Even if he miscalculated there was hardly cause for concern. He and the *Island Princess* had weathered some big ones, ones that would capsize less seaworthy crafts. As he had told Kiri, the boat was strongly built, and while she wasn't particularly fast, she could take almost anything the elements could dish out.

There was a strong wind to push him along, and he should get to the island easily in an hour—long before things worsened, if they were going to.

Even so, he might have turned back. He was confident he could weather a storm, but he didn't particularly care to subject either himself or the boat to a battering unless it was absolutely necessary. But what he had learned in Russell made it imperative that he get back to Long White Cloud as soon as he could.

The boat lurched, and he tightened his grip on the wheel, spreading his legs apart for better balance as he corrected the course and headed directly into the wind. The storm was the least of his worries.

He thought of what Sam had told him, and his lips tightened. He wasn't at all sure how it would affect their relationship, but Kiri had to know what he had found out.

Kiri, her light blue jacket and cotton slacks soaked through, her hair plastered to her wet skin, flung open the door and stood dripping on the tiled foyer. The rain she had thought so far off had hit with a vengeance when she was about halfway home, and although she had hurried the rest of the way, she was a sodden mess when she finally reached the villa.

The weather matched her mood, she thought, as she sloshed to her room, her sandals squishing beneath her toes. Tight-lipped, she stripped off her clothes, then stepped into a hot shower. As the warm water cascaded down her chilled body, her thoughts raced endlessly. Why had Noel left so suddenly? He could at least have let her know he was going. Although perhaps it was better this way. There would be no long, painful explanations. Just possibly he might stay away until she had managed to leave the island.

Back in the living room, dressed in a warm crimson robe and fuzzy slippers, her still-wet hair slicked back with a narrow ribbon, she glanced out the bank of windows at the yard. Although it was still only late afternoon, it was nearly dark. She turned and flipped on a switch, unreasonably relieved when light flooded the room.

She turned on the radio and aimlessly moved the dial. Anything would be better than sitting here alone with her thoughts. The plaintive sound of country music floated out, then a commercial, and she continued dialing.

The weather forecast caught her attention, and she turned up the volume. At the first words, a cold shiver went down her back, in spite of the warmth of her robe. An unexpected storm, the worst in years, the announcer intoned. A tropical system, twisting unpredictably from its course and heading through the Bay of Islands. Already it was battering the outer rim. Residents were advised to stay indoors, batten down. Secure all boats—

Secure all boats. The phrase leapt out at her, and she shuddered, grasping the arms of her chair as though they were a raft and she was afloat herself in the wild sea. Noel might be out in that storm.

The thought that he had left without telling her seemed completely unimportant compared with what might be happening to him. He had said the *Island Princess* was seaworthy, but could any craft withstand what the announcer was calling the most challenging storm of the past several years?

She felt as though a tight band were constricting her heart, and breathing was painful. Noel might be out there alone.

But she mustn't jump to conclusions. He knew the area, he would have heard about the storm. Perhaps he was snugly holed up in some sheltered harbor.

If so, why did she feel this increasing panic? She had never much believed in ESP, but she could *feel* him out there, battling the storm. God, were they already so closely linked that she was tuned into his thoughts? Was it already too late to run away?

What could she do? She couldn't just sit here, waiting, agonizing. Perhaps a cup of tea or coffee—she rose and started toward the kitchen.

When the lights flickered, she knew intuitively what would happen next, and she clutched her robe tightly around her waist, staring out the window into what was now complete darkness. Then, without additional warning, the lights went out, leaving her in blackness.

She stood motionless, unable to make out any feature of the familiar room. Somewhere, she knew, there must be candles, emergency lighting. People who lived on islands were never completely unprepared for the vagaries of nature. She had no idea where to look, though, even if she could have found her way in the darkness.

Her heart hammered in her chest, and her mouth was dry with fear, even as she tried to assure herself there was really nothing to worry about. Darkness didn't harm you. She had only to wait out the storm...

Putting out her hand, she found the wall and began groping her way to the kitchen. Surely she could locate some matches.

She froze, as a fierce gust of wind hit the front of the villa and a blast of air swept into the hall. The front door was open, and she had latched it securely.

Someone besides herself was in the house.

Chapter 14

During the few paralyzing seconds that she huddled against the wall, a dozen thoughts flashed through Kiri's head. Who would brave the worsening storm to come to the villa? Could it possibly be Tainui, and had he only pretended to leave the island? Perhaps Rapauru, taking this opportunity to make good on some of his threats? Or even Noel, changing his mind about leaving and returning to be sure she was safe?

Recovering from the first burst of panic, she decided that whoever it was, she wasn't about to cower in darkness. Summoning every ounce of courage she possessed, she took a deep breath and called out. "Hello! Who's there?"

"Kiri? Where are you? Are you all right?"

Recognizing Neiri's voice, Kiri slumped against the wall, too relieved even to answer. She would never have expected Neiri to make her way through the storm, but she was incredibly glad she was here.

"Kiri?" Neiri repeated, increased concern sounding in her voice. "Answer me. Are you all right?"

The golden beam of a flashlight cut through the darkness, and Kiri walked swiftly toward it.

"I'm fine," she said, raising one hand to shield her eyes from the glare of the flashlight. "The power went out. I was just trying to find a light of some kind."

Neiri reached out and touched her arm, then pulled her into a close embrace. Kiri was too surprised to resist. With the older woman's body pressed tightly against her, she felt the chill of Neiri's sopping wet clothing, but even so the contact was warm and extremely comforting.

Wordlessly, Neiri held her against her chest for a long moment, and Kiri knew that the Maori woman was aware that she was trembling. Somehow it didn't matter—the reserve between the two was melting away. She didn't know how it had happened, but there didn't seem to be any reason to keep up a facade with Neiri anymore.

"The phone went first," she said, finally pulling away. "And then the lights..."

"I was afraid of that," Neiri said briskly, taking Kiri's arm and propelling her down the hall. "The phone is always the first to go, anytime anything goes wrong. Rapauru is having trouble getting through to the mainland on his shortwave radio, too."

How could she find her way in such darkness, Kiri wondered, as Neiri escorted her down the hall, moving as quickly as though it were daylight. But then, she probably knew every inch of the place; she had lived here twenty years. They entered the kitchen and Neiri went unerringly to a wall panel and flicked a switch. Light flooded the room. A little pale, a little sickly, compared to what Kiri was used to, but definitely light.

"We have an emergency generator," Neiri said, anticipating her question. "And butane gas for the stove. I was afraid you wouldn't know how to turn them on. How about some tea?"

Now that there was light, Kiri took a good look at Neiri. Her long hair was wet and tangled, and her flowered dress hugged her body like a second skin.

"You're soaked," she protested. "You must be freezing. Why don't you change into something dry, and I'll make the tea?"

"The stove takes a bit of practice," Neiri replied, filling a kettle, then setting a burner alight underneath it.

Kiri sank down in a chair by the table and watched Neiri bustle about the kitchen, unable to think of a thing to say. In spite of Neiri's unfailing politeness she had always felt the woman resented her, yet she had fought her way through a howling storm to come to her rescue. It didn't make sense.

As though it were the most normal thing in the world to be moving around a kitchen soaked to the bone, Neiri poured the tea and found a plate of scones. She set them on the table in front of Kiri and pulled up a chair.

"There, now," she said. "Eat something. You'll feel better."

Tea and scones. The New Zealand specific for anything that troubled you, Kiri thought. It really wasn't a bad idea. Although there were a hundred questions she wanted to ask, her fright had taken its toll. She munched away and drank the hot fragrant tea, as Neiri watched her in companionable silence. This must be how children felt when they came home from school to hot buns and cocoa, Kiri thought, all snug and protected. It was a first for her.

Lifting her gaze to Neiri's serene countenance, she spoke almost shyly. "Thanks for coming over. I *was* scared, although maybe there was no reason to be. It's just a storm."

As though in defiance of Kiri's facile assessment, a gust of wind rattled the windows and the sharp crack of nearby thunder echoed through the room. Neiri smiled, not at all taken in by Kiri's bravado. "These storms can be frightening if you're not used to them—and this is a bad one." She reached across the table and covered Kiri's hand with her own. "Don't be ashamed of being scared—we all are sometimes."

"You're afraid of the storm?" Kiri's eyes opened wide. "And yet you came all the way here through that horrible weather, because of me—"

"Rapauru would have come, but he was needed to protect the village," Neiri said simply. "We couldn't leave you here alone."

"Alone?" How did Neiri know she was alone? Noel had been here when the Maori woman left this morning. She must have known how they had spent the night, undoubtedly knew that they were lovers, and under those circumstances, wouldn't she have expected Noel to be with her?

"We knew Noel was in Russell," Neiri said gently, perhaps reading Kiri's thoughts in her expression. "We saw him sail by the village this morning going in that direction. When the storm came up unexpectedly, Rapauru managed to radio Russell."

Her brown eyes met Kiri's squarely, full of sympathy and warmth. "He had already left. They said he was on his way back here."

The words echoed in her head—he had already left. Her premonition had been correct. He was out there somewhere in the storm, possibly battling for his life.

As though reading her mind, Neiri tried to encourage her, although her own anxiety was apparent in her worried tone. "Don't worry. He may have managed to duck in some place..."

Neiri didn't believe that any more than she did, Kiri thought, a cold feeling settling in the pit of her stomach. She was just trying to reassure her.

"I hope so. I'm ever so grateful that you came," she continued softly. "But I really don't understand why you did. You knew I probably wasn't in any physical danger— just scared. You came all that way to reassure me. I thought you resented me, wanted me gone..."

Neiri smiled sadly, shaking her head. "Well, of course we did. At first. But after we got to know you...things changed. Perhaps we treated you badly, blamed you for things that weren't your fault..." Her voice trailed away. "I'm sorry Ian didn't know you," she finally said. "He would have been proud."

"I've finally made up my mind about the island," Kiri said slowly. "It was never really mine—not by any criteria that matter. You won't have to leave. I'm going to turn it over to the government—as Ian wished."

When Neiri didn't reply, Kiri gave her a sharp look. She had expected more of a reaction—joy, excitement—anything but the sad, sweet smile.

"You don't seem very surprised," she said.

Neiri shrugged. "You're Ian's daughter," she said simply.

Even after everything that had happened, the woman refused to think harshly of the man! "Aren't you angry?" Kiri burst out. "How can you just accept what he did, ignore the fact that he didn't even care enough to protect you with a will! He couldn't have loved you."

Neiri rose and refilled their teacups, then looked across at Kiri, though she didn't seem to see her. She appeared to be gazing into something unseeable, some secret well of knowing. For an instant Kiri felt that she was peering back into time, absorbing the strength of generations of Maori women, wise and stolid and secure in themselves.

"I believe he loved me," she said slowly. "But that's really beside the point. I loved him. That's the important thing—not whether you're loved, but whether you love somebody. Being loved is a great pleasure—but it's loving that expands your soul, opens you to the wonders of the universe. Makes you more than yourself. Whatever the risk, whatever the consequences, if you love, you are one of the fortunate ones—you have really lived."

Kiri stared openmouthed. She had never expected such philosophical depth from the simple Maori woman. Although why she had ever harbored that impression, she didn't know. There had been myriad clues indicating that Neiri was a complicated woman, which Kiri undoubtedly would have noticed if she hadn't been so wrapped up in her own dilemma.

"But what if you love someone who's not for you?" she whispered. "What if you know what's going to happen—that there is bound to be pain?"

"Even then," Neiri said firmly. "It's the loving that's important. Besides, you can never be sure of what's going to happen. Sometimes the heart is wiser than the head." She stared silently at Kiri for a full minute. The young woman had the uncomfortable feeling that her every emotion was lying bare. Then Neiri smiled. "You love him, don't you?"

"Yes." She whispered the word, then raised her eyes to Neiri. "Yes," she repeated, her voice gaining strength and conviction. There were many things she was unsure of, but loving Noel wasn't one of them. "Yes, I do."

"He'll be all right," Neiri said softly. "Try not to worry. He'll be all right."

The agonizing crack of breaking wood told him the mast was going, and Noel swore aloud. His words were snatched from his mouth, washed away in the gale that had been buffeting him for the past couple of hours. Using all his strength, he twisted the wheel. Keeping the boat headed into the wind was becoming more and more difficult, but if he took a wave broadside, he would capsize for sure.

Any sane man would have stayed in Russell until things cleared up, but what good was hindsight? He'd thought of Kiri, probably frightened, alone, and he'd had to try it. Not that he had ever expected the storm to be this bad.

What he'd learned in Russell seemed immaterial now, compared with his fierce concern for Kiri. This storm was close to hurricane force, and he doubted that Kiri would know how to protect herself in the villa. What if a window blew in? He thought of all the things that could happen to her in a storm this severe, and clenched his jaw until it hurt; even his own precarious situation was secondary to her welfare.

He felt as though he had been standing at the helm for days instead of hours. Every muscle protested, as he straddled the deck and gripped the wheel with hands that were nearly frozen to the spokes. Not that his efforts to steer did much good. With the mainsail gone and the mast down, he was flopping about aimlessly.

There wasn't any use even trying to start his auxiliary motor. It had sputtered and died an hour ago, and he knew it was swamped with water.

For the first time since leaving Russell, he wondered if he would make it. The wind seemed to be strengthening, howling about his ears like a demon, and visibility had contracted to mere feet. Even if he didn't capsize, he might be cast up on the rocky shore, a prospect that wasn't any more pleasant.

A wall of water slapped him in the face and washed back over the deck, further drenching his soaking clothes. Holding the wheel with one hand, he wiped the water out of his eyes with the other. How much longer could this monster last? How much longer could *he* last, for that matter? He was going on nothing but adrenaline.

He tightened his lips and gripped the wheel, as the boat lurched, shuddered, righted itself. What kind of damn thinking was that? He would last as long as he had to, because much more than his own life depended on his getting back to the island. If he were lost, Kiri would never know...

But hugging a useless wheel wasn't helping a thing. In the open ocean he would have gone below, closed the hatch, and tried to ride it out. He would have bobbed around like a cork, but he would probably have survived. Here, he was in as much danger of being cast up on the rocks as capsizing, and he had to be ready to swim for it if he had to.

He stared awestruck at the mammoth waves, as he crested one, then dropped deeply into the trough that dwarfed the boat. Swimming for it was hardly an option, either.

Suddenly Kiri's face flashed before his eyes, every feature so plain he could almost have sworn she was right beside him. Her face was white, strained, her generous mouth was set firmly, and her eyes, shadowed with fear, seemed to look directly into his own. He could almost hear her words above the roar of the water.

"You can make it, I know you can."

The boat shuddered under another wall of water, and Noel skidded against the railing, then righted himself and grabbed the wheel. "I sure as hell hope you're right," he muttered.

As the night wore on, Kiri and Neiri sat together in the kitchen, downing innumerable cups of tea, sometimes in silence, sometimes making nervous conversation to counteract the sound of the storm pounding outside.

The violence outside was more than matched by the upheaval in Kiri's heart. She had always prided herself on her control, her pragmatic approach to problems, but ever since she had come to this island, nothing had been under her control. She'd been tossed around on a sea of emotion: guilt, envy, ambivalence about the future of Long White Cloud, and more shattering than anything else, she had fallen in love with Noel.

Noel, who might never make it back. The thought was so impossible she shoved it aside. He had to come back—she would will him to come back.

She took a sip of tea, wondering if Neiri were at all fooled by her calm facade. Did she guess the hysteria that was close to the surface? Maybe talking would help.

She ventured a weak smile. "You know, I really don't know much of anything about you. What did you do before you met Ian? Where did you meet? Had you known each other long before you came to the island?"

Taking the cue, Neiri told her how her first husband had died in a boating accident, how Ian had come to Rotorua a year later to study the thermal area, and how she had guided him around the various boiling springs. It had been love at first sight.

"Why didn't you ever get married?" Her voice was hesitant, as she wondered whether Neiri would take offense at the question.

"At first, I didn't want to give Rapauru a stepfather—he was so intensely Maori, and my family thought they would lose him if I married a *pakeha*. You met my brother—he's old-fashioned, and didn't believe in mixing the races. Of course, Rapauru came to love Ian so much it wouldn't have mattered, but by that time, I guess we just didn't think of it. It seemed not to matter..."

Both were silent. Was Neiri thinking what she was thinking? It would have mattered for inheritance purposes.

"Did he ever talk about me?"

Neiri gave her a long look. "Yes. Although not often. I think it hurt him to remember..."

"He could have come to see me. Written."

"Yes..."

"When did he meet Noel?"

"Several years ago. They went to the same meetings, fought for the same causes. Noel was younger, trying to establish a niche, and Ian took him under his wing." Neiri's dark eyes met Kiri's green ones. "Kiri, I'm glad you came here. I'd like to think of you as my daughter, too."

Kiri's eyes spoke her sincere gratitude; then, both women lapsed into silence. All Kiri's energy was focused on Noel, on waiting. She had never realized how much energy it took to just wait.

She may have dozed off a few times during the night, when there was a lull in the storm, only to be snapped awake by its renewed assault. She definitely had been asleep when she heard a call from the kitchen door.

She jolted upright, unable for a moment to figure out where she was. Everything was quiet, unnaturally quiet; then she heard the first tentative cheep of a bird. Dawn lighted the kitchen; it was almost eerie in the half-light. Then she remembered—the storm. And Noel.

Neiri was on her feet first. She reached the kitchen door just as Rapauru threw it open. He stood motionless in the doorway, his eyes going anxiously from one woman to the other. "Everything okay here?" he asked brusquely.

"Fine," Neiri said. Kiri couldn't get an answer through her dry throat. She met Rapauru's eyes and she saw sympathy in their dark depths.

"We don't know about Noel yet," he said softly.

The room started to spin; she sat back down at the table. "What was the last you heard? Where was he?"

Rapauru, his arm around his mother, crossed to the table and looked down at Kiri. He seemed uneasy with the role of comforter, but she could see in his expression that he was concerned about her. A vagrant thought whisked through her mind. Had it taken this tragedy to bring her close to the two Maoris? Were the three of them finally reconciled in their fear for Noel's safety?

"We know he left Russell just before the storm hit," he said slowly, as though unwilling to be the bearer of bad news. "I've been on the radio since it blew off up the coast. There's damage—boats overturned, trees down—"

He was skirting around what she wanted to know—had to know. "But what about Noel? Was one of the overturned boats the *Island Princess?*"

Neiri moved closer and put her arm around Kiri's shoulders as Rapauru looked at the ceiling, at the walls—at everything but Kiri. "Maybe."

"Maybe!" She jumped up from the chair and grabbed the stalwart Maori by the shoulders, almost shaking him in her frustration. "What do you mean, maybe?"

He hesitated, then took her arms from his shoulders and placed her gently back down in the chair. "We're not sure.

It's still pretty rough out there, and no has been able to get a boat out. But someone on one of the neighboring islands reported what looked like the wreckage of a sailboat—drifting past.''

"The coast guard! They must have boats out. Or helicopters. Surely they have something!"

"Yes, I've called them. They're searching, but they're looking for a lot of people who got caught out last night. Things blew up so quickly—"

She jumped from the chair and started for the door, but Rapauru's hand darted out to catch her arm and haul her back. "Where do you think you're going?"

"There's the launch. I'm going to look for him."

"The launch is at the bottom of the bay," Rapauru said. "The wind tore it loose and some driftwood knocked a hole in it. I saw it as I came in."

"You mean there's no way at all to search for him?" Very slowly, as though a sudden movement might break her, she sank back down in the chair. Despair sat like a huge rock on her shoulders, weighting her down. It was almost incomprehensible; Noel might be dead. The thought that she might never see him again was almost too much to bear. To think that just a few hours ago she had planned to leave him, get on with her life, because she was afraid! Afraid to love!

She lowered her head to her hands. She had to be honest with herself, brutally honest, as she had always prided herself on being, but hadn't been at all since she'd come to Long White Cloud. She could never leave Noel of her own volition. Although she hadn't been able to phrase it as Neiri had, she had come to accept the truth of what the woman had said. It was loving that mattered.

Finally, she faced the truth; she would have loved Noel as long as he allowed it—and if he left in the end, she would have handled it as best she could.

Rapauru turned toward the door, and she jerked herself back from her fruitless recriminations. "Where are you going?"

"The sea's calming down fast—within half an hour, some of the boys and I should be able to get out in the canoe."

"The canoe! I didn't know it was finished."

"Close enough."

"I'm going with you!"

He shook his head. "You'd only be in the way. We'll let you know as soon as we find out anything."

Neiri put her hand on Kiri's shoulder. "He's right—there's nothing you can do."

"Well, I can't just sit here."

"Why don't you go up on the promontory. You can watch them from there."

The idea was a good one. Kiri rushed to put on sturdier clothing, then hurried out the door and up the hill to the top of the island. She barely noticed the evidence of the storm's passing—fallen trees, gushing streamlets, the air washed clean, as fresh and innocent as though it had never been a howling monster.

She reached the promontory and paused to catch her breath, then looked out at the sparkling sea. The sun was just rising, painting a golden path on the water, and she could make out Rapauru's canoe, a dark, oblong form cleaving to the white-capped waves. In all those myriad islands, those countless shorelines, where would he look for Noel?

All the problems that had caused her so much anguish seemed petty in the face of one overwhelming fact: she might never be able to tell Noel how much she loved him. Only let him return safely, give her another chance.

Ian's abandonment, her own insecurity—none of it mattered. She knew she was being childish, bargaining with God, or Fate. But if given another chance, she would stay in his life as long as she could. Perhaps she never would be first with him—but he would come first with her.

She settled down on a boulder and prepared for a long wait.

Chapter 15

The sea, restless, heaving, its vista changing constantly, nearly mesmerized her as she stared out across it. The whitecaps were gone now, and the water stretched calm and blue under the noon sun. Rapauru's canoe had long since passed out of sight, and only emptiness met her tired eyes.

A rodent of some kind scuttled in the brush behind her and she turned, blinked, then resumed her vigil.

Time dragged on. She had become so used to staring at emptiness that she didn't even notice it for several seconds—the faint gray outline on the horizon. She sat up straighter as it came closer, the shape becoming ever more distinct. Her heart beat a little faster. It looked like a boat. Possibly Rapauru's canoe, with news of Noel.

She lifted her binoculars to her eyes, and her heart seemed to freeze inside her chest, then erupt in a frenzied tattoo. She couldn't breathe. She couldn't believe it. The *Island Princess* was limping painfully toward shore.

She scanned the craft incredulously, unable to see how it could still be afloat. Only a stump remained of the mast, and from that stump a makeshift sail was lashed, so ragged and torn that she didn't see how it could begin to hold the wind. The boat listed badly, and it was barely crawling over the water—but there was no doubt about it. It was the *Island Princess* and it was coming home.

She nearly flew down the trail toward the villa, oblivious to the scratches on her legs, or to the branches grabbing at her hair. By the time she arrived at the pier, panting and gasping, but ecstatic, the boat was already scraping along the edge of the dock.

Noel was leaning against the wheel. She had only a moment to think how pale and exhausted he looked, when he threw her a line. It was a weak throw, but she caught it and tied the craft securely to a piling, then turned to Noel.

He was sagging at the wheel, his last burst of energy apparently used up when he threw her the line. She screamed for Neiri, then scrambled aboard.

"Good catch." He managed a weak grin.

Half sobbing, she tore across the debris-strewn deck and caught Noel in her arms, both embracing him, and holding him up, unable to say a thing except whisper his name over and over. He looked as though he'd been through hell, but he was alive, and that was all that mattered.

She was still holding him when Neiri arrived breathless at the dock. Between the two of them, they half carried, half dragged him up the path to the villa and deposited him on a couch in the living room. He slumped back against the cushions, exhaustion written in every line of his face, as Kiri knelt beside him.

"I had to get here," he whispered, raising his hand to smooth back her hair, then letting his arm fall to his side. "I had to tell you—"

"Not now," Neiri said briskly, returning with a glass of whiskey that she held to Noel's lips. He swallowed and Kiri thought she saw some color come back into his face.

Even before the two women had stripped off his shoes and wet clothing and covered him with a warm blanket, Noel was asleep.

"He'll be all right now," Neiri said. "I don't know how he managed to sail that hulk home—but all he needs now is rest." She put her hand on Kiri's shoulder, her eyes bright with understanding. Kiri suspected Neiri read the love and relief on her face—she felt as jubilant as though someone had handed her a string with the world on the end of it.

"You'd better get some rest, too," Neiri continued. "I'll go on over to the village. Maybe there's some way I can get word to Rapauru, or at least be there when he gets back to tell him Noel is safe."

After Neiri left, Kiri drew up a chair close beside Noel and sat where she could watch his face. Perhaps she was tired, but she wasn't conscious of it. All her attention focused on the man who had fallen into an exhausted sleep. With his eyes closed, his long lashes falling against his sculpted cheekbones, his lips relaxed and slightly open, he looked so vulnerable that she felt as though her heart might break with tenderness.

What must he have gone through? His boat was evidence of the battering he had undergone; so too was the pallor of his face, the spasmodic clenching and unclenching of his fingers as though even in sleep he held the boat to the wind. How could she have ever been ridiculous enough to think she could walk away, ignore what had happened between them? When he awoke she would tell him of her plans for the island. If he gave the slightest indication that he cared for her, she would stay with him as long as she could.

She reached for his hand, then lay back against the chair, preparing for a long wait. Eventually, she, too, fell into a fitful sleep.

She didn't know how much time had passed when she became aware that Noel was no longer asleep. She opened her eyes and found herself looking directly into his deep blue gaze. She was still holding his hand, and his fingers curled slowly around her palm.

Rising to a sitting position, he pulled her toward him. Even before she was fully awake his arms were around her, and he was murmuring her name as he rained kisses on her cheek, her lips, the little hollow at the base of her throat. His heart thudded against her chest, his breath was hot on her skin, and he seemed determined to leave not even a whisper of space between them.

"Oh, Kiri, Kiri..."

"You're home—you're safe..."

"I'd never have made it if it hadn't been for you. You were there, with me..."

"I was so afraid..."

She had no idea how long they babbled on almost incoherently. Finally she drew back so she could see his eyes, and took a deep breath. Now was the time, before she lost her nerve. She had to tell Noel what she planned to do about the island.

"I don't know what I'd have done if anything had happened to you," she began. "I have to tell you—"

"Shhh..." He put his finger lightly on her lips. "I've a lot to tell you, too. But everything can wait for a little bit."

And so it did. She cuddled into his arms, as they stretched out together on the couch. He placed her head gently on his chest, buried his head in her hair, and they both slept.

When they finally awoke, dusk was settling over the island, brushing the living room with velvet shadow. In spite of her cramped position, she felt completely rested. Noel apparently did, too, if she could judge by the enthusiasm with which he was kissing her awake.

In another instant they would be lost in passion. A wonderfully seductive thought, but before that happened she needed to talk to him, find out his real feelings toward her, and let him know what she planned. "I have something to tell you," she gasped.

He kissed her squarely on her mouth, then drew back so he could see her expression. "Me, first," he insisted. "Don't you want to know why I went to Russell?"

It seemed so long ago—she had nearly forgotten her pained surprise when she had discovered he had left so abruptly. She nodded her head, and Noel continued.

"Sam got back from Australia. He called me on the boat. He had some interesting information—something that very much concerns you, Kiri."

"The proprietor of the hotel in Russell? How could it concern me? I don't even know him."

"No, but Ian did." He settled his arms comfortably around her.

"Yes," she said slowly. "You told me they were good friends."

"Sam didn't learn of Ian's death until a few days ago—his son's mine is completely isolated. When he did hear, he came right home—because Ian's will was in his safe."

Kiri sat bolt upright. "Ian left his will in his safe! How is that possible? Why didn't anyone know about it?"

"Just a mix-up all around. They were together one night, just two old friends, drinking a little, reminiscing a little, and Ian began talking about you. It was the first Sam had even heard of you, but Ian couldn't seem to stop talking. He told him everything—his guilt, his regret, his hope that he'd see you again. Impulsively, he decided to write a will right then and there—and Sam witnessed it."

"So you were right about him after all." Kiri lifted bewildered eyes to Noel's face. "But why didn't his attorney have it—or even know about it?"

"Timing. Ian planned to take it to his lawyer as soon as he got back from a week's fishing trip. Sam put it in his safe. Then he got an urgent message from his son—he had to have his help right away. He forgot about the will. Ian had a heart attack—and there you have it."

"And there you have it," Kiri echoed sadly. So much pain for everyone, and all for nothing. Ian had indeed made the provisions everyone had expected. And so much for her altruistic gesture of returning the island to the government—it was all taken care of.

"Why did Sam call you?" she asked. "Why not the attorney?"

"He wasn't exactly sure what to do. He knew I was Ian's good friend," he said softly. "And he heard you were here. He thought someone should bring you the will personally."

"You have it with you?"

"Yes. And there's something else. A letter." He took the slim oilcloth-covered package from his pocket and handed it to Kiri. Her fingers were trembling so that she could hardly open it, but she drew out a thin sheet of paper and unfolded it carefully. A suspicious mist blurred her vision, but she managed to read every word.

My Beloved Daughter,

Never doubt it, Kiri, you are beloved, although I know you have cause to think otherwise. Leaving you was the hardest thing I ever did in my life, but it seemed best at the time. Your mother felt—and she was probably right—that it would only confuse you if I tried to stay in contact with you. So I closed that chapter of my life and resolved never to look back, although you have always been in my heart.

Later, when you were grown, I thought of getting in touch with you, but so much time had passed, and I wasn't sure you would even welcome a reminder of me.

Now I'm not sure I did the right thing—for you or for me. I realize daily how much I lost, and how I must have hurt you. If I could turn back time I would do things differently, but none of us can do that, can we?

I can never atone for having abandoned you. It is too late. But I want you to have Long White Cloud—another thing that is close to my heart. You, Neiri, Rapauru, the island—and Noel, who is like a son to me—are the most important things in the world.

So I am leaving you the island in the sure knowledge that you will do what is best for everyone. I believe the character and temperament are set at birth—and you were always such an honest, loving little girl. You will not have changed. You will do the right thing.

Your loving father,
Ian MacKay

The lump in her throat was so huge she couldn't have spoken, even if she had known what to say. Her father had loved her. All these years, years in which she had been bitter and condemning, he had loved her. Loved her enough to trust her with everyone and everything else he loved.

She didn't bother to look at the will. It really made no difference who owned Long White Cloud. She had been going to make the same arrangements for Neiri and Rapauru that she would make now. Everything else could wait; she knew the most important thing. Noel had known what was in the will, and he had brought it to her, although it could well have meant the end of his dreams.

Mutely, she handed the letter to Noel, oblivious to the tears that stung her eyes and had begun trickling slowly down her cheeks. Then sobs came, deep, wrenching, painful, as the barricades she had erected around her heart, barricades she had thought were made of steel, crumbled like sandcastles at high tide. For the first time in years, Kiri cried for her father. The father who had loved her enough to trust her with everything he had held dear—because she was his daughter.

She cried for her mother, too, the woman who had wasted years in bitterness, not realizing the worth of the man she had refused to follow.

"Kiri, Kiri." Noel flung aside the letter and knelt beside her, pulling her into his powerful arms. "It's all right." He cradled her head on his chest and gently stroked her hair.

Eventually the sobs quieted. She wasn't crying for herself—she was through with what she thought of as years of self-pity. She was a strong, independent woman, and she would reach for what she wanted.

She took a long, quivering breath and drew back from Noel's embrace until she could see his face. His dear, beloved face. She would never get enough of it if she looked at him for the next fifty years. Noel, with his sparkling wit, his deep loyalty, his intense commitments.

Noel, who was so like her father.

"I love you," she said, her voice still shaky with emotion—but not sorrow. Not any longer. She felt a wild, singing elation, as she met his eyes squarely. "I love you, darling. Will you marry me?"

His reply was deeply satisfactory. Surprise and elation flared in his eyes, turning them to blue smoke. He crushed her against his chest, gripping her so tightly she could hardly breathe, then found her lips for a deep, searing kiss that seemed to last forever before he drew back a fraction of an inch.

"I thought you'd never ask," he finally said, his voice husky with emotion. "Kiri, I love you so much."

She snuggled even closer into his strong, protective arms—arms that she knew would always be her shield and her fortress. There would be time later—all the time in the world—to discuss things that must be decided. But for now, only one thing was important.

Ian's daughter had come home.

* * * * *

This is the season of giving, and Silhouette proudly offers you its sixth annual Christmas collection.

SILHOUETTE

Christmas Stories

1991

Experience the joys of a holiday romance and treasure these heartwarming stories by four award-winning Silhouette authors:

Phyllis Halldorson—"A Memorable Noel"
Peggy Webb—"I Heard the Rabbits Singing"
Naomi Horton—"Dreaming of Angels"
Heather Graham Pozzessere—"The Christmas Bride"

Discover this yuletide celebration—sit back and enjoy Silhouette's Christmas gift of love.

Angels Everywhere!

Everything's turning up angels at Silhouette. In November, Ann Williams's ANGEL ON MY SHOULDER (IM #408, $3.29) features a heroine who's absolutely heavenly—and we mean that literally! Her name is Cassandra, and once she comes down to earth, her whole picture of life—and love—undergoes a pretty radical change.

Then, in December, it's time for ANGEL FOR HIRE (D #680, $2.79) from Justine Davis. This time it's hero Michael Justice who brings a touch of out-of-this-world magic to the story. Talk about a match made in heaven . . . !

Look for both these spectacular stories wherever you buy books. But look soon—because they're going to be flying off the shelves as if they had wings!

If you can't find these books where you shop, you can order them direct from Silhouette Books by sending your name, address, zip or postal code, along with a check or money order for $3.29 (ANGEL ON MY SHOULDER IM #408), and $2.79 (ANGEL FOR HIRE D #680), for each book ordered (please do not send cash), plus 75¢ postage and handling ($1.00 in Canada), payable to Silhouette Reader Service to:

In the U.S.
3010 Walden Ave.
P.O. Box 1396
Buffalo, NY 14269-1396

In Canada
P.O. Box 609
Fort Erie, Ontario
L2A 5X3

Please specify book title with your order.
Canadian residents add applicable federal and provincial taxes.

ANGEL

Take 4 bestselling love stories FREE
Plus get a FREE surprise gift!

NORA ROBERTS

Love has a language all its own, and for centuries, flowers have symbolized love's finest expression. Discover the language of flowers—and love—in this romantic collection of 48 favorite books by bestselling author Nora Roberts.

Starting in February 1992, two titles will be available each month at your favorite retail outlet.

In February, look for:

Irish Thoroughbred, Volume #1
The Law Is A Lady, Volume #2

Collect all 48 titles and become fluent in the Language of Love.

LOL192

THE LANGUAGE of LOVE